PLAYING WITH FIRE

The Scarlet Series #3

Toria Lyons

Published by Accent Press Ltd 2015

ISBN 9781783758616

Copyright © Toria Lyons 2015

The right of **Toria Lyons** to be identified as the author of
this work has been asserted by her in accordance with the
Copyright, Designs and Patents Act 1988.

Accent Press Ltd, Ty Cynon House, Navigation
Park, Abercynon CF45 4SN

Dedication

To those who have been there for me. Every little bit of help is much appreciated. You can be certain I'll be passing it on when possible.

And to those in the beds around me at Guy's. May the curries do their work!

Chapter One

Marcus didn't think it was possible to continue breathing with his heart ripped out. But he still lived, and he could even pretend to smile and joke with the rest of the wedding party.

Why had he turned up to Clare's wedding? Why hadn't he made some kind of excuse to miss it? To avoid seeing the only woman he'd ever felt strongly for reconfirm her vows and take herself out of his reach, forever? Maybe he was a masochist. He was ultimately happy for her though – somehow she had tamed the wildest of them all.

Did Alex deserve her? In Marcus' opinion, the jury was still out.

He was relieved that he'd never made a proper pass at her. That would have been really awkward. At least he would still see her next season at rugby training. Well, until she became pregnant like he suspected her friend Sarah would soon be. Just the thought of that made him down another drink.

Sophie was used to being invisible, but she had hoped that Marcus, as her "escort" for the day, would pay her a little more attention. She had spent hours ensuring she looked elegant – the stylish, pale pink halter-neck dress was a stark contrast to how she had dressed during those awkward first months at Harford. Sophie loved the pretty outfit, and the contrasting darker pink ribbon fascinator adorning her pixie haircut. Her natural, light brown shade might hardly have been unique, but it looked so much better than the long, horrible, matte black it had been previously.

Not that Marcus had registered it at all – his thoughts were elsewhere. He hid it well, but she picked up on the odd wistful glance towards Clare, and the forced laughter and smiles. It didn't really matter, anyway: she found him attractive, but he wasn't her type. Far too tall, too blond, too clean cut, too nice? No, that wasn't right.

Sophie frowned and looked him up and down, trying to think what exactly it was about him that day. Apart from his lack of attention. She just couldn't work it out. So she had another drink.

Marcus was relieved when the speeches finished. In a couple of hours, he could escape to his hotel room. Not all of the Harford Park players had been able to travel to Scotland for the ceremony – he was one of a handful "lucky" enough to be invited. A few photos of the Park contingent dressed up to the nines and he would slink off.

He wouldn't even be part of the team for a while – after another season interrupted by injury, he was going on loan to a South African outfit for the summer, and was leaving Harford as soon as the final, end of season whistle had blown. Only a few days to go. Of wishing that he was in Alex's place. He laughed cynically and lifted his refilled glass in time for the final cheer. 'Here's to heartbreak,' he muttered under his breath, and downed the whole flute of champagne.

Sophie's hearing wasn't any better than average, however she could guess Marcus' toast didn't carry the same sentiments as the rest of the room felt. Her own glass had been topped up by the same waiting staff that had needed to return so quickly to Marcus' glass. After that, they just left the bottle on the table. She took another gulp, grabbed the bottle, and refilled both of their flutes to the brims.

'Ow. Ow. Ow.'

Sophie had never, ever had a blinding headache like the one she had at that moment, and a mouth as parched as the Sahara. Why had she had quite so much to drink?

'Arrgh.' She went to lift a hand to her head but something stopped her, pinching and tugging at the back of her hand. It felt like … wires? *What the hell?*

She was lying on her back, her head propped up by pillows. She never slept on her back. Ever. Something was beeping around her, and the soft shuffle of people moving. The smell of … antiseptic?

Her other hand was free and she patted it over to the first. It felt like there was a needle in the back of her hand. Her eyes flew open and she winced at the bright light before she was able to focus.

'*Heita bokkie*, you are back with us.' A rotund woman in a nurse's uniform hovered over her, her brown face alight in a friendly smile.

'Wh – where am I?' Her voice sounded rusty as her throat was dry.

'Here, some water,' the nurse fed her a straw. 'You're at the Groote Schuur, you had an accident in the city yesterday. Just a few sips, please. I'm Thandiwe, but call me Tandy. I am your nurse.'

The nurse had a familiar, clipped accent Sophie just couldn't place. 'The Groot … groot … where's that, please?'

'Why, Cape Town, of course.'

'Cape Town!' shrieked Sophie, and shot upright. The movement made her head feel like it was going to explode, and the world swam around her. 'Ow! Oh, help!'

Tandy grabbed a bowl just in time for Sophie to vomit up the little water she had drunk. 'Sshhh, keep yourself as still as possible. You've had a nasty bang to your head and ribs.'

Once Sophie had returned her head to the pillows, the

world steadied again. She took some cautious breaths as the nausea and pain receded. Tandy gave her a glass of water to swill her mouth out, and the horrible taste began to abate.

She warily eyeballed the room – it was clearly a hospital. 'I don't remember … I live in the UK, I don't know how I got here.'

'Don't worry, it's quite common for things to be fuzzy when you come around. It'll return to you in the next few hours,' reassured Tandy. 'Do you remember your name?'

'Of course, it's Sophie. Sophie Edwards.' She reeled off her London address and phone number, but Tandy wasn't writing it down. 'Don't you need to know who I am?'

Tandy smiled comfortingly. 'Relax now. We managed to find out from your belongings. Your husband will be here soon.'

'Husband?' squeaked Sophie in confusion, and went to move again, but warning pain and disorientation kept her in one place.

'*Ja*, he is *lekker*, a lovely man. He has been sitting with you while you've been unconscious. Look, here he is now.'

Sophie stared at the familiar, well-built figure walking towards the bed. 'Marcus? *You're* my husband?'

He looked relieved to see her conscious and smiled. 'Sophie, love, thank goodness you're awake.'

'But … *you* are my *husband*? I … I'm so confused.'

Tandy interjected, 'Sophie has only just woken up, and she's having some memory problems. This is all perfectly normal with knocks to the head, so don't be worried.' She whispered that she would be back later with some medicine, and melted into the background.

'We've been so worried about you, you've been out for almost a day.' Marcus went to kiss her and she shrank away, conscious of the trace of vomit still remaining on her breath. He looked hurt.

'Marcus, please. I'm sorry, I've just been sick,' she apologised.

He started panicking slightly. 'Are you OK? Shall I call Tandy back?'

'I'm fine, I'm just a little ... confused. Please, give me a few moments.' She took a deep breath and felt a twinge of pain. She looked down at her hands – the one without the needle was bruised purple. She rolled up her sleeve to see the discolouration continue. Her ribs were also tender; it hurt if she took a deep breath, but it was bearable.

Out of the corner of her eye she saw a wall clock with a calendar. She squinted at it, trying to figure out the date. She blinked again. What? She was missing over four weeks!

Somehow, in just over a month, she'd travelled to South Africa, got married, and landed in hospital. Her thoughts were whirring around her tender brain but she sought to pacify him. 'Marcus, my memory's a little fuzzy at the moment. I remember the wedding. I wore pink, but that's it.'

He tried smiling at her, the worry clear in his eyes. 'That's OK. As Tandy said, the doctors warned me you would be a little confused. It may take a while for your memories to come back.'

'But why am I here?'

'You were hit by a passing minibus in Cape Town. You were carrying a copy of the wedding photo and the hospital got in contact after one of the rugby-mad doctors recognised me. I'm afraid your handbag has disappeared, and we can't find your purse, passport, or phone. You're in a private room, my family's insurance covers it.'

She figured out what was missing. 'Did I not want a ring?'

'A what?'

Her voice rose in panic, 'Rings. I have no rings. I can't

be married to *you*, I have no wedding or engagement rings!'

Marcus patted her uninjured hand soothingly and started rummaging in a pocket. Sophie watched in awe as he brought out a couple of glittering rings and carefully slid them on to her ring finger. They fitted perfectly.

'That better? They X-rayed you and didn't find anything broken, but they didn't want to leave the rings on when you were unconscious in case of swelling,' he blathered.

The rings, however tasteful, felt alien on her hand. Sophie frowned, waiting for the jumble of memories in her head to right themselves. The wedding? She vaguely remembered *a* wedding. Maybe a plane journey? A sun-drenched city? She winced from the extra effort.

'Don't try to force things,' instructed Marcus firmly. 'I've had concussion before and it'll just make your head hurt more. It probably thumps enough already.'

Sophie smiled weakly in agreement. 'That's true. So, what have you been up to?'

'Just rugby training. I missed the session yesterday as I was here, but had to pop in briefly today.' He grinned suddenly. 'I'll be starting for the Cup match this weekend, it's a massive opportunity to show what I can do. Hopefully you'll be feeling fit enough to pop along as we planned.'

Marcus was talking as if she would know what he was on about. As she searched her fuzzy memories, her head began to thump again in warning.

Tandy hurried back just in time with a cup of tablets and a glass of water. 'Here, it's time for these.'

Sophie murmured her thanks and swallowed the tablets as Marcus continued, 'I managed to contact your parents. They said they were glad to know you were OK ...' he trailed off, not seeming to know what to say.

'It's that obvious my parents aren't really interested in

6

me, isn't it?' She laughed harshly, ignoring the daggers of physical and mental pain it caused. 'They have their interests, and their erstwhile daughter isn't one of them.'

Surprise and sorrow flashed across his face, but before she could think more of it, Sophie suddenly felt rather sleepy with the medication kicking in. She yawned. 'Marcus, Tandy, I need ... sleep ...' Blackness descended fast and she drifted off.

When she came round, the setting sun was shining through the blinds on her window. No one else was in the room, so she had chance to think. The events leading up to her current predicament were blurred, but maybe she could start with remembering further back, perhaps to when she had moved to London? She dozed for a while, trying to sort through assorted memories. All was fine until autumn, soon after she had started following Harford Park RFC ...

Sophie tripped over the kerb and cursed under her breath as pain shot through her big toe. She swore again as she looked down at her tender foot. Typical. She'd hardly had the coat of nail varnish on five minutes and she'd already ruined the pedicure. The girls would think she was useless again.

This is how they wanted her to dress, but Sophie could not understand why. Her open-toed sandals were too high for her, the skirt she wore was too short, and her cleavage? Well, she'd not inherited her mother's biggest assets, that was for certain.

She looked like a child playing dress-up ... in hooker clothes.

Moving more carefully, she wobbled to the bus stop, shivering as her whitened breath hung in the air. Even in sky-high heels, she was barely past five feet tall, and her slight build made her look even smaller. She was used to people bumping into her, not seeing her. Everything else about her was average.

After taking her shopping, Andrea had frogmarched her to the hairdressers for her nondescript brown hair to be dyed black and cut heavily around her face in one of the latest fashions, which Andrea had insisted suited her. Sophie wasn't convinced, and was fed up of its straw-like texture. It was also a nightmare to style; the dye and constant straightening had dried it out even further, and she was sure the heavy, frizzy fringe wasn't a good look for her. Plus, it was already time to colour the roots.

The bus drew up as she reached the stop. At least one thing was going her way – any longer and she would freeze to death. The bus's route would take her straight to the nightclub where the girls were heading. She swiped her pass as she got on and the vehicle pulled away, seconds later crawling past the entrance to her house. Instead of going out, she wished that she could be curled up at home with one of the books she'd borrowed from the library several hours earlier – hours before she'd departed to shiver by the touchlines of the Harford Park pitch; hours before she'd gone home to change from too-tight jeans to scanty clubbing gear. She stifled a yawn while she found a safe-looking seat by an old lady, and tried to ignore the look of disgust directed at her skimpy outfit.

The bus trundled on its way, the seconds and minutes ticking away frighteningly fast. Andrea was going to kill her: she wasn't immaculate, and added to that, she was going to be late – even though it wasn't physically possible to travel home, change, and get to the club by bus in the time given. And taxis were too expensive while she was saving for her dream holiday.

Not for the first time, she wondered what her life would be like if she hadn't known Andrea from school, if she hadn't responded to a message on that social networking site. Probably a lot more peaceful.

She actually enjoyed the rugby games they went to, and

was trying to learn the rules. Or was it laws? None of the other girls had the slightest interest in the game; they just liked to watch the men in their skin-tight kit and discuss which of them had the best body, the best face, the best technique in bed. And bitch about everything else.

Sometimes, she gazed enviously at the sensibly clad supporters who gathered every week, laughing and joking together. Although the vast majority of the group were male, there were a few women, not much older than she was, who joined them. A few of them were in relationships with the players. Andrea had been very annoyed about this, particularly as one of them was rich as Croesus and the other was an ex-bedpartner of hers who she was convinced found her irresistible. Some days, Sophie's envy of the happier group became so bad she purposely blocked them from her mind and view.

Her phone beeped with a message and she cringed when she saw it was from Andrea.

Change of plan, we're at Jester's in Harford. Hurry up. A.

Great. Her bus was headed in completely the wrong direction.

An hour later, she was hidden behind the others in the crowded bar, watching the coats and drinks again, and wincing as, wobbling, she shifted her weight from one foot to another. Once she had defrosted, her feet had really started to hurt. Moving didn't make the shoes any less painful, so she bent down to rub one foot.

Just as she lifted a strap away from her reddened skin, she was barged slightly. 'Eek!' she squeaked, tottering and desperately trying not to fall on her face.

'Sorry.' An arm steadied her. 'I didn't see you down there!'

Sophie carefully stood upright, to meet a broad, shirt-covered chest wearing a Harford tie. One of the players.

'That's OK, it's my fault for wearing such stupid shoes,' she acknowledged wryly, daring to take a peek up at him through her long fringe.

'I wouldn't call them stupid, but being comfortable in what you're wearing is far more attractive. You look like you're in pain,' bluntly observed the blond player.

She vaguely recognised him in the dim light. *Something beginning with "M"? Marcus!* As she remembered, he smiled kindly at her to soften his remark, and carried on his way through the bustling crowd towards the bar.

Wow! He was lovely. Andrea would be spitting feathers if she saw them talking: she'd been after him for months. He was rather shy and very good at escaping.

A few minutes later, he passed by again with a tray of shots, smiled at her, and handed one over. 'Here, you look like you need it.'

Sophie took the glass, nervously muttering her thanks. As he disappeared, she took a sip. And coughed. 'Bloody hell!' The tipple caught the back of her throat, but the burn was strangely enjoyable. She downed the rest, stifling further coughs.

A few minutes later, the girls returned and without a word of thanks, grabbed their drinks and bags. Sophie muttered about going to the loo and escaped their inane, tipsy or bitchy chatter.

The cubicle was blissfully quiet compared to the bar, and Sophie took her time, pulling out her phone and checking the updates on a rugby forum she'd just joined. Her handle and avatar didn't identify her as female – she quite enjoyed the anonymity of asking questions about the rugby she'd watched and getting some knowledgeable replies along with a fair bit of banter. She giggled, the alcohol kicking in as she posted a couple of cheeky responses.

After she'd dawdled as much as she could, she left the cubicle and spuriously washed her hands before repairing her make-up. Thankfully, for once, it had mostly stayed in place. She couldn't say the same for her mop of blackened straw. The bright lights leached even more colour from her cheeks, making her look anaemic. She had no idea why Andrea had insisted on that hairstyle.

Bracing herself, she pulled open the door as two girls barrelled in, barging her slender frame to the side. More people who didn't notice her in real life. 'Excuse me,' she muttered.

Sighing with regret – a night with her newly-borrowed books would have been far more enjoyable – she started making her way back. The girls were still standing gossiping. They didn't even acknowledge her return, but within minutes had left her alone with the drinks again as they trooped off to the loos themselves.

'Still here?' Marcus was passing with yet another tray of shots. 'Here,' he handed her another small glass.

She smiled, ignoring her automatic reaction to refuse, and downed it in one, hiding the reflexive cough. She grinned with a flush of success.

He laughed at her and handed over another before continuing on his way.

Sophie downed that one too. Her bravery made her giggle; this was most unlike her. She began swaying to the music and humming. Her feet had miraculously stopped hurting.

She didn't even mind terribly when the girls returned and immediately left her again. In the shadows, she could happily sway around. The shots had given her just enough buzz to relax and enjoy the music and people-watching. Time flew until the girls reappeared, and she decided to wander off again, this time to have a look at the different levels of the bar. She'd never really had a chance or even felt like looking around before, but was curious about where Marcus had disappeared to, and wanted to buy him a drink.

On the top level, the group of Harford players were difficult to miss, their muscular frames towering over many of the club's other punters. She couldn't see Marcus, so she decided to pop to the bar first to buy a few shots for him. She even got a couple for herself. He still wasn't there when she carefully returned with a tray. Uncertain what to do, she nibbled her lip in frustration, standing on tiptoe to see if he was hidden, sitting on the low sofas.

'Hello there, sweetie.' A bold arm slid around her waist. 'Looking for anyone in particular?'

Sophie turned her head to look up at her accoster, one of the massive props. 'Ummm, Marcus? I'm looking for Marcus. He gave me a few drinks earlier, and I … I thought I'd return the favour,' she answered, hesitatingly.

This bemused her new friend, who raised his voice. 'Hey, lads, I've found the answer for the missing shots. Marcus has been charming this cute little sprite. Wait for it, she actually bought the next round!'

Sophie was dumbstruck. Before she knew it, the shots had all disappeared from her tray. 'Ummm,' she started.

'Wow. A girl getting the drinks in? Tidy. Are you single?' An absolute mountain of power towered over her.

Sophie shrank back and squeaked, 'Eep!'

'Awww, be gentle, she's shy. Yo, Alex? Look after the nymph until Marcus gets back.'

Before she knew it, she was perched on another player's lap, awkwardly trying to keep her dignity, and pulling her skirt down and top up. The air rang with wolf-whistling and raucous cheers, but luckily, the lap on which she balanced didn't belong to an octopus. Instead, he was quietly talking to the lad sat next to him and drinking a bottle of lager. She recognised him as the scrum-half, Alex, with whom Andrea had apparently slept the previous season. Andrea had planned to reel him in, while he hadn't been keen to repeat the experience.

A tall, iced glass of something clear was handed to her,

and she sipped at it cautiously, tasting only refreshing lemonade and a hint of something else. A couple of times she tried to stand, still looking for Marcus, but there was nowhere for her to go. Large, powerful bodies were packed tightly around her. Then she realised she didn't know what to say without the shots to give him, and sighed.

'You OK?' asked the owner of the lap.

'Yes, thanks … ummm, Alex,' she blushed, tugging again at her skirt. 'I can't see Marcus and I need to get back soon, the girls will wonder where I am.'

'If you insist.' He shrugged his shoulders and helped her up, parting the crowd and walking her down the steps to the main bar, his arm protectively around her shoulders to prevent further upset.

As they got closer, she saw Andrea and the rest of the girls gossiping. The tall blonde glanced her way and her eyes widened when she saw Sophie with Alex. Sophie inwardly cringed and dipped out from under his arm, expecting her to be furious. Instead, Andrea smiled and beckoned her over.

'Ooh, looks like Alex likes you,' she cooed. 'He couldn't take his eyes off you.'

Sophie tried to stammer something in response, failing to think of anything to say apart from 'Really?'

'Well, some lucky woman will catch him some day, so why not you? Fancy some Dutch courage?' Andrea whispered something to one of the other girls and within minutes, she was handed another tall glass.

Sophie coughed after one sip, 'I don't think –'

'C'mon, Sophie, be brave,' encouraged Andrea. 'Besides, it's not *that* strong.' She tipped the bottom up slightly so Sophie was forced to drink half of it.

Shortly afterwards, everything began to blur, and she didn't realise what was happening when the group started moving up towards the Harford crowd, in time to hear them finish singing a vaguely familiar tune.

'Now we've never met a nice South African,
And that's not blaadie surprising, mun.
'Cos they're a bunch of arrogant bastards,
Except Marcus 'cos he's actually Irish!'

They raucously cheered the last line instead of singing it.

Sophie giggled at the rugby boys' version and the way Marcus responded, looking resigned to the attention. The way he benignly cuffed the main perpetrators, he must have heard it more than once before.

She tried to catch his attention, but her height let her down again and his eyes were elsewhere, on a group at the other side of the bar.

She felt someone stop by her, and glanced up to see Alex again. 'That's an old one. I think it's from before I was born,' she commented.

'The best rugby songs are the older ones,' Alex observed, 'Plus they tend to be the saltiest.' He winced as the boys launched into another tune with lots of four-letter lyrics. 'Have you ever been to South Africa? I went there after uni. Things were still changing after apartheid.'

'No, but I'd love to go. I hear it's beautiful. I want to go on safari too, and see the elephants and hippos and rhinos and lions and those tigery things that aren't tigers.'

'Tigery? Leopards or cheetahs, you mean?'

Sophie wrinkled her brow. 'Ummm, it sounds terrible, but I'm not sure. Both, maybe?' She brightened up. 'I want to see the springboks too.'

'Animal or human?' he grinned at her.

'Both, again,' she giggled as she was handed another drink. She took a sip to refresh her mouth and this time didn't taste the alcohol.

'Why were you wanting to speak to Marcus?'

'I can't remember.' Sophie frowned and giggled again. Everything seemed to be getting more and more farcical.

14

'You OK?' asked Alex. 'Need some fresh air?'

It was so nice of him to ask. Andrea must be right about him liking her. She didn't disagree when he led her out to the dark night, ignoring the catcalls and whistles.

The next moments were a blur: her swaying into him, him lifting her onto a wall, lifting her chin and asking if she was OK, her deciding that he had a nice mouth and she'd quite like to kiss it. A wave of nausea and a now-familiar male voice groaning, 'It's my fault, I didn't realise she was such a lightweight. I'll take her home.' The same person holding her hair back as she retched up whatever she'd had to drink, and seeing her to bed before she passed out.

Chapter Two

Sophie's eyes shot open as she realised *Marcus* was the man who'd seen her home and tucked her up that night! She groaned in embarrassment: that next morning she'd woken wearing only underwear. How would she face him when he returned to the hospital?

'So, you are awake, Mrs Coetzee?' An elderly man in a white coat stood over her. 'I am Doctor Van Zyl. I need to run some tests to check your responses.'

Although he was clearly addressing her, she didn't recognise the name, 'Mrs ...?'

'Coetzee. I understand you are having some memory problems?'

'Some.' She rubbed her temple with her free hand. 'It's coming back to me slowly.'

'*Gut.* You are a very lucky woman. You are not the first foreigner to be knocked over by a minibus taxi; the last had a nastily broken femur and was here for weeks. Not a *gut* holiday, *né?*'

Sophie murmured her agreement as the doctor began examining her, commenting sporadically in medical terms to a nondescript white-coated man a few yards behind him.

'So, you were sick when you came around?'

'Yes,' confirmed Sophie, 'but I've been fine since, and I'm really hungry now.' The growl of her stomach confirmed her words.

'Excellent. We will arrange food, and if you continue to improve, in the morning we will take the cannula out. Tomorrow, we will discharge you.'

Having satisfied himself as to her condition, he wandered away, muttering something about lucky tourists. A few minutes later, food appeared and a ravenous Sophie tucked in. Shortly after, her eyes began fluttering shut again.

Several weeks after the disastrous night at Jester's, Sophie still flinched at the memory of waking up clad only in underwear, her meagre outfit neatly folded over the foot of the bed, shoes lined up underneath. Andrea had been uncommonly nice to her, and no one had laughed in her face. However, she had avoided many of the nights out afterwards, citing headaches, a poorly tummy, or non-existent family visits.

That week, she had received the general email directive Andrea sent before any home game, 'Time to up the pressure, short skirt time. It's warm enough.'

Sophie had cringed at this. Yes, the sun was shining, but there was a wintry chill to the air. Nevertheless, she'd missed going to the live matches so she followed orders. Her welcome was less than cordial: from the moment she arrived, Andrea started sniping at her. There were several other girls who had ignored the dictate and worn jeans, but despite Sophie acquiescing, Andrea still carped ... and continued to drink heavily.

Matters came to a head at the end of the match. Andrea cast daggers towards a happy group of supporters and a few players on the other side of the club. 'Look at them. That shouldn't have happened!' she railed drunkenly at a shaken Sophie. 'You're bloody useless. You're a mess, look at your roots! You never attract any men and you couldn't even seduce Alex. It was pure luck that his fiancée jumped to conclusions.'

Sophie blanched in horror. 'He's getting married? I didn't know that! You said he was single and liked me.'

'Stop playing the innocent, did you really think you had

a chance with him? It was a set-up; she was meant to see you with him! It nearly worked too! I could've earned a fortune.'

'A set-up?' The other girls were smirking at her, seemingly enjoying her dressing down.

'Look at them. How could you not notice them together before? Have I not taught you anything, you stupid, gullible fool?'

Sophie glanced over to the other side of the club, where the group stood. Alex, the man she vaguely remembered trying to kiss, was smiling beatifically down at the happy blonde in his arms. Even from that distance, she could see how close they were.

She couldn't take any more, so she grabbed her handbag and fled. She heard some of the girls cackling with laughter as she left, and Andrea's drunken ranting continued. Just as she reached the main doors, a group of players entered, blocking her escape. One of them was Marcus. He glanced her way, the smile turning into a scowl. He rolled his eyes at a friend. That hurt even more.

Instead of pushing past, she dived into the ladies' loo, just in time for the impending tears.

Yet more rejection. How much more could she take?

She locked herself in a cubicle and grabbed a handful of tissues to muffle the sobs. Her mind spinning in circles and not knowing what to do with herself, she eventually flipped the toilet lid down and collapsed on top of it, giving way to the wave of despair that had built up inside her. She cried for an age, stifling the sobs when she heard women enter, until the tears died down and she was left in a stupor.

Sophie sat on the closed lid, trying to gather her thoughts and stem the sniffles of self-pity welling up. Andrea's acidic comments echoed round her brain, etching themselves into her already-battered self-esteem. She felt like the fool she'd been called; there was no way she could ever show her face again with them laughing at her. And what damage had she caused to Alex's relationship?

With a sigh, she stood and flushed the loo to cover her lack of usage. She shivered and pulled her short skirt down as much as possible, although the lightweight clothing on her upper body meant she wasn't going to warm up any time soon. She slid the bolt back carefully with shaking fingers and peeked out, not wanting to meet anyone by the sinks. Fortunately, it was empty. With a sigh of relief, she washed her hands, lifted her hair away from her face, and started to repair the damage her tears had caused.

The door opened and a familiar-looking, pretty blonde entered. An expression of shock crossed her face, but she smiled politely at Sophie and went into a cubicle.

Sophie looked back at the mirror. No wonder she was shocked – in the bright light it looked like she was wearing a clown's mask. Well, swollen eyes coupled with light brown roots showing through her crow's hair and bright lipstick? She looked more like some horror writer's idea of a nightmare clown. Enough was enough. It was time to go home; she wasn't sticking around to be mocked.

She soaked a wad of tissues and began to wipe the painted mask off, scrubbing vigorously. Once down to bare skin, she smudged on some foundation to help cover the pink remnants of her crying, blusher for colour on her pallid cheeks, a touch of mascara, and lip gloss to look normal. The light veneer looked better on her, until it was mostly covered again by her mop of blackened straw. It was enough having to run whatever gauntlet there would be on her exit, without giving them extra ammunition.

Water ran and the blonde came out of the cubicle. Sophie's heart plummeted as she realised that the blonde washing her hands was Alex's fiancée.

'You look much better now you've got that mess off.'

Sophie jumped at the soft words. 'Th … thank you,' she stuttered. A breeze of cold air blew through the open window and she shivered. Her crow's nest of hair fell further forward over her face.

'Are you OK?' the woman asked with concern.

'I've just realised I've been a fool. And I'm so sorry.'

'For what?' The confusion was clear in her voice.

'For ...' It was time to come clean. 'I just found out it was all a set-up. I didn't do it on purpose. She told me he was single and liked me.'

The woman's brow creased in confusion. 'You'll have to rewind, I'm not with you.'

Sophie turned to fully face her fate. 'It was me who ... who you saw with Alex at Jester's. But we didn't do anything, he wouldn't even kiss me,' she added quickly. 'I was very drunk, hardly able to stand, and I didn't know he was engaged. And I've just found out it was a set-up. I'm so sorry.' She looked down at her feet and braced herself for a caustic response, unable to hide the tremors of combined shock and cold running through her slight body.

Moments passed. The woman had stopped drying her hands with the paper towels.

'I won't be coming here anymore,' gabbled Sophie. 'I've started to really enjoy the games, but now I've found out ... what I found out. I just wanted t-to apologise before I went.'

'I'm Clare. What's your name?' the woman asked softly.

Sophie lifted her head in bewilderment. 'S-Sophie,' she stammered. The sympathy on Clare's face made the brimming tears spill over. 'Oh God, I'm so embarrassed about it all and I'm so sorry. Please, I hope it didn't damage your m-marriage.' She swiped at her eyes with one hand.

'Here,' Clare passed her a tissue. 'Dry yourself up and we'll find a quiet room to ourselves.'

'A room?'

'Yes, you need to tell us everything you know.'

Sophie had never been in the memorabilia-covered function room before. In fact, she'd never been in any of the rooms at the back of the club. While Clare went to fetch a friend who wanted to hear Sophie's story, she wandered around, fascinated by all the rugby pictures on the walls. What amused her most was a line of photos from nearly a hundred years before, the dated outfits the players were wearing so different from modern times. She wrapped her jacket closer around her to ward off the chill from the cool room, and bent to examine a picture of a dashing young man posing with a dark leather ball.

'He was the founder of the club.' Clare re-entered the room carrying a bundle of cloth. A tall brunette holding three glasses followed her.

Sophie jumped, turned and blushed. 'Sorry, these are really fascinating.'

'Don't apologise, it's nice to see you're interested. This is Sarah.' She gestured towards the brunette. 'And this is a warm coat. You're making me feel cold in that outfit.'

Clare handed over the long, black garment and Sophie shrugged it on, almost sighing in delight as the woollen fabric immediately started to warm her body. It swamped her, but she could huddle into its capacious folds. 'Thank you.'

'And this is a decent drink. I'm assuming a tot of whiskey wouldn't go amiss?'

Sophie blushed and nodded, taking a tumbler and a large swig. She began coughing at the burn in her throat, ''Scuse me, I'm not used to drinking.'

'We'll soon cure you of that,' joshed Sarah. 'If it wasn't for summer, we two would be a pair of lushes by now.' She pulled some chairs around the table and they all sat down. 'So, tell us about yourself.'

Sophie gazed at the two women, not sure why these

22

strangers were so interested in her, and expecting to see mockery. Instead, she saw genuine interest. She began haltingly. 'I'm twenty-four, I'm from the south coast. I inherited a house from an aunt a few months ago, so I decided to move here as I have no ties elsewhere.' She shrugged, hiding long-suffered hurt. 'I've been doing some temping in an office in the City. That's when I met up with Andrea again.

'Andrea?' asked Sarah.

'She's the tall blonde with the deep tan and loads of make-up. Really long nails. The Queen Bee. We went to school together, she heard that I'd moved to London, and messaged me. I don't know why she contacted me, we were never friends in school,' Sophie shrugged, 'but at first it was nice to know somebody here who I could meet up with.' She had been awfully lonely in the house by herself every evening and every weekend, despite her piles of books.

Clare nodded in understanding. 'I know what it's like to move to the city without knowing anyone. What happened then?'

'We met for drinks, she asked me loads of questions. I got terribly drunk and confessed I liked sportsmen. Well, she said I did but I … my parents never let me drink and I could've said anything that night. Next, she invited me to a game. I turned up in comfortable clothes and she laid into me, said if I wanted any friends I would have to dress like them.'

'And you did?'

'I did. She insisted on going shopping. I mean, I thought about not going back, but she kept messaging me and I didn't know how to make friends elsewhere.' She cringed at how pathetic it must have sounded. 'It was easier just to go along. We have – *had* – some fun nights out. Yes, I'd end up looking after the coats and bags and drinks, but it meant I was out instead of sitting at home, alone.' Sophie shrugged, 'It just carried on like that and though I was cold watching the games, I started enjoying them.'

'So, what happened that night?' Clare prodded.

Sophie related what she could recall of that night, faltering in detail after they had gone outside. 'I can't remember much more than that, although I remember puking into a bush. Someone helped me get home, I don't know who. All I remember is a male voice and someone holding my hair back.'

'He didn't take advantage of you?'

Sophie flushed. 'I woke up in my underwear. He was a real gentleman, whoever he was. I think he had some kind of accent.'

'A mystery knight in shining armour?' mused Sarah. 'It must have been someone from the club who recognised you.'

'I don't know; it's all a blur. The next week, Andrea was really pleased, but after that it went back to normal until today. She was in a foul mood when I arrived and after full-time she started drinking. She said I was useless, a laughing stock, and a f-fool.' Sophie ended on a sob and began crying, hiding her face behind her hair.

Clare wrapped her arm around her, hugging her. 'You're not at all. You're a much nicer person than she is.'

Sarah leant forward, patted her hand and handed her some tissues. 'Forget Andrea's personal comments, we've established she's a bitch. You mentioned it was a set-up. What made you think that?'

'She told me it was my fault she wasn't getting the money. I suspect she was getting paid to engender a split between you and Alex. I'm so sorry if I caused problems.' She placed her head in her hands and Clare hugged her again.

Sarah spoke directly to Clare, 'Are you thinking what I'm thinking? Or more precisely, who?'

'Monica?'

'Bingo.'

Sophie lifted her head. 'That's the name Andrea said; Monica was pissed off it hadn't worked and she wouldn't get her share. Who is she?'

Clare rolled her eyes, 'She's my father-in-law's soon-to-be ex-wife, and my soon-to-be hubby's evil stepmother. She's after family money, but she's not getting any of it.'

'Good,' asserted Sophie with a sniff. 'If that's how she operates, she sounds like a diabolical woman who doesn't deserve anything.'

'And you sound like a woman after my own heart – if I wasn't straight and totally in love with my husband,' laughed Sarah. 'Do you mind if Clare and I have a quick chat?'

'Not at all, I'll just … try to stop crying,' she hiccupped.

Clare gave her another hug before getting up and following Sarah out of the room. Sophie stared at her hands and tried pulling herself together. She couldn't believe the women were so forgiving that they had actually comforted her. Her. Sophie. She couldn't remember the last time someone had hugged her, apart from Aunt Agatha who had left her the house. How she missed her.

She dabbed at her face and took some deep breaths, closing her eyes and clearing her head. Minutes later, she opened them to find Sarah and Clare patiently waiting for her to pull herself together.

Sarah smiled sympathetically at her. 'You OK?'

Sophie nodded. 'Sorry about all that.'

'Sophie, are you free next Saturday?' asked Clare

'I'm free all Saturdays from now on, I … I don't know anyone else in London.'

'Well, you can come with us on an away trip. You'll get to know some of the regulars. It'll be fun.'

'Away trips are great,' confirmed Sarah. 'They're

25

better than home games when there's a good group of you. For now, I'll take you out the back way and get one of the boys to drive you home. We don't want Andrea to find out we're on to her.'

'Oh, OK.' She was bewildered that they hadn't blamed her or called her a fool.

Clare frowned. 'One last thing, though.'

Sophie held her breath, waiting for the axe to fall. She knew it was too good to be true. What were they going to ask of her?

'Wear some bloody warm clothes for once: lots of layers, a hat, scarf and gloves. The whole shebang.'

Sophie smiled in relief. 'No problem.'

A few minutes later, after exchanging phone numbers, she was shepherded out to find Marcus Coetzee waiting in his car. He was tapping the steering wheel impatiently and she muttered her apologies to him along with her address. 'It's just off the high street,' she finished.

'I know where your road is,' he said, and zoomed off.

Sophie huddled in the passenger seat as he deftly drove her home. Several times, she opened her mouth and took a breath to say something innocuous, to ask why he'd scowled at her earlier, but on glancing at Marcus' stony features, she opted to keep her mouth shut.

Despite his mood, she felt safe with him as he was concentrating fully on driving.

Eventually, she felt she had to break the awkward silence. 'You're South African, aren't you?' she blurted. 'You don't have much of an accent.'

'I've lived over here for years and my mother was Irish. I'm told the accent comes and goes.'

They exchanged no more words while the vehicle was in motion. She just watched him surreptitiously. He was really attractive, even the scowl didn't disguise that. The short, blond hair was just a little spiky and looked softly tempting to touch. She couldn't see the colour of his eyes, and the beams from passing streetlights only highlighted the prominent Germanic cheekbones leading to a strong nose and well-shaped mouth. He had only the faintest shadow of stubble, he must have shaved not so long ago. His muscular forearms swung the vehicle effortlessly around the corners, wide shirt-covered shoulders tapered to a narrow waist, and his broad thighs were undisguised by the relaxed jeans.

As she watched him, something started to coil lower in her tummy, some kind of anticipation. What was it about him?

While she was thinking, the car drew up outside her house and she tore her eyes away before fumbling with the door handle.

'Stay,' he commanded, getting out of the car and jogging around to her side to pull the door open.

She was unused to such gentlemanly behaviour, belatedly remembering to keep her legs together as she clambered out of the car. 'Thank you.'

He walked her up the path to the front door and waited until she had taken her keys out. 'Nice house,' he commented gruffly, looking over the Edwardian exterior.

'It was my aunt's. She left it to me last year. We were quite close – she never had children. I miss her a lot.'

'I'm sorry for your loss,' he hummed automatically.

She nodded in response. As he turned to leave, she blurted, 'I'm sorry for anything I did that night. I was drunk, I can't really remember it.'

Marcus turned back to her and exhaled heavily. 'It was my fault for getting you drunk.'

Sophie shook her head decisively. Despite her natural reticence, straight-talking was becoming addictive. 'No, it wasn't. I felt great after those shots, I had a nice buzz. It was the drinks Andrea gave me, they did the damage. I don't know what was in them, I didn't recognise the taste.

I'm not good with alcohol. Stupid of me, I know.' She shrugged and hung her head, waiting and biting her lip nervously. He didn't respond, so she awkwardly turned back to the door, opened it, and flicked the porch light on.

She glanced over her shoulder. He was still standing there. What colour were his eyes? Blue. His eyes were definitely blue. 'Would you like to come in?'

'No, I should be getting back to the club.'

'Oh.' She covered her pang of disappointment by looking down and realised she was still wearing the borrowed coat. She quickly unbuttoned it, shrugging it off. Her jacket came too, leaving her clad only in a light, revealing top and short skirt. The corners of his mouth twitched up.

She handed the coat over, 'If you're going back to the club, please could you give this to Clare with my thanks?'

His softening expression hardened again, 'That's one hell of an outfit, and your hair looks like shit. You look like a cheap hooker.'

She recoiled in shock at his blunt comments. 'I'm sorry. I won't dress like this again.' The tears threatened to return.

He looked contrite. 'I'm sorry. It's nothing you've done, it's something else and I'm taking it out on the wrong person.' One tear welled up and he started to panic at the sight. 'I really didn't mean it! You look nice apart from baring too much skin, and the shoddy clothes are a bit tarty. Well, the hair … that's still dreadful.'

She unexpectedly hiccupped with laughter and he laughed too, relieving the tension.

'I'm going back to my natural colour, or as near as possible,' she declared, wiping the stray tear away with the back of her hand.

'Good.'

They stood awkwardly, her on the higher doorstep, him holding the coat.

'Well, thanks again.' She felt like she needed to make some kind of gesture, lifting a hand up.

He must have thought she was going to give him a farewell cheek kiss and moved towards her. They collided, and as she lost her footing on the step, his arms caught and wrapped around her in an awkward hug.

He was so warm and his body felt great, pressed against hers. He felt safe. She had to stop herself from extending the contact. More than one hug in a day, wasn't she lucky?

She lifted her head, intending to disengage and step back. Instead, she took a deep breath. Ooh, he smelled exceptionally nice too. Kind of tangy but male at the same time. What was that? She began snuffling at his collar, her lips inadvertently brushing against his neck.

'What on earth are you doing?' he asked bemusedly.

'You smell really good. Like, really, really good. What is it?'

Marcus laughed and she felt the vibrations run through her like a shock. That coil residing below her tummy tightened.

'I've no idea, I borrowed someone's aftershave today. I'll have to find out.'

'Please do, it's really good on you.' With difficulty, she lifted her head up, away from the tempting scents. 'Thank you for the unintentional hug. I'm so clumsy but I do love hugs.'

She intended on bussing his cheek with thanks but somehow, her mouth landed on his. He hissed at the contact, tried to talk, but his lips were too close to hers and instead, they kissed. Slowly, luxuriously. Their lips parted, their heads angled for the best contact.

Oh, he tastes as good as he smells, thought Sophie vaguely as her arms squeezed him tighter, her hands running over his shoulders and his back.

She wanted more contact with him, and leant into him even more, trying to mash her body into his. That peculiar feeling was growing within her, a swelling and a melting at the same time. She wriggled closer, continuing the kiss, her clutching hands ensuring he didn't escape.

He groaned, his arms moving leisurely down her body, suspending her with feet off the ground. Her legs parted, wrapping around him, as he hoisted her further. Her skirt rose up and his warm hands cupped her almost-bare cheeks. The feeling of him holding her there sent shockwaves through her body and made her want more. His fingertips were so close to where she wanted something – some solidity, heat, contact. Her pelvis rotated, looking eagerly for that something. A growing hardness pressed into her mound, the rough jeans rubbing against her skimpy silk pants, and the fever flared higher.

She hazily felt herself being carried inside and lowered onto smooth, cool wood. She refused to unlock her legs from around him, instead pulling him closer and slipping her hands under his shirt, running her hands up his torso to draw it off. She helped him haul her top over her head, and they continued to kiss as he undid her bra, murmuring in pleasure and encouragement as his hands cupped and firmly squeezed her small breasts.

His mouth left hers, travelled down her sensitive neck to her chest, and licked then sucked a begging nipple. She couldn't restrain a cry of anguish at his slow suckle; it just felt too good.

Her skirt was nothing more than a belt around her waist, her knickers covering very little, and despite the attention to her breasts, she was missing that delicious pressure lower down. The want was building within her, the ache intensifying despite their leisurely pace. She tried to grab at him. 'Up. Up,' she mumbled.

She succeeded in pulling him back to her level, and she grasped the prominent bulge, massaging it firmly as one of his hands danced along the seam of her underwear.

A finger stroked her lightly and she gasped into his

mouth. He flicked at her, and it felt like a pleasurable electric shock. She wriggled her hips closer and mewled into his mouth. She clutched at his clothes and tried to find the zip holding him prisoner from her.

Her fingers located and grasped the small metal tab, tugging it down. The metallic rasp resounded over their panting and brought Marcus to his senses just as her fingers delved in. He leapt back, leaving her fingers grasping thin air. 'Good fucking God, girl, you're not safe to be let out!'

For several moments, she didn't realise what had happened, missing the contact, but spellbound by the treat of his toned chest, lit by beams from the porch light.

Seconds later, realisation and embarrassment washed over her for the umpteenth time that day – she was sitting on the dresser in the hall, practically naked. 'Oops,' was the best she could think of, followed by, 'I don't know what happened there. Sorry.'

She crossed her arms across her chest, covering her breasts, damp, erect nipples rubbing against her arms. She shivered at a shot of pleasure.

'Sorry? I …' He snatched his shirt off the floor, also picking up the coat he had dropped. 'I'll … um, see you around.'

The front door slammed behind him. Sophie heard the bark of an engine being maltreated and the car noise quickly faded, leaving her cold and coming to her senses.

Chapter Three

'Morning, sleeping beauty!' A cheerful Tandy was bustling around Sophie's bed, drawing the curtains open. 'Here, some lighter painkillers for you. We will take the drip out now you're awake.' She efficiently removed the needle from Sophie's hand, freeing it up.

Sophie swallowed the tablets as directed, not strong enough to argue. The night had passed uneventfully; she'd slept on and off, woken by nurses to check her vital signs. Her head pain was quickly ebbing, although the jumbled memories still hadn't sorted themselves out.

'If the doctors think it's OK, you'll be discharged later today for Marcus to take you home. Lucky you. And lucky me – I'm coming with you for a couple of days.' Tandy grinned in excitement. 'I don't get out of the city much, and his family, your in-laws, have a beautiful vineyard.'

Sophie smiled and agreed, as if she knew what Tandy was talking about.

A few weeks after her chat and mini-breakdown in front of Clare and Sarah, Sophie finally felt like she had found a place she belonged. Before the away game, she had texted Sarah, asking for a hairdresser recommendation to strip the awful black out. Sarah had replied and arranged to meet her and hold her hand. The hairdresser had taken one look at Sophie's dead hair with its split ends, proclaimed it was a lost cause, felt her skull, and proposed to cut it all off. Sophie had been left with a few guiding pictures to make her mind up, and she had gone for it. Now she had a pixie haircut, which many had told her made her brown eyes pop and flattered her face.

This time, the mirror told her the same thing. At last, she felt a little more confident.

Sarah had helped her find thermal underwear to survive some of the colder games, and she had asked the stylish woman for everyday clothes help. Sarah and Clare came round to her house one evening, and with the help of a couple of bottles of wine, showed her how to make the most of her existing wardrobe and shop for a few more basic items. They hadn't spent too much money, but all the pieces they bought were good quality and suited her petite build.

Her head lifted high as people started telling her how great she looked.

Every weekend, Sophie skipped along to the match, whether home or away. She got to know many of the other supporters, including some more of the women: high-flying Lindsay who was similarly petite, but had the authoritative presence of a six-foot Amazon, and curvy Sian who went out with Rob, one of the Harford props. She'd had a few drinks with some of the women's team and was even thinking about trying to play. She needed to get stronger first though; she felt far too slight and unfit for such a physical game. Plus, if she attempted to consume the vast quantities of alcohol they regularly downed, she would soon be taking a trip to the nearest A&E.

Another positive was that Andrea had disappeared. Sarah had hinted that her husband, Tom, had spoken with the club bigwigs and they had made it clear she wasn't welcome on the premises. Some of the other girls still came along, and another named Kelli had taken over the mantle of Queen Bee. Or "Queen of Bitches", as Clare drolly tagged them. Not that anyone paid them much attention, anyway.

The only fly in the ointment was Marcus. He was off

the injury list, playing again, and playing well at that. He had lovely hands, which in his centre position were vital – they could straighten a line and offload long, accurate passes into the wingers' hands. She loved watching him play; he was so graceful.

However, in the club afterwards, he acted like she wasn't even there, never acknowledging their awkward clinch. He had absentmindedly smiled at her a couple of times but essentially treated her like a stranger. They hadn't spoken again. Another blow to her feelings.

Unfortunately, matters were much worse elsewhere.

Sophie sat at her desk and cringed as her manager yelled at her for something else going wrong which she hadn't even had a hand in.

'Why the hell didn't you pick that error up?'

Because three people with more extensive qualifications had already reviewed it? You told me to email it to you as soon as it came in.

'You made me look like a fool!'

You did that yourself by not checking the work before presenting it as your own.

'You'll have to stay late to complete this project. It's overdue.'

As you've been sitting on it for the last fortnight.

'I don't know why we even employ you!'

Your last five slaves walked out. I'm the only one who'll take your shit and not go running to HR.

Her manager strode away, muttering about incompetence, and Sophie exhaled. She only had a few weeks left on her contract and needed a decent reference, otherwise she would have quit already.

With relief, she saw that an email had arrived from Clare. The weekend rugby matches had become the only time she was treated like a human being with feelings.

Hi Soph, I'm glad you can make it to the re-wedding. If

35

you're not bringing a plus one, would you mind being paired with one of the single men for the wedding breakfast? Cx

Hi Clare, As long as he keeps his hands to himself, it's fine with me. Soph x

Hah! I got together with Alex at Sarah's wedding to Tom; you'll never meet anyone with that attitude ;) Cx

Yep, I'm a hopeless case. Off down Battersea tonight for this Crazy Cat Lady Starter Kit. See you tomorrow. Soph x

Sophie chuckled as she attached a picture of a box of kittens to the message, and quickly closed her computer down. She'd had enough. She didn't get paid overtime and it was a Friday and well past time to go home. Everyone else had left apart from Sophie and her manager, and she'd stayed late every evening that week.

She heard the lift coming, grabbed her backpack, and ran to catch it. The doors opened and her heart sank – there were already three large, florid, suited men in there, looking the worse for wear. They must have been drinking with clients.

One of them sneered at her, 'It's a pixie. Do we have room for a small one, boys?' They moved around to make space. It would be a tight fit.

'Don't worry, I'll wai –' Sophie heard the heavy tread of her manager returning, and dived into the lift, pressing the down button and exhaling in relief as the door swooshed closed. Inside, the fumes of alcohol, stale cigar smoke, and aftershave were almost overwhelming. She breathed cautiously through her mouth and hoped the lift would pick up speed.

'Change your mind, or are you avoiding someone?'

sniggered one of the three.

Sophie gave him a brief, tight-lipped smile and fixed her gaze on the floor. *C'mon, lift.*

'Discretion, I like that. Wanna go for a discreet drink?' The youngest looking one placed his hands on the wall either side of her, caging her in.

She shrank into herself with her backpack clutched to her chest, refusing to look up, and was relieved to hear the ding of the lift opening. She ducked out from under her propositioner's arms and scurried out of the building, to the echoes of drunken laughter.

Why did she let so many people intimidate her? The only time she was assertive was when she was on her bike, commuting to and from work, and that was only because if she didn't take the lane when needed, she would be squashed flat by impatient drivers.

She couldn't wait to get home, and she couldn't wait for the next day – a home game at Harford. Despite Marcus' form, they had suffered some unexpected losses recently against the top sides and it was a relief to be playing lower-league opposition for once. Not a guaranteed win, but a better chance.

It was grim on the pitch. Much worse than expected. Harford Park just couldn't open up the visiting team's defence, they were getting knocked back in contact and their heads were going down.

'Tom's despairing. They just can't catch a break,' Sarah sighed as the forwards began to congregate at a lineout.

'So's Rob. He's working his arse off out there,' added Sian. 'All the scrum dominance coming to naught every time.'

'When they do that backrow move with Alex coming in at an angle, the defence are going to smash him. They're already lining up for it now.' Sophie shook her head and cringed into her pint of stout.

Seconds later, the crowd gasped as Alex was pulverised into the ground. It went quiet around her.

'How did you know he was going to do that?' asked Sarah cautiously. 'It's a new move, they've only tried it a couple of times.'

For one moment, Sophie panicked as she saw everyone staring at her. Her nascent confidence vanished and she wanted to disappear on the spot, retract into her clothes like a turtle into its shell.

Then she realised they weren't nasty stares – people actually looked curious. She chewed on her lip for a moment. 'I thought it was obvious: the number eight always clasps his hands together before a move he's involved in, and the openside cricks his neck and glances at the player he's passing to, in that case, poor Alex.'

There was copious swearing around her. 'No wonder the defence has been predicting so many of our attacks recently,' groaned Sian.

'I thought you knew?'

Most around her shook their heads.

'And the lineouts?'

More negative shakes.

'We used to stand behind the posts. Andrea insisted it was always a good position for watching their arses. I noticed they were doing these weird things all the time. The worst offender is Gavin, who –'

A hand was clamped over her mouth. 'Shush,' ordered Sarah. 'We don't want anyone to overhear. You need to speak with the coaches. If these habits have been spotted by the other teams, it would help explain some of the recent defeats.'

'How would they know?'

'They send people to watch, sometimes get copies of entire matches.'

'Oh, I had no idea. I don't know how that side of things

works.'

The whistle blew for a penalty, and Sarah latched on to Sophie's wrist, coaxing her towards the Harford coaches sitting in the stand. 'C'mon, I'll take you to Tom, you need to tell him what you know. Please,' she added. She waved at her husband, who noticed her signals straight away.

Sophie was impressed. Even in the middle of a match when the coaches didn't need to be distracted, Sarah had captured Tom's attention immediately. She felt twinges of self-doubt – what if she was wasting their precious time? 'Do we have to tell him now?' she whispered.

'They need to know. The match is at risk. Harford haven't been able to replace the former performance analysis guy, that's probably why this was missed.'

They reached the row and Sarah bent down to murmur into Tom's ear. He first blinked at Sarah, mouthing a swear word, then gestured at Sophie to take a seat beside him.

'Would you mind sitting up here with us?' asked Tom quietly. 'I'll give you a teamsheet on a clipboard and you can briefly note down all the major tells you can recall.'

Sophie blushed. 'Do you … um, want the opposition stuff as well? I'm not as certain, but I've noticed a couple of things.'

His eyebrows raised, 'Yes, please.' He thanked and kissed his wife, who patted Sophie's arm reassuringly and headed back down the stairs to the rest of the supporters.

Within five minutes, Sophie had covered the teamsheet with scribbles and a few of the Harford setup were hanging over her shoulders, making their own notes. Tom was consulting with the head coach, Chris, about half-time changes; they were debating whether to take some of the worst offenders off.

At half time they all stood up, and Sophie chewed her lip, not knowing what to do.

'Come with us,' instructed Tom. 'We're going into the

changing room to sort some of this out.'

She followed, wanting to clutch the clipboard to her chest as security, but a couple of the coaching squad were still reading her writing. They entered by an unfamiliar route, under the stands and down a corridor with grubby, white breeze-block walls darkened and scarred with dirt. The rubber matting on the tiled floor was scattered with clumps of mud and discarded pieces of tape. She followed Tom and the others, feeling completely lost and out of place as they pushed open a red door marked "Home".

Sophie had never seen anything like it. The room was full to bursting with male bodies, some partially undressed. There was an almost overpowering smell of embrocation, and a cacophony of men swearing and kicking inanimate objects in frustration. She hid behind Tom, peeking out every now and again for a glimpse.

So much muscular male flesh! Her heart was doing a tango in her ribs, and something else was beating lower down. Men! Fit, sweaty and half-naked men. Her eyes must have been on stalks. She had to tear them away.

One massive bloke started stripping completely. He was down to his underwear and had his thumbs pulling the black, tight-fitting shorts down when she decided that was too much for her. She started to edge towards the door, only to see a shirtless Marcus walking in, fussing with some strapping on his shoulder. She gaped at him. His chest was as great as she remembered. Mmmm, she thought, it would be nice to touch it again.

'What's she doing here?' grumped Marcus to Tom.

'She's helping us with some tactics.'

'But there's no way she knows anything more than the square root of fuck all.'

'She's already been more use than the last analyst. Right, boys, we're going to make some changes. Starting with Gavin: if you have to wipe your hands on your shorts at every lineout when it's your ball, can you do a few decoy-wipes too, please?'

Redhead Gavin groaned and sank his blushing face in his hands as a few of the boys started lampooning him. That was one of the worst habits Sophie had noticed, and meant the opposition knew exactly who the ball was going to most of the time, therefore where to compete and how to defend.

Tom raised his voice. 'No one, I repeat no one, takes the piss, as very few of you are innocent. We'll work on this next week. For now, we're just going to sort out the most important. We can beat this side easily if you get your fucking heads in gear!'

'Sophie, any way you could take a couple of days off work to go through the tapes with me and a couple of others? We've only had time to touch the surface today.'

'Ummm, my line manager ...' The fear showed in her eyes, and in the involuntary cringe.

Tom frowned with concern. He knew from his wife that Sophie struggled to assert herself, and how much pleasure Sarah was taking in helping the diminutive and shy young woman come out of her shell. He had been blown away by her keen observational and analytical skills, despite her lack of in-depth rugby knowledge or sports qualification.

After Nathan left, as a temporary measure, they had contracted a consultant to produce match analyses, but Tom and Chris had been increasingly unhappy at the lack of finer detail they were receiving. So, they had started doing it themselves, with the help of a couple of players who were keen on learning new skills, all the while looking for someone more permanent.

By employing her, he'd kill two birds with one stone by making his wife happy and hopefully halting Harford Park's recent run of poor results. It was highly unusual to pull someone in from outside the sport, but Tom rarely did things by the board. Many of the details Sophie had picked

41

up on were completely new to them; her fresh eyes could be invaluable. They had eventually battled a win on the pitch, but Tom knew his players were capable of so much more, so he'd arranged to have a word with her in his office.

That much fear wasn't normal in response to such an innocuous question. 'What's your job?' he asked gently.

'I'm a data analyst temping at a stockbroking firm in the City. It's only a short contract, but it comes to an end soon and I need a good reference to get more work. I'm saving up and I can't afford to upset anyone. I'd love to help Harford Park, though, after all you've done for me.' She worried at her lip, a habit he'd noticed she had when she was unsure of herself.

Tom smiled. He still had contacts in the City and could pull more than a few strings. 'Don't worry, I'll sort it out. I'll give you a job and references myself if it comes to that.'

There was a knock on the door, and Marcus popped his head in. 'You wanted me?'

'Yep. I need you to show Sophie here how the match analysis equipment works, and go through today's tapes. You also owe her an apology. It was mostly down to her that we managed to turn it around today.'

'Sophie? That's you, the girl Alex ...? I didn't realise ...' he trailed off, staring intently at her. 'Your hair?'

She avoided his eyes. 'It was too damaged to strip the colour out. I had to chop it off.'

'It suits you. You look different now I can see your face and you're even shorter than I remember when we ...'

Tom watched in amusement as they both blushed. Interesting.

Marcus stumbled on. 'I just thought you were a girlfriend or a sister of one of the players who'd sneaked in, that happens every now and again. I'm sorry.'

'No problem,' she acknowledged diffidently.

'Great, now that you've kissed and made up, as it were, go show Sophie how to do her stuff.' Tom ushered them away.

He closed the door and grinned fiendishly. He wouldn't normally have allowed anyone outside of the coaching setup anywhere near the changing room, but he wanted to check how Sophie reacted. He trusted Sarah's judgement, yet still needed to see for himself if she was as green as his wife had said. It had been pretty amusing to watch her try to hide behind him, wide-eyed and blushing and unable to look at anyone.

What was unexpected was the awkward frisson between her and Marcus, and he couldn't wait to tell Sarah about that development. She would be happy, and a happy Sarah made for a happy and contented Tom. He started hardening at the thought of his reward.

Sophie was relieved that skyscraper heels at rugby were now a thing of the past. She was shorter and had little hair to hide behind, but that didn't seem to matter to the friendly supporters. She hadn't realised she was virtually unrecognisable, or unmemorable. Ouch. That stung.

She had thought about the intimate clinch in the entrance to her house, had dreamt it had gone further, had woken up slick between her legs. If she was working with him, she would have to clamp down on those feelings and ignore the buzz in her body whenever he was around.

She followed Marcus to another office door. He brought out his keys and unlocked it, flipping the lights on so she could see the several screens with pieces of computer hardware strewn around.

'This was Nathan's office, the performance analyst here until a couple of months ago.' He pressed some buttons and lights flashed, booting up the machines. 'He insisted he needed all of this expensive equipment, then handed in his notice shortly after. Tried to take it with him, but Tom wasn't having any of it.' Marcus laughed dryly, 'Nathan's now at another club in our league, and I'm pretty sure he's given away all our secrets to the opposition. We've had to completely change all our calls, tactics, everything.'

'That seems really … dishonourable.'

'Yeah, all the boys are pissed off and we've already lost to his new team this season. Badly. We'll play them again in a month, so in the meantime we need to improve.' Marcus entered a password, then pulled over two chairs. 'For a basic analysis, the match is uploaded then tagged or coded and a stats sheet created with a highlights reel. Something like "lineouts completed versus lineouts lost". The basic stats are rather dry as they don't account for individual circumstances, just a rough guide.'

'Like someone dropping a ball due to a bad pass? Or being turned over in a tackle and losing the ball, or getting penalised for not releasing because there was no support?'

He smiled, visibly impressed. 'Yeah, along those lines. Although sometimes players get turned over as they run away from support, or the support is too slow, or the wrong player's there, so there may be a myriad of causes.'

Sophie was relieved she'd manage to blag that; all the posting and reading on rugby forums had been time well spent. 'OK, show me how it's done.'

Marcus went through the basic functions he'd learnt, but within half an hour she knew more than him. 'You're so fast at this!' He watched in awe as her fingers flicked the keyboard at lightning speed.

Sophie hummed distractedly as she continued isolating clips for the coaching team to review. 'I've used similar software before; it's easy once you know how.' She sat back in the chair and pensively tapped her fingers on her lips. 'You can leave me at it if you want to go join your mates.'

44

'I'll go for a drink. Want anything?'

She glanced over to see his eyes were on the plump lips she was drumming. Her body thrilled briefly, until she decided to ignore it. They were to be work colleagues, after all.

'Just a juice and soda or something, thanks,' she smiled. Her attention returned to the screens.

A short time later, she was repeatedly and frustratedly rewinding and playing the same clip. She couldn't figure out what they were trying to do. She muttered under her breath and frowned at the screen, leaning closer. 'What was that about?'

A voice over her shoulder intruded. 'Backs move.'

She shot upright and clutched her chest. 'Bloody hell, Marcus, you scared the life out of me!'

He sat back down next to her. 'Sorry. I'll knock next time. I was supposed to be running on to the ball at an angle, but I fucked up when I was caught at the last breakdown. No one spotted it until it was too late. It's actually a basic, schoolboy move.' He had a pint of beer in one hand and a pint of something crimson in the other.

'Well, I don't know many moves, schoolboy or otherwise.'

'Tom's going to put you on a rugby coaching course.'

That was news to her. 'Really?'

'I've just been speaking to him. If you can make it, there's a foundation session tomorrow morning in the very basics, which I'm helping deliver. Afterwards, we'll watch the women play and I'll point a few things out. There's an RFU Level One coaching course over a few days next week. You can pick up some of the techniques in no time. If that goes well, in a couple of months, you can attend the next level up.'

'But ...'

'Don't worry about work, he has that in hand already. He says you needn't return to that firm: he's spoken to a

45

friend there and the club will take over paying your salary as of Monday. If that's what you want, of course. Tom doesn't want to force you into anything, it's your decision. He made that clear.'

'Ummm …'

'There's also work you could do for Tom's company in the City. They're always in need of good data analysts. Either full-time or, once you're trained up here, you could work part-time at both. What do you think?'

'I-I don't know what to say.' Relief that she didn't have to return to see that manager again was rushing through her and she felt almost lightheaded. However, it was a big step and it felt slightly out of her control. She chewed her lip in contemplation.

His eyes went to her lush mouth and heated for a moment. He looked away and gulped down a mouthful of beer, then stared at the crimson pint in his other hand. 'Sorry, this is for you. Cranberry and soda OK?'

'Fine, thanks.' What was that look about? She took the glass. 'Back to this course next week, who's doing it?'

'Some of the boys, that's why it's spread over a few days to fit between training sessions, and a few of the women who could take time off.'

'I've never played rugby.'

'You don't have to have played, although it helps. You've been watching for several months, so you'll be surprised how much you already know. I'm coaching the women Monday night. Come along and you'll pick up some practical experience.'

Chapter Four

Sophie giggled at her reflection in the changing room's age-spotted mirror. The borrowed cotton twill rugby shorts were so big they could have fitted a prop, but there was nothing smaller in the bin of odds and ends. Thankfully, she had a pair of cycling shorts underneath, and someone had found a pair of kids' boots for her. The jersey on top was massive too, the neckline almost hanging off her, and she was wearing one of her base layers underneath with a sports bra flattening her chest down. With her short hair, she looked like a young boy playing dress-up.

'Ready?' Mel, the captain of the women's team, had helped her get ready and was quelling a smile.

Sophie straightened her face and nodded. 'Yep, but I've no idea what I'm doing.'

'No worries, Marcus said you were just here to learn the basics. He does shout at us sometimes, he can be quite fearsome, but he's always patient with the newbies.'

Except me it seems, she concluded a couple of hours later. On running out, when someone had chucked her a rugby ball, she'd remembered why, apart from cycling to commute and keep fit, she didn't do sports. Bad coordination. Dismal coordination. Pathetic coordination.

She felt like a clown. She had already been stifling giggles at her outfit, and they broke loose when it became apparent how disastrous she was. All the girls were laughing too, but in the nicest possible way. Marcus was just shaking his head in despair – he had given up trying to teach her a pop, gut, or any other type of pass.

The red and black training gear and extra level of authority suited him, and the running-tights-under-shorts-look outlined his gorgeously muscular legs outrageously. Every time he bent over to demonstrate a technique, she had to bite her lip to stop herself sighing. And the close-fitting base layers and jersey on his top half did nothing to disguise his muscles. Every time she remembered what his bare torso looked like, a thrill ran through her. She was surprised the other women weren't gawping as much as she wanted to, instead they were just getting on with it.

With his focus on the drills the women were practising, she found his assertiveness a bit of a turn-on. This didn't help her concentration either. He had shouted at her a couple of times, but the incredulous girls had just shouted back at him for being mean. She'd even started to exaggerate her uselessness and clowning around. Just a little bit, not to waste valuable training time.

Marcus was so deliciously easy to wind up. She'd never teased anyone before, it just wasn't something she ever thought of or had the confidence to do, but ways of breaking his stern composure kept coming to her. She'd seen him smother a few smirks shortly after she'd fallen over a tackling pad and landed face first in the deepest pool of mud on the pitch, and after the girls had lifted her so high in the air, she'd unintentionally squealed. And she'd screamed and shot upright when she'd tried out the prop position and the second row was a little too enthusiastic in binding between her legs, grabbing more than just shorts. Her comment about doing her own depilation, thanks very much, had even made him snigger.

When he'd bound on to her as a demonstration, having him so close to her had blown her mind and she'd tripped over her own feet, forgetting to release him as she fell and pulling him down too. He'd lain on her only briefly before pulling himself away, but her shaky legs on standing weren't entirely due to the impact with the ground. She had restrained herself from pulling him even closer, to satisfy the want growing inside her. There was no way she could train with them again and come out intact, mentally or physically.

However, in the showers afterwards, she started to wish she'd been better at it. The girls were such great company, but she couldn't disrupt their sessions all the time. Nevertheless, she'd learnt a fair bit, not least how much it could hurt hitting the ground. She had been genuinely intrigued by how the set pieces of the scrum and lineout worked, and how moves were put together, even though she couldn't do them herself. She loved it when things slotted into place in her head like jigsaw pieces, and she began to understand the whole picture. She had always been good at observation, and her understanding of what she had been watching every weekend had already increased a hundredfold.

Tom and Chris had been very happy with what she had done so far, and there was a pile of discs waiting in the office for her to "work her magic on". Marcus had been designated as her helper with Rob, the prop, and a techie wizard as her IT backup if needed. Tom had even lined up some work for her in his company if she wanted to supplement her income. Everything seemed to be coming up roses.

The following Saturday, she was already regretting her decision. Sitting with her laptop between a grumpy Chris and an even grumpier Marcus at the top of a windblown stand somewhere in the north of England, even her new thermal underwear couldn't keep her from shivering.

'Here, you're making me feel cold.' Marcus passed over a thick jacket. 'It's a spare, I brought it up from the subs' bench but it's not as cold up here as I thought.' He had twisted a knee in the first ten minutes and had been taken off as a precaution.

'Really?' She accepted the coat gratefully, huddling into the fabric as it swamped her.

'Yeah, when it rains it's like being pelted with icy needles.'

As she warmed up, she was able to concentrate more on the action. She felt under pressure to point something out, highlight some aspect of play, but the gale-force wind was wreaking havoc on any throw or kick, and the whole match was a close-fought scrap. The teams were evenly matched apart from the Harford scrum, which was inexplicably struggling. The scrum-half would feed the ball between the two packs, the hooker would get a foot to it, but before it could be whisked away, the opposition were heaving Harford backwards at a rate of knots and winning penalties.

Sophie was staring at a screenshot of the scrum, trying to figure out why the opposition looked a little strange and was so powerful. She knew from her own experience that the two second rows should have their inside arms around each other, but where were they?

'Marcus, where are the opposition second rows' arms? Is that legal?'

He took one glance and swore, 'Those cheeky fucking buggers! No, it isn't legal, but this ref probably won't notice, his attention is focused on the front row. No wonder we're going backwards on our ball.'

'Is it dangerous?'

'Can be. Their hooker can't strike for it as their arms are between his legs for a more powerful push. Plus they can use either hand to sneakily punch the opposing player and the ref won't see a thing.'

Sophie bit her lip. 'What can we do?'

'Make sure the boys know. They'll want to have a quiet word with the ref and play some tricks of their own.' He grinned and spoke a few words into his mouthpiece.

'Watch this.'

At the next break in play for running repairs, the water carriers spoke to Alex and Rob, who smirked and nodded. The next scrum was shortly after. Alex conversed with the ref just after it set and Harford managed to tear their scrum apart, the ref awarding them the ball. He also rummaged in his pocket and flourished a yellow card at the guilty second row players.

'Cool.' She exchanged smiles with Marcus.

'They may be more powerful going forward, but it's easier to split their scrum if you're conversant in the Dark Arts of scrummaging like Rob. He probably would have noticed soon himself. I'm surprised he didn't, but in the heat of battle, or in weather like this, some things aren't always so obvious.'

The game was effectively over in ten minutes, after Harford, with fifteen men against thirteen, had scored two quick tries.

At the end of the match, Sophie nibbled her lip again as she concentrated on finishing spurious notes, and sighed in exasperation as she closed the laptop.

'What's up, imp?' asked Marcus.

'I don't feel I've helped much today. I need to learn more before I can make a difference.'

On her other side, Chris interjected, 'It was good work, you two. Little differences all add up. Tom and I have the experience to sort the big picture out.' It didn't sound like much of a compliment from Chris, but he was known for keeping his counsel.

She glanced at the head coach and he tried to smile back, his downturned mouth unused to it. Sophie suddenly realised he wasn't as old as she'd assumed, only around his late-thirties – his wild hair and weather-beaten skin made him look older. His shrewd blue eyes were surrounded by the thickest lashes she'd ever seen, and he had dimples.

51

'You have dimples,' she blurted.

He smiled a bit more and the dimples deepened before he gingerly stood up. 'Yep, don't remind anyone, they take the piss.'

Wow. The dour coach was actually quite a heartbreaker. He was also rather slow making his way down the steps. Some movements looked painful and by the time he reached flat ground, his smile was long gone. Sophie winced for him.

'He has joint problems, and early onset arthritis,' breathed Marcus in her ear. 'He had to retire from playing in his early twenties. Some days he really struggles to get around. Won't accept any help though, so don't offer it. Lives by himself, single, rugby is his life.'

Sophie felt a lump building in her throat. 'That's rather sad.' She started packing up her things to leave.

'Yeah, he's a damn good coach, everyone learns a lot from him. I brought the coat for him. I didn't know how cold he had got and he struggles more on some days.'

'Oh shit, and you gave it to me?' She flushed guiltily.

'Don't worry, it needs to be colder before he'll show any weakness. It was good you took it; next week we can do the same and he'll be more likely to take something if you do too.'

'OK, deal.'

They smiled at each other until Marcus cleared his throat. 'Of course, by "we" I mean some of the boys, I don't plan on getting injured next week.'

'Of course not. Let's get out of here.' On standing, Sophie found her legs had gone strangely weak. 'I'll see you on Monday for the analysis?'

'Yeah, that'll be cool. Hang on, you're going on the supporters' coach back instead of the team coach? You can come with us.'

Sophie wrinkled her nose. 'I'd rather not, it's more fun with the supporters. They have wine and loads of goodies and singing. You lot only have protein shakes, beer and strange habits.'

'What? Wine? I'm jealous!' laughed Marcus as they continued down the stairs and towards the exit. 'And goodies? Err, what kind of goodies?'

'It depends what we've all brought. Usually cake and cheese and biscuits, that sort of thing. Sarah made some chocolate brownies this week. Having nibbles means the coach doesn't always have to stop for food on the return journey.'

'Brownies also? Any way I can sneak on?' Marcus gave her puppy dog eyes.

Ooh, those weak legs again. 'Ummm ...' She didn't know if he was serious or not; she'd never seen any players not take the coach back. 'Isn't it compulsory for players to stay on their coach?'

'Yeah, I guess so. But I have to put up with Rob-the-hypochondriac – he's convinced he's getting a cauliflower ear and won't shut up about it.'

For someone who was supposed to be observant, she was confused by him. 'If Sarah will let me, I'll sneak you a brownie before the coaches leave.'

'Awww, thanks.'

Sophie yawned, and carefully turned over in the hospital bed. The pain had continued to ebb and her head continued to clear as she recalled countless matches, both away and home. Until the end of the season when Harford, after a disastrous start, had finished a respectable third in the league. Sophie had met up with a radiant Clare just about to depart for her belated honeymoon.

'So, you're off to "Sith Effrica" next week?'

Sophie grinned. 'Yep, and just in time to get away from a wonderful British summer.' They both grimaced at the torrential rain pelting the street outside the bar.

'It's dismal out there. I'm sooo looking forward to Italy. I'm nearly packed already. How's your holiday checklist coming along?'

Sophie brandished her phone. 'Not far to go, according to this … I just need to sort out travel insurance and order a new rucksack tonight. A zip broke on mine when I test-filled it this morning.'

'Don't forget your insurance, we've all seen how accident-prone you are,' laughed Clare.

'I know, it's so embarrassing.' Sophie rolled her eyes. 'Look at my new handbag-slash-day bag, it's got hidden pockets for valuable stuff. So I don't lose anything. I've bought the smallest, slimmest, most basic phone to fit in there, and a neat little purse too.'

'Ooh, lovely.' Clare spent a few minutes admiring the design and testing the pockets, before she gave it back. 'I need one of those for away trips – very useful, and stylish. I'll have to drop some heavy hints to Alex. Good find, well done you.'

Sophie flushed with pleasure – she didn't often discover things other people really liked too.

'Since you're flying out there and you'll see Marcus, can you take his copies of the wedding photos please?' Clare carefully pushed their glasses of red wine and the remains of their late lunch to one side and handed over a large, stiff manila envelope. 'It's open for Customs anyway, have a look.'

Clare had a strangely expectant air, so Sophie carefully untucked the flap and tipped the contents onto the table. Right on top was a glossy, unguarded shot of Sophie and Marcus together under the wedding arch, Sophie smiling serenely down at Clare's bouquet. Marcus was smiling down at her too, a gentle smile full of love.

'Gosh.' Her heart twinged at the perfect photo.

'I know, he looks besotted. Do you think he likes you?'

Sophie hooted with laughter. 'Hah! I've no idea what

made him look like that, he barely had time for me that day.'

'I dunno, you were giggling like two schoolkids later in the night.'

'It's a fluke, a trick of the light. The photographer must have taken loads to come up with that one.' She frowned in thought. 'I think we were talking about stuff, his family and returning to South Africa. After the speeches is a bit of a blur. I'm never drinking champagne again.'

'Yeah, yeah, we all say that.' Clare rolled her eyes and giggled. 'That was a spectacular catch of my bouquet, not klutzy for you at all.'

'Oh, good grief, did I catch it?' Sophie groaned, 'That's Marcus. He insists no one could be as useless as I am, and he refuses to admit defeat. Therefore, he's been chucking things at me in the office. I'm getting quite used to ball-shaped objects flying towards me.'

'And … what's that sparkling on your hand?'

'Huh?' Sophie studied where Clare was pointing, where her image's hand was half-hidden by the bouquet 'I've no idea, must be another trick of the light. It was getting dark by then.'

Her friend's attention stayed on the photo. 'Despite the alcohol, he still looks interested.'

Wistfully, Sophie positively yearned for someone to look at her that way in real life. She steeled herself. 'Clare, I know you're an incorrigible romantic, but there's nothing going on between the two of us.'

'Are you sure? You spend enough time together at the club.'

'Yep, we're just friends. We get along OK, and I can relax with him. He's the only person I've ever felt like I could tease.'

Clare smiled in reflection. 'You know, we kissed once, at Sarah and Tom's wedding, but he left for home and Alex made his move shortly after. In fact, I think Marcus flirting with me probably pushed Alex into action. And he was brilliant when Alex did his disappearing act. I do hope he finds a nice girl to fall in love with, someone who deserves him.'

Sophie inwardly cringed. She couldn't really tell Clare who Marcus was already in love with – it would upset her or make her feel guilty – and to say Clare had a heart of pure mush was an understatement. Sophie sometimes wondered how she hadn't had her heart broken a thousand times before she'd met Alex.

Despite being several years younger, Sophie felt ancient in comparison to such unbridled cheer and optimism. She knew Clare had been through hell and come out the other side with a gorgeous husband and a re-established relationship with her mother.

Perhaps she was happy because she had experience of how bad it could get and was grateful for the good?

Perhaps that was the secret of it all? Being happy and positive like Clare, being assertive and self-assured like Sarah, with the commanding presence of Lindsay, belying her small stature? Sophie had the feeling she was on to something.

'Here's Sarah, and she's brought bubbles!' whooped Clare.

The arriving brunette grinned, carefully placing glasses on the table. 'Thought we'd have a few drinks to celebrate the end of Harford Park's rugby season and Sophie's imminent departure. Ooh, nice handbag. Are these the photos?'

The waiter following her began filling the glasses then placed the bottle in a bucket of ice as the women claimed their drinks.

Clare began giggling again. 'Sophie's just said she's never drinking champagne again, after my wedding.'

'Clare, you said the same after my wedding, and remember those glasses you downed before you stomped off to shag Alex for twelve hours?'

'Well, at least Sophie didn't sleep with Marcus that night.'

'True, neither of them were in a state to do anything. Remember the dancing?' All three of them began chuckling. 'On the tables too!'

Sophie shielded her face, red with embarrassment. 'Please don't remind me of anything I did under the influence, you know I'm a total lightweight.'

'So is Marcus, at least you have that in common. Tom saw him to his hotel room and I dropped you off at yours before hubby and I commenced our marathon sex session. I don't know what it is about staying in a hotel, we both get as randy as can be and have to christen all the furniture.' Sarah sighed happily. The giggling gradually calmed down. 'You're looking thoughtful, Soph,' she remarked.

'I've just realised that I have the power to do whatever I want, to be whoever I want to be.'

'Sounds fabulous. How are you going to do that?'

'This holiday, this trip, I'm going to reinvent myself and become a new Sophie. Someone who doesn't cringe, who doesn't let people walk all over her or speak down to her. Someone who's not "wet". Sophie version two-point-zero, with upgraded software and improved graphics.'

'What? You've lost me.'

'I'll need to modify my behaviour and continue your makeover.'

'Err ... OK. Just let me know if we can help.'

Sophie hummed distractedly. 'I'll do some investigation, figure out where to start.' She had to attack it like a project, do a full analysis and investigate possible outcomes.

'You know, there may not be as much to change as you think. You're a braver person than you realise. And you're certainly not "wet".'

Clare nodded in agreement. 'You approached me, put yourself at risk of being slapped down, and now you're doing what very few people do – travelling a different continent by yourself.'

'Not really by myself. I'm meeting up with Marcus. He said he'd show me around the Cape and I'll see some of his matches.'

'One person on a whole continent? That works. Perhaps you'll have a holiday fling with him?' suggested Clare.

Sophie snorted. 'Hardly. If we've managed to keep our hands off each other working together in the same office for the last six months, we're not likely to suddenly jump into bed, are we?'

'Would you like to?'

'We're just friends.'

'Sophie, that's not answering the question,' Sarah scolded playfully.

'OK, so I find him attractive, but he's not my type.' She shrugged, hoping they didn't notice her reddening cheeks.

'What *is* your type if it's not tall, blond, and gorgeously fit-to-fuck?' teased Sarah. 'Short, fat, and balding? I'll have to let any single, front row vets know they're in with a chance.'

The three dissolved into giggles again.

'At least you'll get to see his family's place, I hear it's rather spectacular.'

'The vineyard? Marcus reluctantly showed me a couple of pictures, but that's it.'

'Reluctantly?' interjected Clare.

'He's from money, but keeps it quiet according to Tom.' Sarah seemed to know a lot.

'Why's that?'

Both Sarah and Sophie shrugged.

'By the way, what made you decide on South Africa?'

Sophie smiled into the distance. 'My Aunt Agatha, the

one who left me the house, did a lot of travelling. However, mostly due to apartheid, she never toured Southern Africa. She made me promise to go and to spread a pinch of her ashes on some wild mountainside.'

'And you're spending several months there?'

'Maybe longer, it depends how long my holiday funds last. I plan to travel up north, maybe as far as Malawi or Kenya. Go on safari, see all the beasts Aunt Agatha dreamt of. I haven't booked much yet, I'll decide where I'm going on the hoof.'

'Wow!' Clare looked impressed, 'That sounds great.'

'I'm quite envious too,' added Sarah.

Sophie almost hopped in her seat with anticipation, catching her rocking glass in time. 'It's the trip of a lifetime, I've been saving for it for most of my life so far. And it may change the rest of my life, if I can successfully reinvent myself.'

'A toast to Sophie's holiday,' proposed Sarah.

The three women chinked their glasses and chorused, 'To Sophie's holiday!'

As the plane took off a few days later, Sophie was feeling chuffed with herself. She had done her research. She knew what to say, what to do. She could fool people she was a confident, outgoing person instead of a timid mouse. Her checklist boxes were all ticked. What could possibly go wrong?

Chapter Five

Sophie went through a battery of tests to ascertain she had recovered enough to leave the hospital. Her head still banged, but the nausea had subsided somewhat. Another white-coat-wearing, middle-aged doctor with a complicated Dutch name confirmed she could have a touch of amnesia, but otherwise, she was fit and healthy. He droned on, 'Obviously, it is a little early to be discharging you, and you are still having memory problems, but we've arranged for an experienced nurse to attend you.'

Tandy was happily grinning away behind the doctor, and Sophie had to restrain a giggle.

Marcus arrived, freshly showered after training and pushing a wheelchair. 'Come on honey, time to go home.'

The three of them made their way out to the car park, and Sophie was transferred to the passenger seat of a silver BMW. She didn't resist or ask questions; she was still trying to sort the jumbled memories flicking through her confused, aching mind. She dozed in the semi-reclined seat, leaving Marcus to drive and an excited Tandy to sit in the back seat.

An hour later, Sophie carefully sat up to view the scenery, the regimented lines of leafy vines blanketing the gentle slopes. As the sun sank behind a distant mountain, they passed a gatehouse and drove down a wide, tree-lined road, approaching a huge, gleaming white, Dutch-style house with fancy gables and a thatched roof.

'It is so beautiful. Do you remember it?' asked an awestruck Tandy.

Sophie frowned. 'I-I don't know. I can remember pictures but I can't tell if they are true memories. How long have I – we – been staying here?'

Marcus glanced quizzically at her. 'Not long at all.' Curious.

He drew up on the drive in front of the main doors, switching the engine off and getting out. As Sophie fumbled with the door handle, he scooted around and opened her door, undoing her seatbelt and hoisting her carefully in his arms.

'I'm sure I can walk,' protested Sophie weakly, as Marcus carried her towards the front door.

Tandy tutted. 'Sophie, let your husband look after you.'

'Yes, Sophie, listen to your husband.' There was a strange edge to Marcus' voice. 'You're light as a feather, anyway.'

Sophie glanced up at him, but was unable to detect what the undercurrents meant. The imposing black door opened before Marcus and his burden could reach it.

'Marcus, I was wondering where you'd got to, love.' The soft Irish twang coming from the elegant brunette in the cream linen suit seemed out of place in the staid surroundings. 'Oh, you've been to collect … Sophie.' The woman's brow wrinkled slightly, betraying her mature years. 'Hello. I've had the room next to Marcus' made up, for you to have some space while you recuperate.'

Sophie wasn't great at reading feelings, but she didn't think she was just imagining the slight frostiness in the woman's voice when she turned her cool green eyes on her, a contradiction to how she'd addressed her son.

'Thank you. I'm sorry to put you out.' She tried to smile a little, but the chilly gaze had moved on.

'Jakobus and I are off to the airport now, we'll see you in a couple of months.'

His mother bussed Marcus' cheek and gestured behind for her husband, a stoutly built, grey-haired chap. He patted Marcus' shoulder and gave Sophie a fleeting smile as they slipped past, down the steps, and into a sleek black Mercedes, which purred down the drive and out of sight.

As Marcus continued carrying her into the house, Sophie felt even worse. She had always thought when she married, she would get to know his family and hopefully get on with them. Perhaps have the parental relationship that was missing from her own life? However, it seemed his parents didn't want to know her at all.

Whatever had made her get hitched so soon? What had happened in those missing weeks? Her head started thumping even more.

'I'm off to find my husband!' she whooped, grinning wildly as she skipped down the stairs and through the reception.

The concierge laughed as he opened the door for her. 'Gek lady, in that outfit you're skop, skiet en boom klim*!'*

'What?' Sophie turned her head, but continued walking towards the taxis.

'You're going to have an adventure – watch out!'

For the next couple of days, all she did was rest in the bland but tastefully decorated bedroom. She slept for most of the day and night; her head hurt too much to concentrate on the TV and although she had a tablet in amongst her belongings, she didn't switch it on. There were a couple of glossy books about South Africa on the bedside table, and she looked at the pictures and read some excerpts, hoping she would get to see at least some of the highlights. Tandy helped her shower in the en suite, and fed her some light soups and salads. The lingering headache and nausea fortunately abated.

She had heard Marcus in the room next door. He had popped his head around the door a few times. He helped her make some calls to arrange for replacement bank cards to be issued from the UK, and asked for a list of what was likely to have been in her missing handbag.

On the third day, after Marcus had gone to training, she decided to venture out of the room on jelly legs. Tandy hovered in the background as she cautiously negotiated the main hallway. 'You take care, Sophie, you've done well to get dressed.'

Sophie winced. 'I didn't manage to put a bra on, my ribs are still too sore. Do you think I could get some fresh air?' she asked. The outside was calling her as sunlight streamed through a couple of windows.

'You have a wander around the garden, then you can sit on the *stoep*,' allowed Tandy.

'The shtup?'

'Outside, there.' Tandy pointed through the windows to a vine-covered porch area. 'I will get some blankets for you, it's not as warm as it looks. Don't go too far.'

After a wobbly trip back to her room for suitable shoes and sunglasses, Sophie stepped out of the house into the bright sunshine. Despite Tandy's comments about the temperature, it was still like a British spring: warm in the sun, and chilly in the shade. The sky was a pure shade of blue, with cotton wool clouds scurrying across in the light breeze. There was snow on the distant mountain tops, beyond the regimented vineyard rows covering the hillsides.

She stepped off the *stoep* and into the white-walled gardens surrounding the house, wandering for half an hour around the many bushes and the pool, and eventually, out of a gate into part of the vineyard. She saw figures working in the distance who waved at her. She waved back. One of them broke off from the group and trotted towards her.

'Hello, my name is Joseph. I am the manager here.' He smiled, his white teeth gleaming in his dark face.

Sophie held her hand out, 'I'm Sophie Ed – just Sophie. I'm visiting from the UK.'

Joseph held his gloved hands up, 'Nice to meet you, Just Sophie. Sorry, I will not shake your hand, I've been using some chemicals.'

'Oh. OK.'

'Be careful when you wander around the vines – snakes sometimes bask on the paths.'

'Snakes!' squeaked Sophie, stepping back towards the house.

Joseph laughed. 'Don't worry too much, it's winter and we remove them regularly. Be careful anyway – the puff adders and cobras are very poisonous.'

'Thank you.' She heard Tandy call her. 'I'm over here!' she answered.

'What did I say about not going too far?' Tandy's haranguing was brought to a halt at the sight of Joseph. 'Oh. Hello.' She smiled awkwardly, and Joseph smiled back.

Sophie felt like an interloper. 'Have you two met?' she asked. 'I'll, ummm, head back to the sht … sht … porch thingy.'

She left, circuitously making her way back, trying not to be paranoid about any leaves that moved in the breeze, or crevices where something could hide. 'Be brave, Sophie,' she chanted.

As she returned to the *stoep*, gingerly shook out the blankets and lay tiredly across a chaise longue for a nap, the thought occurred to her that dangerous situations could be good practice. Training to become the new, confident Sophie. She would have to explore the vineyards and brave the snakes more often.

'Sophie, will you marry me?'

Through the champagne haze, she could just about see an earnest-looking Marcus on bended knee, gazing up at her. The glittering diamond on the bed of red velvet contrasted sharply with his black tuxedo.

She laughed. 'Yes, Marcus! I'll marry you!'

The ring slid smoothly onto her finger, and she stared at it in awe. It was just a little loose, so she crooked her finger to keep it in place. He stood, towering above her, and grasped her around the waist, swinging her in a circle. She threw her head back and laughed joyously. 'I'm engaged!'

'So am I!' Marcus' laughter rang out too, echoing against the stone balustrades enclosing them.

She stopped laughing and gasped. 'Sssssshhhhh!'

He stopped laughing too. 'Why's that?'

She brought her head closer to his to whisper, 'Because no one here can know!'

'OK,' he whispered back conspiratorially.

They looked at each other and giggled, then shushed each other. Sophie tried to stick her beringed hand over his mouth, but ended up stroking his parted lips. He licked her fingers and a shiver went through her, 'I s'pose we should kiss to seal the deal? That's what engaged couples usually do, isn't it?'

'Mmmm,' Marcus tried to speak around the fingers. 'Hokay.'

Her head dipped towards his, their parted lips meeting, and they kissed sweetly ... for about a second, then they both groaned in pleasure and the kiss deepened. Sophie felt her body sing with delight, her arms wrapping around his broad shoulders, legs wrapping around his hips.

As hands started to slip under clothes, vibrations and facile tinny tunes interrupted them, along with some voices.

'Marcus? Sophie? Where have you two pissheads gone? Answer your damn phones, we need you for the photos!' yelled a female.

'Marcus? Sophie? Sarcus? Mophie? Where are yoooooou?' giggled someone else.

The combined intervention of their names being called

and pesky technology broke their intimate contact. They stared at each other.

Sophie touched his lips again, and hers. 'Wow, that was fun, Sarcus.'

'Sarcus?'

'Mophie, then?'

They both began giggling again and the moment was broken. She was let back down on to her feet and they shushed each other before stumbling back through the shadowy garden and towards the summoning voices, sniggering over their names.

'What about Sarcophiecus?'

'Yuck, sounds funereal. Mopharcusie?'

'Ha! I'm sure that's a politician.'

'I think you're right.'

'I'm always right, most of the time.'

'All right, smart arse. Whatever happened to the shy Sophie who wouldn't say boo to a goose?'

'Boo, Mr Goose.' She made some quacking noises and flapped her arms. It was enough for them to dissolve into more howls of unexplainable laughter.

Marcus returned mid-afternoon, visibly tired after a morning of hard training, to find Sophie sprawled across the sofa in a room downstairs with Tandy whistling cheerfully upstairs.

He dabbed a kiss on the top of Sophie's head. 'Hey, *cherry*, how was your day?'

Sophie carefully glanced up from the mind-numbing American soap on the TV. 'Good, thanks.' She grinned. 'I've been outside for some fresh air, seen the vines, and wasn't bitten by snakes.' She didn't mention her memory straightening itself, or the puzzling scenes she'd recalled.

'Great,' he smiled back. 'You're looking much better.'

Sophie self-consciously went to dab her face, but stopped before her fingers touched skin. 'The bruising's coming out really well. Tandy and I did some make-up experimentation earlier to disguise the discolouration.'

'Your head was OK with that?'

'Yeah, and the ribs and arm too. Look how colourful it's gone!' She excitedly pulled up her top to show the dramatic purpling covering the side of her ribcage.

Marcus stared for a few seconds before he tore his eyes away, colour rising in his cheeks.

Sophie suddenly realised that in being carried away, she'd flashed him the lower half of her breasts. Her bare, braless breasts, and she flushed too. Pulling her top back down, she tried to cover the awkwardness. 'Ummm, but you must be used to seeing bruises like that on a rugby pitch.'

'Yeah, of course, all the time ...' He sniffed, 'Do I smell dinner?'

'Tandy insisted on making a stew and potatoes. She's set the table in the dining room for the both of us.'

'She's not joining us? She's welcome to.'

Sophie grinned again. 'Tandy's going out for a meal with Joseph tonight.'

'Joseph, the vineyard manager?'

'Yeah. Is he a nice guy? I don't want her hurt, she's been an absolute angel to me.'

'He's a great guy. They'll struggle to keep a relationship going with her living in the suburbs of Cape Town, though.'

'Isn't it a bit early for that?' Sophie sighed. 'Give them a chance to enjoy their first date, please?'

Sophie spent the next morning wandering around, watching the workers expertly pruning the vines, retying the trunks, and training the branches or "canes". She offered to help out, but Joseph laughed and said she would need to study viniculture before she would be able to assist. Instead, she helped clear away some of the dead and pruned branches, with Tandy energetically mucking in also.

That afternoon, she was tired from the unaccustomed work so she dozed on the *stoep* while a downbeat Tandy packed. The nurse was leaving the next day, having babysat for long enough.

A stranger stuck her blonde head around the door. 'Oh, hallo. I'm Bridget, Marcus' sister. You must be Sophie?'

Must be brave. She squared her shoulders. 'Yes, I am. You've heard about me?' She gave a beaming smile, not wanting to be appear like a mouse in front of someone so self-possessed and elegant.

'Not as much as I want to.' Bridget perched on a seat next to the chaise longue, crossing her jean-clad legs and fussing with the Celeste silk scarf visible under her jacket. She smiled ruefully back. 'Not even a rumour of my brother's *skelm*, yet he is now married.'

'*Skelm*?'

'A lover he keeps quiet, a secret. We have mutual friends in London and they hadn't heard about you.'

This was strange. Sophie didn't know whether she was being insulted or not. 'We've known each other for a while, but how we got together?' Sophie shrugged, 'It's still all a bit of a blur.'

'*Ja ja*, the accident, of course. Any idea why you were at that hotel in the City?'

Sophie frowned. That was a good question. 'I don't know. Perhaps …' Her head gave a warning throb and she rubbed a temple. 'Ow! This damn head won't let me remember. Every time I try to figure something out, the pain returns.'

'I'll do the thinking for you, then. He didn't say anything to us, his family, although he's been distracted. He didn't say anything to our friends. He was surprised when you turned up, but attentive. He rushed to the hospital. This isn't the behaviour of someone who would

69

desert his wife, and I know my brother well. Or I thought I did.'

Sophie stopped rubbing her head. What Bridget was saying, albeit brusquely, made sense.

'We hoped he had met someone when he came back last summer, he was quite excited about a woman he'd met through the club. I take it that was you?'

Sophie's heart dropped. She was pretty sure it wasn't her. In fact, she was pretty sure she knew who it was. She began to redden with embarrassment.

'Ooh, didn't you know? I'm sorry, I've made you blush.' Bridget looked away for a moment, then back towards Sophie. She looked solemn. 'Can I ... can I ask you one thing?'

'What's that?'

'Please ... please don't hurt my brother.'

Sophie gasped. 'I wouldn't!'

'Because it did occur to me ... the only reason I can think of for him leaving is if you cheated on him.'

Sophie's horror-struck reaction must have mollified her.

'I'm sorry to doubt you. Anyway, I'll be off now, I just came by to pick up an invoice. I'll see you at the *braai* in a few days, and we'll have a proper chat then. Don't get up, I'll see myself out.'

A reeling Sophie smiled stiffly in agreement, and the whirlwind Bridget left with a wave.

She sank back onto the chaise longue. Despite the questions and doubts Marcus' sister had raised, and her strange, slightly aggressive attitude, she felt she had responded naturally and with confidence instead of being a shrinking violet. At least that was successful.

Her shoulders relaxed as she thought about the issues the forthright Bridget had voiced. Her head began clearing, and events were finally slotting together, starting to make some sense. Sophie dozed lightly in the sun as she waited for Marcus to return.

The two of them had sneaked away from the wedding breakfast with a purloined bottle of champagne, and hidden below a step in the garden, in an intimate area with outside heaters keeping the chill away.

Sophie was teasing some of Marcus' background out. 'What? They give you that much hassle?'

'Yeah, my sister's gay, so she won't be having children any time soon. I'm their only hope. My parents won't be there, they're off to Ireland to visit family, but they'll still be calling me, setting me up on blind dates and having single daughters of people they know "drop in" unexpectedly. Do you know how awkward that is, especially when you're soaking naked in the hot tub?'

Sophie gurgled with laughter. 'OK, so we pretend we're going out, even married, and that'll get your family and friends off your back?'

'Really? Would you do that for me?'

'As long as you show me around the Cape while I'm there.'

'Deal!'

They shook hands and grinned.

Marcus oohed. 'I've just thought of something, back in a couple of minutes.'

He jogged off, up the stairs, leaving Sophie swigging from the bottle and humming a distant tune. She must have dozed off as Marcus had to shake her awake.

'Sophie, I'm back!'

Her eyes opened and she blinked sleepily to clear them, seeing two of him on bended knee in front of her.

'Sophie, I'm back.' The front door slammed.

She blinked – it was all starting to make sense. She had to confront him. 'Marcus, pop out here.'

His blond head poked outside, and he smiled to see her

on the chaise longue. 'Hi, honey.' He came over and kissed her on the cheek, taking a seat next to her. 'Tell me about your day.'

'Marcus, I've remembered the wedding. Clare's wedding.'

His face fell, his eyes darted back and forth, and his cheeks began reddening.

'I remember flying over, and I wasn't married then, but everyone seemed to think that we were hitched in the UK. I was staying in a Cape Town hotel by myself, not here.' All the data was adding up to one conclusion. 'Marcus, are we actually married?'

He looked sheepishly down at his feet. 'Ummm, not really,' he admitted.

'Not really?' she echoed incredulously. 'How can one be "not really" married, unless we're not?'

He ran a hand through his spiky hair, leaving tufts disarrayed. 'We're not, but ... ummm, some people think we are.'

'Who does? Why on earth would they think that?' she fumed.

'It was that photo. They assumed we were bride and groom. And your comment to the concierge.'

I'm off to find my husband!

That was what she had said to that cheerful fellow, the last thing she remembered before waking up in hospital. Realisation dawned upon her of how her original misunderstanding must have occurred.

'Marcus, pass me your phone.'

He pulled it out of his pocket and passed it over. She squinted at the date and her suspicions were confirmed. She hadn't lost any time at all. The hospital clock had been wrong. There was no amnesia, no missing scenes. Just a touch of misunderstanding and confusion. It finally made sense.

'You had been muttering about your husband when you

were brought in, about finding him. They contacted the club, and someone from admin shouted across the gym that my wife was in hospital. I spoke with the doctors and they said not to correct you as it would be too confusing while your head recovered. Somehow, the story became muddled, and they thought we were married for real.'

'But why not tell everyone else the truth?'

There was no way anyone could blush harder than Marcus did then. 'Because it was convenient for me. The boys on the team have stopped ragging me about not having a girlfriend or calling me gay and my parents are no longer trying to fix me up with a *mooi meisie*, a nice girl. Everyone's leaving me alone because they're so shocked that I kept the marriage secret and deserted you before returning here. And, well, it was your idea in the first place.'

'My idea?'

'At Clare's wedding, after the speeches, we got talking and I said I wasn't looking forward to the hassle from my parents. You said something about me needing a pretend girlfriend. One thing led to another, and there happened to be selection of rings in the gift shop of the hotel, and ...' He shrugged. 'You didn't seem to remember it the next time we spoke, and you'd already lost the engagement ring off your finger that night. The hotel returned it to me.'

'Oh. Good. Grief.' That explained the fuzzy flashbacks.

'And, well, you needed someone to pay your hospital bills.'

'Don't be silly, I have travel insurance. Someone as clumsy as I am would never ...' she trailed off and frowned. It must have been ticked off on her checklist, otherwise she would have had a reminder. The details would be on her phone. But her phone was gone, and the checklists with it. She couldn't recall buying insurance, and she couldn't recall seeing anything in her travel-related emails about a policy. 'How much was it?' she asked faintly.

'You don't want to know.'

'I do. Tell me,' she demanded.

'Hang on.' He disappeared for a few minutes and returned, presenting her with an invoice.

It took her a few moments to convert the rand figure into pounds, and she winced at the sum. Apart from travelling funds, she had some savings, but they were all tied up. She couldn't pay Marcus back for several months, probably not until after she returned to work.

'You were treated privately at the hospital, they assumed you had full holiday cover and South Africa doesn't have a reciprocal healthcare agreement with the UK. You were unconscious for some time, they had to do some really expensive scans, plus you needed round-the-clock care. They only discharged you as Tandy was willing to come to keep an eye out for warning signs.'

'I'll check my email, but I can't remember actually booking the travel insurance,' acknowledged Sophie as she rubbed her aching head. So much for her checklists, and everything else in her lovely, new-but-gone handbag. 'So, what do we do now?'

'The doctors said to let you recover in one place for a couple of weeks. I thought you could do a bit of travelling after that. You'll head back to the UK about the time I do, and a few months later, I can tell people it fizzled out.'

'All so simple?' Sophie wasn't sure whether to be mad or not.

'Yeah, it'll take at least eight weeks to get a new passport and visa. We'll fly up to Pretoria next week to sort it out, then you can do some travelling, maybe see the Kruger Park and meet me at the away game there. In fact, you can come on away trips and do some sightseeing while you're there. We can do trips around the Cape area so your time's not wasted.'

She remained silent.

'It's quite nice here, honest. It's secure, you can chill out. It's more comfortable than my flat in the suburbs. It'll be us three until Tandy goes, then just you and me. Apart from the vineyard staff, and they don't enter the house.'

It didn't sound so bad, but she still didn't respond.

'You'll miss the trips you've already organised, you won't be able to cross multiple borders without a valid passport. It's either stay here, or get a temporary travel document and go home. If the doctors will let you fly.'

And have to wait until next year to return, if at all. She didn't voice her thoughts just yet, but what he was saying could be possible. She had no job to return to until autumn, plus her house had been rented out. She had nowhere else to go.

'Klaus, my best friend and flatmate in the City, he guides overland tours. One of them's to Victoria Falls in Zimbabwe, through Namibia and Botswana. Once you have your new passport, I can get you on his trip. You'll love it, you'll get to see loads of wildlife and the most spectacular scenery.' He fell silent too.

The wordless gap lengthened.

'And the *braai*?' Sophie eventually asked.

'Ahh. Ummm. Well ...' Marcus appeared uneasy. 'You just need to act as my wife for that, in front of my friends and teammates. I'll be there, though, and I've told them not to grill you too much, that you can't remember and it's a touchy subject for me. You'll have met most of the players and their partners by then anyway.'

'Huh? Met them how?'

'You are coming to watch me play on Saturday? The *braai* is on Sunday.'

Something else slotted into place. She had wanted to see some rugby while she was there, and a couple of his games had coincided with her visit. 'Are you still starting?'

'I think so.' He grinned, happy the conversation had

75

moved on to firmer ground. 'I've been training there all week. It'll be good to get decent match time – it's been a long time since I've played regularly.'

'How is the shoulder?'

'Like new. I've been able to really push the weights these last few weeks, and it's stronger in drills, plus the physio is excellent, better than the last guy at Harford.'

'Yeah, Tom said he was looking for someone full-time for next season.'

There was an awkward pause and Marcus swallowed. 'There is one more thing, about the *braai*?'

She really did not like the sound of that.

'Ummm, some of my friends will be staying overnight, the night before and after. We're a bit short of rooms and we *are* supposed to be married so … ummm, you'llhavetosleepwithme.'

'Sleep with you?' echoed Sophie.

'Well, in the same bed for two nights. We can put pillows between us if you like, and I'll try not to snore,' he added hopefully.

Put that way, what harm could it do? Sophie acquiesced, 'OK, deal. But you can't leave me for ages by myself, I'll need you there for support.'

'Deal. Seal with a kiss?'

'Don't push your luck. I'll take a gentle hug though.'

Chapter Six

After a tiring morning outside, it was time for lunch when Sophie heard a knock from the kitchen door. 'Hang on!' she called, and winced as her head banged. 'Tandy, would you mind finding out who that is?'

The nurse looked worriedly at her patient rubbing her head. 'If it will stop you being silly, yes.'

She was back within moments and stuttering. 'It is Joseph, he needs to speak with Marcus. He's worried about the latest grafts, he thinks he found some mildew.'

Sophie checked the time. 'Take him the house phone and call Marcus on his mobile, he'll be having lunch so should be able to talk.'

'OK.'

The nurse still hadn't returned a while later, so Sophie walked towards the voices to find Tandy at the door, talking with Joseph who was smiling at her. Tandy held some flowers in her arms and was shyly stroking a couple of the blooms.

'Those are beautiful flowers,' commented Sophie.

'Joseph grew them himself, in a greenhouse around the back.'

'Around the back?'

'The other side of those trees,– the barn, and other buildings.'

'Oh.' The grounds had been landscaped so well, Sophie had forgotten the vineyard had agricultural buildings.

While she was distracted, Joseph waved goodbye. 'I must return to work. I will see you tonight, Tandy?'

'Of course.'

Sophie said goodbye too, then waited for the back door to close. 'I take it your date went well?'

Tandy stared at the flowers. 'It was … magical. He took me to the top of the vineyard, we had a picnic and watched the sun go down, and we talked and talked until the stars came out. Then we were silent, but a comfortable silence. I don't get to see the stars in the city, not like that.'

'Will you see him again, when you return home?'

A tear trickled down the dark-skinned woman's cheek as she put the flowers down by the sink. 'I cannot. My job is in the city. Joseph's job is here. He loves the vineyards, it wouldn't be fair on him to ask him to leave. So maybe we will meet again. Probably not, as it would upset me too much.'

'Have you thought about leaving Cape Town, moving elsewhere?' Sophie pulled out a chair to sit at the small kitchen table and Tandy joined her.

'I cannot leave. I cannot gain a reference to find another job,' she answered dully. 'I spent years saving to study to become a nurse, and I was the best in my class. Not many black women succeed. But in my second year, a doctor made a pass at me. He would not accept "no", he damaged me.' Her shoulders shook.

'Oh, Tandy.' Sophie held her hand.

'I was hurt, the police were involved, and hospital management too. Nothing was done, I was poor and female, he was rich and male. I had no proof it was him, and his wife gave him an alibi.'

Sophie couldn't do anything except continue to clasp the nurse's hand.

'He didn't get away with it completely. He tried it again, but this time he was interrupted by the woman's husband.' Tandy smiled wryly. 'He lost some things which were very dear to him. He won't be doing that again. He can't walk, for a start. His wife, who lied to alibi him, now has to support him. He refuses to divorce, so there is justice. And no female nurses are allowed near him. But now, even though I was right, I am now a troublemaker in some people's eyes.' She shrugged. 'So I will not be promoted. All that training and money wasted. Is a shame.'

Tandy was so matter-of-fact, and Sophie's heart was breaking for her. It was more than a shame – it was downright unfair.

The nurse stood and wiped her eyes. 'I must thank you and Marcus for giving me this break, you did not need me for so long. I will say goodbye to this place tomorrow, and hope that you have better luck in the future. I must put these flowers in water.'

Sophie resolved to speak with Marcus, thinking there must be something they could do to help.

'I was talking to Tandy this afternoon, and she told me her story. It was so undeserved.' When Marcus returned that afternoon, Sophie related what had happened.

He shook his head. 'I've seen her and Joseph together, they were holding hands and looking so content. He lost his wife and daughter to a drunk driver years ago. I've never seen him interested in anyone else since. Tandy would be ideal.'

'Yep, but she says she can't get work anywhere else.'

'Joseph deserves to be happy. Call Bridget tomorrow, she has contacts in healthcare and will get to the bottom of it, maybe even pull some strings. If Tandy qualified so high up in her class, the local hospital here may be interested. We can at least ensure she has decent references to begin elsewhere.'

'We could do that?' Sophie felt like crying in relief. 'She's been lovely to me, and has taken so much joy in being here.'

'We could try.' Marcus awkwardly patted her on the

back.

She really wished he would hug her again. And more.

Tandy was all packed and ready once Marcus returned that Friday afternoon from training. He was taking her back to her place in the city, but Tandy looked sad and reluctant to go. Sophie hadn't heard back from Bridget, so just repeated the invite for her to return when she could. It was barely a week since they had met, but she felt like she was losing a friend.

That evening, as Marcus and Sophie were sitting down for supper, the house phone rang. It was Bridget in lawyer mode. Marcus put the speakerphone on so they could both hear.

'I spoke to a contact at the hospital. Apparently she's been one of the best nurses there for years. Not a bad word to say about her. They don't want to lose her.'

'So, why have they treated her so badly?'

'Because they could? I don't know. She has been turned down for every promotion she's applied for. '

'Bloody hell,' sighed Sophie. 'The poor woman.'

'It appears they had a rogue in their HR department with a petty grudge, they're looking into it. In better news, they've agreed to backdate a pay rise, so she'll have a little windfall, and give her a proper reference when she asks.'

'Really?'

'I've also had a word with a friend at a Cape hospital, less than twenty miles from the vineyard. They'll take her on if she's interested.'

'Ooh, brilliant.' Sophie began dancing on the spot while Marcus watched bemused. 'She'll be able to afford to move, and she can see if the relationship with Joseph goes any further. Thank you so much, I love you!'

Bridget laughed, her brusque composure broken for a moment. 'It was a pleasure to kick some administrative butt and do some good. I'll get my friend to give her a call, offer her the job. Right, got to go, I'll see you on Sunday for the *braai*?'

'Yep, definitely.' They both said their goodbyes, and Bridget hung up.

'Woohoo! We did it!' Sophie flung herself at Marcus and he twirled her around. A sharp spike of pain brought her back down to earth. 'Whoa, not great for the head and ribs.'

'Oops.' He settled her back on her feet and his arms slowly released her. 'You OK?'

The pain had gone and she couldn't help noticing how good he felt against her. How would she manage sharing a bed? 'My fault, I got carried away. It's fine now. I just forgot for a moment.' She was reluctant to leave his arms.

Her thoughts must have been well hidden as he solicitously helped her to the table to enjoy the cooling meal. She was puzzled by a shopping bag sitting by her plate, 'What's this?'

'Your handbag hasn't turned up so I got you a new one.'

'Really?' She had rarely ever received presents, as her parents didn't believe in them. Excitedly, she tore through the pink tissue paper and squealed when she saw the red leather shoulder bag. 'It's a bit like my old handbag at home, but nicer.' Much nicer. She didn't recognise the designer's name but the leather was soft as butter. 'That's unbelievably thoughtful of you.'

'I got … well, Bridget helped me pick up some basics going from the list of what had been in there. Make-up and stuff.' He looked almost embarrassed that she was as excited as she was.

'This is brilliant.' There was a little bag with all kinds of potions, including a small bottle of her favourite perfume, plus a matching red purse containing a couple of thousand rand. 'I'll pay you back once my new bank cards arrive.'

81

'No rush. No phone yet, we'll sort that out next week.'

'You didn't have to do this. Thank you so much.'

She locked eyes with him, and something passed between them, something which made her forget the handbag, which left her short of breath and yearning for something.

The ringing of his phone broke the moment, and she concentrated on wolfing down her food as he held a staccato conversation with whomever was calling.

As she ate, Sophie reflected on how much stronger Marcus' accent had become since he'd returned to South Africa. He even dropped in some Afrikaans expressions every now and again. For some reason, she found that really attractive. She glanced at him between mouthfuls, at the man she would be spending so much time with, and wondered how much of him she didn't yet know.

As Marcus drove into the rugby ground, Sophie was giving herself a pep talk. The thought of meeting so many strangers was making her want to sprint in the opposite direction, return to the safe haven of the house in the vineyards.

'You've gone quiet, Soph. Are you sure you're OK with this?'

Fearless Sophie. Shoulders back, chin up. If you can brave snakes in the vineyard, you can do this. She gave Marcus a confident smile. 'Just thinking, I can't believe it's Saturday already, almost a week since I got out of hospital. I'm feeling fine though, thank you. Really.'

He didn't look convinced. 'Well, if you're sure. We won't stay too long after the game if you feel tired.'

She smiled again and nodded, her throat too dry to talk. The imposing white stand looked much larger than Harford, and there seemed to be more people hanging around. Big people, tall people making her feel small, despite the semi-high boots she wore with her jeans and a smart jacket. In recent months, she had always dressed down and worn trainers to matches, but she wanted to make a good impression.

She pulled down the visor to check her make-up covered the worst of the purplish bruising on her forehead. A shadow was visible, but it didn't look too dramatic.

While she dawdled, Marcus jumped out and opened her door for her. As she climbed out, he grabbed his kit bag from the boot. 'I'll take you to the bar where the women usually hang around. Then I'll have to go and warm up. You'll have some lunch with them, and you can join them in the stand.'

'Great.' The women. Lovely.

Marcus frowned at her. She really must need to practise being cheerful.

Sophie soon realised she was a touch … bored. At first, she had been treated as a novelty, the "secret amnesiac English wife", but her answers about having concussion and not remembering, coupled with the fading bruises, deflected the most intrusive questions. The small group of players' partners had been welcoming and friendly enough, but they were busy catching up with each other and Sophie had very little in common with them. She was distracted by the warm-ups, watching intently to see how much was different to back in the UK. The ground was certainly a lot firmer.

The other women, though mostly knowledgeable, weren't really interested in the in-depth tactics that the men were playing. Sophie was so used to sitting and working with a laptop that she felt slightly lost not having anything to do.

She excused herself, and found a quiet couple of seats, opening the capacious handbag Marcus had procured for her and pulling her tablet out. She was relieved she had brought the device with her. Fortunately, it had been amongst her belongings back at the hotel rather than in her missing handbag. With what little she had, she could do some analysis. Something inside her eased as she observed play and began making notes. She took some shots of the action, the blue shirts of Marcus' team not terribly clear due to the distance, but good enough for her notes.

Sitting in the warming sun by herself was rather restful, and for the first time since waking up in the hospital, she felt at home, settled.

Marcus was having a decent game of doing nothing spectacular or inspiring, but nothing disappointing either. His usual, really, as he was for Harford Park. He played so gracefully with the ball in hand, and defended solidly, with the robust, bone-juddering tackles she was seeing all over the pitch. As Sophie watched, she started picking up other interesting things, including a couple of gaps in the defensive patterns, some tell-tale habits, and slow covering. She bit her lip, wondering if it was worth letting him know, but when they went a couple of scores down, the decision was made for her. She had nothing to lose.

When the whistle blew for half time, she trotted down to the hoardings and tried to get Marcus' attention, standing on tiptoes, with no luck. Everyone was too tall – he was totally surrounded as they headed for the changing rooms.

Despairing, she glanced around and saw a ball boy fussing with a spare ball, 'Hey, can you do me a favour? Tell that guy there that his wife needs a word please?'

'What's it worth, lady?' The youngster grinned up at her, his fingers making the international sign for money.

Sophie groaned at being scammed by a kid. She rummaged in her bag, handed over a few rand, and the lad scampered off to tug on Marcus' shirt. He pointed in Sophie's direction and Marcus jogged over as his teammates continued inside.

'I've been looking for you up in hospitality, not down

here!' His eyebrows lifted when he saw she had her tablet out. 'Don't tell me …'

Sophie nodded, grinning excitedly. 'I have a couple of cherries for you to pick. See this?' Sophie drew a line. 'If you step up early, you have a chance for an intercept. And this one, they're leaving gaps here and here. Watch their defensive line, there's usually a mismatch here.'

As he looked at what she pointed out, there was a call from one of the players going past, '*Yoh*, Marcus, now's not the time to be looking at holiday snaps.'

Marcus waved him away and concentrated on the pictures. '*Bladdy hell*, Soph, this is great.'

'Oh, and watch for the opposition doing these.' Discreet actions accompanied her words, and he briefly questioned her further on a couple of moves. 'That's about it for now.' She beamed at him.

He grinned back, then leant forward and placed a swift kiss on her mouth. 'Thanks, Soph.' Marcus jogged to join his curious teammates already returning to the pitch, and began whispering in their ears. He glanced back, and gave her a thumbs up.

As she rubbed her lips, a few people were staring at her. She ignored her natural instinct to shrink and gave them neutral smiles before returning to her vantage point.

This time, she had company. The lad she thought was a ball boy trailed her back and sat a couple of seats from her, glancing over at what she was doing as the match restarted. He didn't disturb her, so she ignored him and concentrated on play.

It was warm in the sun, so she shrugged off her jacket to bare her shoulders while squinting at the screen and at the pitch. His team were defending in their half, and Sophie suddenly realised Marcus was stepping up like she had told him. As the ball was being delivered to the yellow-clad backs, a streak of blue shot between them, catching a wayward pass.

'Yes!' Sophie watched with glee as Marcus dashed up the pitch, and the opposition backtracked too late. Without slowing, he touched the ball down under the posts, and pumped a fist in delight as the referee blew to award the try. He jogged back to the halfway line, grinning but visibly gasping for breath, to receive pats and slaps on the back from his teammates.

That took his team closer. Sophie continued to make notes, but after barely minutes, Marcus had intercepted another ball. This time he offloaded it to a flying winger, who escaped desperate hands to dot the ball down and go ahead. There was a longer break before the next score when, after a period of attacking pressure, Marcus dodged a labouring forward to feed the ball out to the same winger.

His confidence was increasing in leaps and bounds. Usually a steady player, that day he was using more than Sophie's feedback – it was as if he was preternaturally reading the opposition's minds. It was a whitewash.

'Lady, are you a witch?'

'Huh?' Sophie glanced away from the pitch to see she had gathered a small following of young boys and girls who were trying to glance at her tablet.

'You cast a spell on that player, he is magic now.'

She laughed, 'No, I'm afraid it's a little more geeky than that.'

'What?'

As there was a break in play, she played some of the clips she'd recorded, pointing out what she'd noticed to the fascinated youngsters. They began shouting things at her they had seen, and she agreed or asked more questions about play on the field. Time flew, and she couldn't believe it when the referee blew the whistle for full time.

'Will you be here for the next match, Soff-ee?' asked one boy, as his baggy jersey fell off a skinny shoulder.

'I hope so.' Without a passport or money, she couldn't

travel too far.

'*Aweh, kiff lady*. Bye bye.'

The ragtag bunch of kids departed and she realised there were also some adults who'd also come closer, to hear what they'd been talking about. She smiled awkwardly at them as she put her tablet in her handbag, and began walking down the steps towards the celebrating home team.

Marcus saw her coming, jogged to her as she reached the hoardings, and swept her off her feet, smacking a kiss to her lips. His lips lingered, and they touched again. And again.

Ohhh, he smelled good. She placed her hands around his sweaty shoulders to steady herself.

He lifted his head to stare at her, the tension growing.

A slap on his back broke the moment. 'Marcus, sorry to interrupt your ... hug, but you're needed to receive the Man of the Match award from the sponsors.'

Marcus reluctantly let her back down, and she gestured for him to go with the suit. He smiled a guilty apology.

She didn't know what to do with herself when he walked away. Her front was damp from his sweaty shirt, her lips buzzing from his kiss, and her knees distinctly wobbly. She watched and clapped as he was presented with a bottle of something, then shivered, and realised she'd left her jacket behind.

As everyone headed back towards the bar, the changing rooms, or home, Sophie returned to the stand, finding the jacket which had dropped behind her seat. It was warmer in the wind-sheltered stand – the rays of the sun still reached the higher seats – so instead of heading inside, she decided to stay out there and complete some kind of match summary. It didn't take long, but she was so comfortable, she dozed off.

A shadow falling across her woke her up. 'I have been looking for you *everywhere*!' exclaimed Marcus. His hair was clean and damp-looking, his shirt and tie spotless, and his chinos smartly creased.

Sophie rubbed her eyes, feeling bedraggled in comparison. 'Sorry, I dropped off.'

'No matter. We really do need to get you that phone. I have a spare handset, I'll pick up a SIM card on Monday.'

She stood, grabbed her things, and began walking with him. 'No sign of my handbag?'

'Nope. Same for your purse or passport. They're long gone, sorry.' He smirked, 'You've caught a bit of sun.'

'Really?' Sophie checked her shoulders, which were looking a bit pink. 'Oh hell, how is my face?' She crossed her fingers and hoped the SPF in her moisturiser did what it said on the pot.

'Not too bad, just a bit of a sun blush. Goes nicely with the bruises. C'mon, I'll introduce you to some of the boys.'

They had reached the doors of the club and she groaned, 'Please give me a few minutes to tidy up.' And to pull herself together to be "confident Sophie". 'I'll meet you inside.'

'Cool.' He looked down at her awkwardly. Was he going to kiss her again? 'Thank you for today, it was just the boost I needed.'

'No problem, it was fun, and nice to be useful. If it helps, I've written some more notes.'

'Great. Definitely.' It was as if he didn't know what to do with himself.

'So, I'll see you in a couple of minutes?'

'*Ja, ja.*'

As she entered the ladies, Sophie was chuckling at Marcus swapping between British and typical Afrikaans xpressions, but gasped in horror at the sight that greeted her. Her "sun blush" was more than a little bit pink and some of the make-up was wearing off, leaving the vivid bruising visible. She rummaged in her bag. Luckily, she had brought enough kit to soothe the incipient tightness and tone down the discolouration.

Once her face was fixed, she closed her eyes, took a deep breath, and centred herself, thinking of the exercises she had practised: posture, carrying herself like she was a foot taller; smile, friendly and open; calm and cheerful. This was her first major test – she didn't count meeting the other halves earlier.

With a confident stride, she exited the ladies and headed towards the bar. Marcus was visible just beyond a wall of smartly dressed people, and she bit her lip thinking of how best to join him.

'So, you're Sophie?' The gruff drawl came from her side and she had to prevent herself jumping or shying away.

'Yes.' She gave a confident smile to a tall fellow in a fawn lounge suit, with darkly tanned skin and wild, white hair. 'I'm Sophie.'

'You're also damn good with kids, a couple of ma boys learnt as much from you today as they did at last summer's training camp. Drink?' He picked up a bottle on the bar, filled an empty goblet to the brim, and passed it over.

Sophie accepted the glass of white wine, taking a cautious sip before composing her response. 'I'm glad they enjoyed it. I've never spent much time with kids.'

'No nieces or nephews?'

'I'm an only child of only children.'

He harrumphed. 'If you ever feel like babysitting, gimme a call. Where are my manners? I'm Todd Duncan.' He offered a large paw.

'Sophie Edwards.' She shook, and was surprised that despite his size, he didn't crush her fingers.

'Visiting?'

'She's with me.' An arm was wrapped around her waist, tucking Sophie into Marcus' side. 'Hi, Todd, how's business going?' He shook Todd's hand, but it looked a little more challenging than Sophie's experience.

'Grand. This li'l lady's yours? I was 'bout to pinch her to be the boys' new mama.' Todd chuckled. 'That was good work she did earlier.'

'She'll be a bit busy with me for the foreseeable future.' Marcus bared his teeth in a semblance of a smile.

Instead of taking offence at Marcus' hostility, it only served to bemuse Todd and he hooted with laughter. 'Good boy, I'm glad you've finally found someone worth keeping around. Well, I'll leave you the rest of this bottle to enjoy, I sure fancy a bourbon. See you tomorrow for the *braai*!'

Todd sauntered away while Marcus picked up the bottle he'd been pouring the wine from. 'Hah! He's finally got the club to carry his wine. Well, well.' He poured himself a glass and took a sip. 'Not bad.'

'It is quite nice, but what was that about?' Sophie was rather confused, and slightly disturbed by Marcus' body pressing against her.

'Todd's a bit of an interloper. He could be happily growing grapes in Napa, but that would be too easy for him. Instead, he decided to take on a rundown vineyard here bordering a rough area and make a go of it. That was one of his adopted kids who got my attention earlier.'

Sophie watched as Todd Duncan clapped a stout, well-dressed man on the back and gestured profusely.

'There's a whole crowd of them that he's found, fed, and homed. Says he's "gonna make some rugby players out of 'em". Not sure how successful they'll be at that, but Joseph was one of his first projects – he trained him up and let him go. I suspect the reason it's taken so long for his vineyard to become successful is his staff are always headhunted by others.'

'Including you?'

'Yeah, but he approached us to take some staff on. Joseph was part of the deal – he needed a change of scenery after losing his family.'

'Interesting character.'

'He is. Likes to kick up a fuss in the wine growers' meetings too. Anyway, I do agree with him that you're great with kids.'

'Really?' Sophie raised her eyebrows at him. 'I've never spent any time with them.'

'I've seen you explaining complicated tactics to some of the kids at Harford. Perhaps that's why they like you – you don't talk down to them?'

Sophie shrugged. 'They were very bright, and challenging. And curious – absolutely full of questions. I like that.'

'Good.' They smiled at each other, and Sophie remembered the near-kiss on the pitch, the near-kiss the night before, and her body's keen urge to get closer to him. Her lips buzzed. She licked them and his eyes dropped to her mouth.

Someone hollered, 'Oi, Coetzee!' and they glanced over at the other side of the bar to see gesturing arms.

'Come on, the boys want to meet you.'

Sophie took a gulp of wine and followed him to the large crowd of men and women.

'Hey, everyone, this is Sophie.'

Marcus followed with a list of names, but Sophie didn't register any of them: she was too busy tamping nerves down. Breathe, smile, 'Hi, everyone,' she chirped.

As Marcus was dragged away by someone, she recognised some of the women from earlier, smiled, and fluttered her fingers back at a couple of them.

'Hey, tablet woman. I'm Gert, if you didn't catch it. Thanks for giving that *oke* a *poes klap* earlier.' The player who'd made the holiday photo comment at half time grinned at her, his white teeth bright in his olive-skinned face.

Sophie took a second to guess vaguely what he meant.

91

'No worries, he did most of the work himself, though.'

'Got any more tricks up your sleeve?'

Sophie laughed. 'Give me a chance, I can't do much analysis with a tablet compared to the gear I use back in the UK.'

'Hey? You do that for real?' Gert distractedly scratched a hand in his dark hair.

'Performance analysis? I started at Harford Park this past season, but I'm still learning. Marcus had been doing some of the analyses with me.'

'*Jislaaik*, he never said anything. Wait till I tell the boys. We'll see you later, anyway, we're dossing over for the *braai*.'

'I'll be there.' She mentally kicked herself for such a facile comment – where else would she be?

They were joined by another giant, a mirror image of the first but with blond hair and lightly tanned skin.

'The mystery woman, *isit*?'

'Am I?' Sophie grimaced, 'There's nothing mysterious about me, honest.' She managed to catch Marcus' mimed question asking if she was OK, and she nodded reassuringly back at him. 'I just had a little bang on the head and ribs, and a touch of confusion. Everything's fine, really.'

'Let's see.' The second giant lifted her chin with a gentle finger, and they both leant in to examine the bruising. 'Not bad. Colouring nicely. '

'There's also my arm, and look at my ribs!' She pulled up her top and showed them her bruised midriff.

They both winced and Gert commented, 'Jan, she bruises better than you. Nothing broken?'

'Luckily, no. Just bruised.' Sophie pulled a wry face. 'I'm just a complete klutz. Marcus tries to teach me to catch a rugby ball and fails miserably. I have no coordination at all.'

Jan shook his head. 'You're doing well today. Many

people would still be tucked up in bed with injuries like that.'

'I didn't want to miss the game. Turns out I'll probably be here for another few matches as it'll take a while to get a new passport.'

'A woman who loves rugby, too. I knew Marcus would find someone a little different.'

'"Little" being rather apt, I'm a short-arse.'

'You look perfectly in proportion to me,' the first colossus added with admiring eyes.

'And the short hair is refreshing, makes a change from all that long stuff getting in the way.'

Sophie lifted an eyebrow. 'I don't look like a boy?' She'd been afraid of that kind of comment since chopping it off.

'*Nooit*, no way, it's very sexy on you.'

'*Ja*, Marcus is a lucky man, to have caught a *bokkie* such as you.'

The two were very friendly and engaging, almost too friendly. She wondered what they were calling her. She'd heard it before, 'A *bokkie*?'

'A *bokkie*, a little doe-eyed creature. Like you.' Marcus wrapped her up from behind, smooching kisses into her neck.

Sophie's eyes fluttered closed as tremors ran through her. She gasped as his hands wandered a little further, lighting up nerve endings. He pulled her back against him, one warm hand going under her top, fingertips nearly brushing her breast. She wanted the hand to move closer, to cup her bare skin.

'I thought I would rescue you before these two spirit you away. Gert and Jan like to team up for threesomes,' he murmured into her neck between kisses.

'We've never had any complaints.'

'*Ja*, apart from when we haven't wanted to repeat the experience.'

93

'But we won't have any success with you. The heat between the two of you is incredible, I feel scorched just watching.'

Sophie was finding it hard to concentrate, surrounded by Marcus and the other two not holding back heated stares. No one else could see past them, at what Marcus was doing to her, and he didn't seem to mind them watching as his hands travelled.

'C'mon, it's about time I took you home,' he whispered in her ear.

She had to hold back a whimper. It wasn't fair to be this turned on and not able to do anything about it. Her legs felt like noodles. She ached with need for some kind of sexual contact. That night, they would share a bed. How was she going to cope? She was ravenous for him, and he wasn't even going to touch her.

Chapter Seven

Leaving the bar was a blur. She was vaguely aware of saying goodbye to people, the giants included, but her attention was on the fellow next to her.

There were strangers sitting in the driver and passenger seats of his car – another tall, blond chap and a woman with long, black hair and gorgeous mocha skin. They smiled a hello.

'Sophie, this is Piet, and his girlfriend Kara, they're staying with us tonight. Piet's driving as he hasn't been drinking.'

Sophie distractedly said hello as Marcus helped her into the back seat. She wasn't sure if she imagined his hands lingering on her, or whether it was wishful thinking. Her body burned with anticipation either way, of his hands venturing further up her thighs or chest.

Once the car swept out of the ground and on to the road back to the vineyard, Kara turned to them with a smile. 'Sorry, we didn't get to meet earlier. I was a bit late and you'd already been surrounded by Todd's kids.'

She took a moment to rein in her wayward thoughts. 'Yeah, that was fun. They're really keen to learn. Todd seemed nice too.'

Piet chuckled. 'You met our local mad American? He's a good guy. Everyone thought he must have been running from something when he arrived and that he wouldn't stay, but he settled in and no one has a bad word to say. *Bladdy* good staff he trains, too.'

'Marcus mentioned it.' She used that excuse to touch

the man-in-question's thigh, and left her hand there.

'Takes them in, educates them, trains them up, and ships them out. In exchange for favours from other vineyards, usually. Donated equipment, that kind of thing.'

'I still don't know how he manages financially,' mused Kara. 'Lots of goodwill, mostly.'

'He's no fool, despite his good-ol'-boy image. Anyone he takes on has to work damn hard, and have the ability and desire to learn.'

As Kara and Piet continued talking, Sophie found her hand was rubbing Marcus' thigh. She was leaning towards him and him towards her. The hand ventured further, feeling the muscles contract. His palm came down lightly on hers and stopped it moving so much, but he threaded his fingers in between hers, up and down, as if in imitation of another far more intimate act.

The touch was soothing as well as arousing, and Sophie felt her eyelids begin to droop as the day caught up with her.

'Sssshhhh, she's had a long day.'

Sophie felt herself being picked up in someone's arms. She snuffled into his neck – it was definitely Marcus – and murmured contentedly, winding an arm around his neck. A few minutes later, she felt herself being placed on a bed, and groused as she lost contact with him. But the bed was lovely and soft and smelled faintly of Marcus, so she stretched out and drifted off.

A while later, she woke, with remnants of disturbingly erotic dreams fading away. She was feeling a little better, apart from her teeth needing a brush, and being a bit uncomfortable fully dressed. She sat up cautiously, finding herself the only one in the bed. Marcus' bed.

A quick freshen up in the bathroom and she changed into a pyjama shorts set, slinging a light cardigan over the top to cover her bare arms. It wasn't late, so she followed the sound of voices downstairs.

They were sitting at the table in the kitchen, swigging from bottles of beer.

Marcus grinned. 'Guess who's missed all the hard work?' He pointed his bottle at her.

She blushed. 'Sorry.'

'Hah, ignore him,' contradicted Kara, 'You needed a break. Those bruises look painful, hey?'

Sophie had forgotten that the shower would wash away her make-up, and her hand went to cover the bruises on her head. 'It's not too bad, actually. The ribs are the most tender.'

'Ribs?'

Sophie carefully lifted her top, remembering the time she'd done it and inadvertently flashed Marcus. This time she took care to tuck the fabric under.

Kara winced and bent down to examine her ribs. '*Eina.*' She lifted the top further up. '*Blerrie hell*, you were lucky you didn't break anything. You can definitely have a pass from doing anything tonight or tomorrow.'

'What am I not doing?'

'Getting the food ready. It's not been much work doing the salads and shit, because with these boys it's mostly meat.'

'Meat,' added Piet.

'Meat, and more!' They all joined in with Marcus to chorus, 'Meat!'

'Why else do we have *braais*?'

There was a sound outside, and the kitchen door burst open. In strode Gert and Jan, arms full with kegs of beer. '*Waar wil jy die bier*?' Both of them laid eyes on Sophie in her nightwear, top still held up and legs bare.

'Yum.'

'Double yum. Want help getting to bed, Soph?'

Marcus blocked their view. 'The bar's set up outside,

the beer can go there.'

Sophie zoomed back upstairs to put on normal clothes –
a pair of leggings and a loose T-shirt – plus the tiniest bit
of make-up as her vanity wouldn't let her be bare-faced in
company. She trotted back downstairs to find them all
sprawled on the sofas, still drinking.

'Beer?'

A bottle was passed to her before she could object and
brief introductions made. The room had filled with more
of Marcus' friends and fellow players, bringing the
number into double figures. She looked for somewhere to
sit.

'Oh, you covered up. Spoilsport. But it doesn't matter.'
Gert patted a small piece of cushion beside him. 'Come,
join me here.'

Next to him, Jan smiled and patted the same area. 'Or
me here.'

There was nowhere else. Even a couple of the armrests
had people straddling them.

Kara was sitting across Piet in one of the single
armchairs. 'Sophie, you can sit on your man's lap, can't
you?' She nodded at Marcus, also in a single-seater, who
opened his arms for her with a soft grin.

'If not, she can sit on mine.'

'She can sit on anything of mine.'

It was either Marcus, or braving the attentions of Gert
and Jan. She went for the known risk of her supposed
husband, lowering her weight carefully onto him. She
slouched back and whispered into his ear, 'Sorry.'

Only then, as Marcus nuzzled against her and she
smelled his beer-laden breath, did she realise he wasn't
exactly sober. His arms wrapped around her, one hand
resting on the inside of her thigh. His fingers didn't stay
still, softly caressing her.

Despite appearing drunk, his actions were arousing as
their bodies melded closer. Perhaps a hand was travelling

up and down her legs because he wasn't clear-headed? And something felt suspiciously like an erection digging into her. She wiggled slightly to check. It was.

Marcus murmured something, and the other warm hand intruded under the loose T-shirt and wrapped around her waist, his thumb and fingers lightly stroking the band of her bra. She was sure something brushed the underside of a breast too. There it was again. She barely withheld a moan.

Her body was buzzing for escape or relief, but she couldn't think of a single good excuse to move off his lap. A lap with an alluring erection. She became conscious of fidgeting slightly, and that her hips were making tiny pushes in his direction.

He began kissing her neck, her eyes fluttered closed, and a moan escaped that time.

'*Jou maaifoedi*!'

'*Ag man*, do they have to do that? *Dit maak my so fokken jags.*'

'Jan, you're always horny.'

'Kara, your *broekies* must be wet too, *nè*?'

'*Voetsek*, Gert. Can't you two stop pretending you need a woman and go fuck each other?'

The burst of laughter brought Sophie around, to see everyone staring their way. She felt her cheeks flame, and quickly gulped a mouthful of beer. 'Sorry.'

'No need to apologise,' soothed a grinning Gert. 'It will give us lots of ammunition to tease Marcus with tomorrow.'

'You would think that with an Irish mother he would be able to drink, but he's more likely to be asleep in the corner after a few beers.'

Marcus grumbled, continuing to nuzzle against her, then his hands slowed and he appeared to doze.

'He's always been a bit of a lightweight with the drink and the women. I'm glad he has sorted the women side of things out.' Piet shook his head in mock disgust as Kara elbowed him.

Cradled by Marcus, Sophie felt secure enough to partake in the light-hearted conversation, which generally consisted of ribbing the others around them during a continued consumption of beer. After her third bottle, she waved away several more, knowing that her clumsiness was bad enough as it was, without the added challenge of vast quantities of alcohol.

Besides, her body was still humming at being in such close contact to the man beneath her. Every now and again, she would shift position and he would stir and hold her closer to him. His subtle, spicy scent permeated the air, and she breathed it in. Something about it seemed to relax her.

Eventually, he stirred and woke, looking around at Sophie and his friends and smiling dazedly.

'Welcome back, Sleeping Beauty.' Piet handed him a beer.

After a few sips, his eyes began to clear, just as the others started to make a move for bed. '*Yoh*, give me a hand to tidy up before you go. Bridget will freak if the place is a mess when she arrives tomorrow.'

'Your sister is coming with her girlfriend?' asked Kara.

Sophie restrained a snigger at the way some of the men's ears pricked up at that.

'*Ja*, and some of her friends.'

There were several audible groans and curses at that. 'Tell them no lectures about being politically correct,' someone muttered.

Gert nodded, '*Ja ja*, we're perfectly happy being sexist dinosaurs.'

'At least they can't accuse us of being racist,' grumbled Piet. 'It's a *bladdy* rainbow nation in here.'

It was true. Yes, the early arrivals had included quite a

few tall, white Afrikaaner-types, but the rest of the drinking and chattering bunch had a blend of the darkest black skin, to chocolate, coffee, light tan, and olive.

Sophie counted at least twelve people. 'Where is everyone going to stay tonight?' she wondered out loud.

Gert pulled a torch out from somewhere. 'The lucky ones get to camp outside, the unlucky are in the house. Kara and Piet are in the room next to you.'

'Unlucky?'

'It's cold outside, but the stars? Incredible. Especially from the hot tub. Plus, we'll stay up for a while longer around the fire tomorrow night.'

'Hot tub?' she asked. 'There's a hot tub?'

'Next to the pool. Marcus hasn't been treating you?'

'I didn't know ...' She flashed back to the drunken wedding night, about him having unexpected visitors when he was naked. She groaned, 'It's another thing I must have forgotten about.' The prospect of seeing Marcus naked was really something she shouldn't have forgotten.

Marcus cleared his throat. 'The doctors said no hot baths for a few days, so I assumed it was out. It'll be ready for tomorrow though, and the pool's been cleaned, filled, and heated up a bit too.'

'Ooh, that sounds great, I love swimming!' She squirmed happily on his lap until his hands stilled her. She enjoyed the heat through her clothes.

As people started clearing out, Sophie wriggled off Marcus' lap, his hands dropping away. She missed his warmth straight away as she busied herself, picking up empty bottles and taking them through to the kitchen. A massive yawn caught her unawares as she stacked them in a box.

'Time for you to go back to bed, *isit*?' Gert winked.

Sophie remembered at that moment she would be sharing a bathroom and bed with Marcus. She flushed, heat rebuilding through her body. He'd seen her in nightclothes when her head was bad, it seemed different now she was better.

Gert gently ruffled her hair and grinned. 'You go get ready for him, we'll finish tidying.'

Get ready for him? More like wrap up and ensure they slept separately! Sophie waved goodnight to the rest of the crowd making their way outside.

'I'll be up in a bit,' Marcus winked at her as he followed them.

It only took her a couple of minutes to get ready, although it took several more to give up on finding a spare pillow or something they could put between them. All the spare pillows had disappeared, she assumed for the visitors to use. She admitted defeat and turned the light out, still thinking about how Marcus felt under her. She knew that was an erection poking into her when she sat on him. In the darkness of his bedroom, her hand went between her legs, and she felt the wet heat still there. Her hips jolted as she stroked herself. It wouldn't take long.

Just as she was about to come, the door creaked open. She bit her lip, holding back a swear word, and froze in place, with her hand still on her mound.

Marcus stumbled into the bathroom, the door was shut, and she heard the shower turn on. Hurriedly, she continued stroking herself. Seconds later, the shower cut off and she heard him brushing his teeth. That didn't take very long either and infuriatingly, just as she was about to come again, the door opened.

Through mostly shuttered eyes, she saw him wobbling out wearing just a pair of shorts before the light switched off.

She felt him get into the bed and lie down. Frustrated, she smoothed her breathing out, pretended she was asleep while her hand still slowly worked between her legs.

She held on for several minutes, waiting for his breathing to settle down too, and turning her face so she

102

was breathing into the pillow.

She had to come before she could sleep, the hot, swollen itch was really getting to her. His breathing seemed deeper and she hoped he was asleep. It didn't matter that he was in the bed, next to her, under the same bedclothes.

Marcus. In bed. With her. Almost naked.

She strangled her moan into the pillow as she came, her legs reflexively kicking out.

As she fell asleep, still throbbing, she heard an almost-soundless whisper, so quiet she could have imagined it. *'You know, I could've helped you with that.'*

Sophie slowly woke, so comfortable she didn't want to move. There was something warm behind her, holding her, a familiar masculine smell around her, and a delicious poke into her lower back that she could feel through her skimpy pyjama shorts. She wriggled a bit, up and down, and the thing moved from her lower back to between her thighs.

Oh, that felt good. Perhaps moving a little bit would work?

She wriggled around for a bit more, enjoying the sensations generated by the feel of the strong man behind her. Her shorts were pushed down and away and they were skin to skin. That was even better. She could feel an ache growing between the legs.

Her movements must have woken him too. A warm hand slid down her stomach to between her legs, teasing her, circling her. Her breathing deepened and her hips began squirming. Her hand slid down to join it, to show how she liked to be touched. He caught on very fast, the increasing slipperiness aiding the exploration. Up, down, across, the odd flick, and little squeeze or pinch.

All the blood in her body felt like it was congregating between her thighs. The hand was building up a delicious heaviness, a growing knot of desire, of need for something. For the solidness beginning to push into her.

As that was under control, her hand ventured back up her body to squeeze her neglected breasts. There was blood rushing there also, the increased sensitivity adding to the pleasurable pain.

Which feeling was better? The teasing fingers, or her own hands? She wanted more of everything. Especially that delicious pressure burrowing into her. 'More,' she whispered hoarsely.

He pressed in, she pressed back, and he breached her entrance. She moaned loudly, 'More. More.'

He surged deeper, the hand on her mound helping him get closer. It still wasn't enough. 'More!' she pleaded.

His hips worked against her, becoming rougher and rougher as she threw her own pelvis back towards him. 'That's it!' Her unseeing eyes flew open and she buried her head in the pillow to muffle her rising cries.

He turned her body so she was face down on the bed and took control, lifting her hips, going deeper and deeper into her. Filling and stretching. His hands controlled her, one steadying her body, the other delving around and discovering what made her go wild.

She rewarded his powerful drives by squeezing his cock tightly, writhing sensuously and clawing the sheets, moaning at the exquisite sensations generated by the hardness inside her.

The thrusts quickened, ignited by her actions, the knot inside her imploded, and waves of ferocious heat swept through her body. As the tide began to recede, she felt him push harder, faster, and yell as he came inside her. She sighed with delight and subsided onto the bed, his body settling next to hers.

Seconds later, she heard him move, and swear quietly … then she realised what she'd done. What *they'd* done.

She'd just had sex. With Marcus.

She'd just had *great* sex with Marcus. Wow.

She waited for guilt, embarrassment, or any other emotion to hit, but the only thing she felt was another enjoyable spasm between her legs. She felt *fabulous*. She felt *epic*.

Sophie stretched like a cat on the bed, the pleasure still reverberating around her body. 'That was guuuuuh-oood,' she laughed, as another delicious aftershock hit. She lazily turned herself so she could see him.

A cursing Marcus didn't appear so chuffed. 'Shit! What have we done?' He rubbed his hands over his face, sniffed them and groaned.

For once, Sophie felt free. 'Please don't burst my bubble.'

'Bubble?'

She lifted her head to look him in the eye. 'Post-coital glow, muppet.' She squirmed as she throbbed slightly and her gaze dropped to the cock, lying on his thigh. She wondered how long it would take for him to become hard again, and licked her lips.

His cock twitched and he pulled a sheet over it. 'Don't do that.'

'Do what?'

'You look like you want to eat me up.'

'Not eat, lick and suck definitely.'

The hand with the sheet started moving slightly

'And swallow, I want to know how you taste.' The rampant devil inside her that Marcus seemed to spawn was egging her on, seeing how strong his willpower would be.

His hand moved a bit more.

She ran fingers up her body and to her lips. 'I wonder who tastes better, you or me.'

One light tug from her and the sheet was gone. Beneath his hand, she could see twitching. Her hips gyrated lightly against the mattress and she licked her lips again. 'Most of all, I want you inside me again, thrusting and stretching me.'

Between her legs she still felt swollen, so one hand returned to explore down there while the other rubbed her breasts. She was so wet, from him and her, and thrust a couple of fingers inside herself, echoing how he had felt.

She glanced his way. He was fascinated by the hand lower down. That made her hotter. Made her whimper and gasp. He was enthralled as she rubbed herself, pinched herself, arched into the sheets and gradually made herself come. It was even better than the previous night, as she didn't have to hold herself in check.

Knowing his eyes were on her made her feel even sexier, and she writhed in pleasure on the sheets.

As she came down from her solo climax, she could see him twitching, beginning to enlarge. She'd never seen a man swell like that before, not from the beginning. She wriggled over so her face was less than a foot away, with her breath whispering on his sensitive skin.

He tried to cover himself again, but she gently pulled his hand away and pinned it lightly on his thigh. 'I want to see. Please let me see.'

He swelled further as she watched, fascinated. This was what had felt so outrageously great inside her. Her hand kneaded his thigh, his fingers forgotten. As his manhood flushed darker and harder, a drop of fluid oozed from the head.

Before she could stop herself, she ducked her head and licked it off. 'Mmmm.' The taste was indescribable, sweetly addictive. Her tongue swept across him again, her lips kissing the velvety skin.

He swore and twitched. 'Soph!'

Her tongue burrowed in, searching for more as it oozed out of him. She murmured with contentment as the nectar trickled out. Her hands began to work his shaft, generating more of the succulent juice. On and on, she slowly began

106

taking him further into her mouth.

She looked up at him. His eyes were on the lips stretched around his cock, and the sight must have been enough to tip him over the edge. She felt him harden in her mouth, then pulses of salty liquid began hitting her tongue. It was different to the earlier taste, but still enjoyable. What a treat.

There was a long period of awkward silence as they lay on the bed and stared at the ceiling. The sun's rays gradually penetrated further into the room. Marcus eventually pulled away and stood, grabbing jeans slung over a chair and pulling a T-shirt over his head. He fussed with another pile of clothes while she watched.

'You OK, Marcus? I didn't hurt you?' She tugged at a sheet to partially cover her body.

'Huh?' He gaped at her, 'How on earth would you have hurt me?'

She blushed fiercely. 'I'm not very experienced with this stuff.' He continued to look puzzled. 'You know, intimate relations? And what to do afterwards?'

'Sophie, we had incredible sex, you brought yourself off in front of me, and then you gave me a fantastic blow job!'

'That wasn't a blow job! I just wanted to taste you and I got carried away. And was the sex really that good for you? I've certainly never come like that before, or been so horny.'

Marcus groaned and threw away the shorts he was holding. 'Could you stop saying this stuff please?' he yelled in a hushed voice. 'I knew what you were doing when I came to bed, you had me hard all night just thinking about it. The sight of you coming is implanted in my head already. All I can smell is you! Just when I've settled down, you go and do or say something which makes me raring to go again.'

Her eyes dropped to his crotch. Sure enough, it was bulging. She licked her lips.

'Fucking hell, not again.'

She was shoved back onto the bed, the sheet stripped from her as he unbuttoned his jeans. In seconds, he was thrusting inside her, and she was clawing at his T-shirt, pulling it off over his head.

He felt different, chest to chest, but no less good. Finally, she could wrap herself around him, force him closer into her, see his face as he tried to regain some control, and how he lost it, how they both lost it when she squeezed him as tightly as she could.

As they lay sweaty and sprawled on the bed, there was a loud bang on the door. 'C'mon you guys, enough of *die fokken*, it's time to get up now, hey?'

Sophie didn't know whether to laugh or curl up in a ball and die of embarrassment. Marcus had hidden his head under a pillow, cursing profusely. She nudged him. 'Well, they definitely know we're sleeping together now.'

She pushed away the remaining covers, rolled out of the bed, and wandered into Marcus' en suite bathroom. Her toiletries had been placed with his, so she grabbed them and showered. Her body felt great, pleasantly sore with no echo of the headache or sore ribs.

'Will you be long?' asked Marcus through the door.

'Just finishing,' sang Sophie. 'Come on in.'

The door opened and Marcus entered with a towel around his waist. He kept his gaze fixed away from the shower, grabbing a toothbrush and vigorously brushing his teeth.

Sophie stepped out of the shower, dried herself off, and began moisturising, still naked and feeling no reason to cover up. She caught his eyes darting away. Every few seconds he would be staring at her despite his best efforts to keep his eyes averted. As he passed her to enter the shower, she pulled his towel off and giggled.

'Sophie!'

'Sor-ry, I just wanted to watch your buns. Lovely buns.' The way they flexed, they made her mouth water. And other parts.

He turned around to stop her watching his backside, so she could see his cock instead. It still wasn't even totally limp, despite their recent bout. She found herself running her hands up and down her legs, massaging her curves, her breasts with her lotion-slickened hands.

He was trying not to stare at her, swiftly soaping up and rinsing off, turning and twisting under the water. 'Shouldn't you be getting dressed?' he suggested.

'And miss this view? Not likely.' His naked and toned, muscular body looked even better with water running down it.

The water snapped decisively off. In two steps, he was towering over her, rubbing a towel over his chest. 'You're always pushing me, always just a little bit too smart.'

'I don't know why I feel braver around you, I feel I can be myself. I like teasing you.' She cupped her breasts, lifting them towards him.

He grabbed her wrists, propelled her back against the wall, and leant into her. He breathed heavily into her neck. 'While I don't feel like this nice guy everyone thinks I am. Some days I want to fuck you into the ground. I want to thrust inside you roughly, have you clawing at my back, do all those nasty, nasty things to you. Fuck knows how I haven't so far.'

Sophie felt like she had been thumped in the groin by a hot iron. She felt she should be angry at him, that was what he must want from her. Instead, heat was flashing through her, weakening her knees.

He lifted his head up and focused on her face, on the lips she was licking. 'Every time we were in that analysis room, I wanted to bend you over the desk and fuck you. Or feed my cock into your mouth. Your mouth has been giving me wet dreams for weeks. Months. Yesterday and last night were fucking torturous for me, but you finally won this morning. I awoke halfway inside you and there's no way even a saint could've stopped. I totally forgot about your ribs and head, are you OK?'

'I feel better than I've felt in weeks.' She lifted a leg and twined it around his.

'Sophie, please. I've never felt like doing this … stuff before. Everyone thinks I'm this sweet guy, but I'm not. When you tease me, I want to spank you. I bet you're horrified.'

'I'm not. I'd like you to pounce on me. It all sounds good.' She suggestively licked her lips and purred, 'Come on, do what you've been thinking of.'

Another bang on the bedroom door interrupted whatever Marcus was about to do next. 'C'mon, you guys, there'll be no breakfast left and Marcus needs his protein.'

A faint voice could be heard giggling in accompaniment, 'Sophie's already had hers.'

Marcus released her and spun to hold the sink with whitened knuckles. '*Fuck*!'

'Wow,' Sophie panted, trying to catch her breath and rein in her body. She picked up a towel and wrapped it around her. The rough fabric only irritated her breasts, so she discarded it and returned to the bedroom to dress and think.

Marcus followed slowly after, dressing in silence while Sophie hummed cheerfully as she pulled on a denim skirt and form-fitting T-shirt.

He was reaching for the door knob as Sophie applied a little make-up. 'Stop, Marcus. Please.'

He did, his head slumping downwards.

'Look, we both want to try things. Why don't we use this as experimental time, get to know what we like? No pressure. We can have some fun, then, as you planned, finish when we return to the UK. I'm on birth control, so there won't be any repercussions. No strings, just fun.'

Marcus chanced a glance over his shoulder, 'Fun?'

Confident Sophie. Shoulders back. Slight smile, though she was buzzing inside with nerves, with fear of rejection. 'Yep. Fuck buddies. Friends with benefits. Whatever. There'll be no one here to judge us, to force us to behave like a couple.'

'That's true – my parents won't be back from Ireland for a couple of months.'

So they had the house to themselves. Useful. 'Plus, some of what you've said intrigues me.'

His eyes flared at that.

'I've never been brave enough to approach anyone for just sex.' She shrugged. 'I wasn't a virgin, but I've never slept around. As I mentioned, I'm on birth control, the coil, but if you want to make sure there isn't anything else, we can have tests done next week.'

Marcus studied her and slowly began smiling, his shoulders relaxing. 'OK then, agreed.'

'Just give me one second. I don't want to go down alone.' She swiped some lip gloss on. 'There. Do I look presentable?' She spoke to Marcus' reflection in the mirror as he looked her up and down.

'If you looked any less presentable, we'd never get out of this room.'

Sophie glanced down at boosted cleavage on display at the V-neck of her tight T-shirt as she walked towards him. 'Hah! It's mostly padding.'

'It just reminds me, you have a nice little handful, a couple of teacups.' As she reached him, Marcus dabbed a kiss to her cheek, then quickly and brazenly sneaked a hand down her front and under her bra, squeezing a breast and pinching a nipple. 'That's enough for me. Let's go.'

Sophie gasped as he opened the door, chuckling under his breath. Cheeky bugger! His moods changed like lightning, she didn't know if she preferred him cheeky or assertive. She had to ignore that the contact had set her body alight again.

Chapter Eight

Venturing downstairs together, they were the recipients of many curious stares.

Kara gestured for them to sit down. 'There's just about enough left for you, we were beginning to think you'd never leave your room. Sleep well last night?' She tipped half a pig on to Marcus' plate, and didn't put much less on Sophie's.

'Very well, like a log, thanks,' answered Sophie politely. Marcus muttered similar observation.

'And this morning, isit?' asked Jan with a wicked grin.

There were some sniggers and Gert added, 'It sounded like you're both morning people.'

Sophie blushed fiercely and dug into her food.

'Ignore them,' consoled Kara. 'They're just jealous.'

'*Ja, ja*, I can't remember the last time I got it up more than three times in a row,' sighed Piet.

'Well, it definitely wasn't after you had concussion, we couldn't fuck for weeks without you getting a headache.'

Everyone snorted.

'It was only a few days,' Piet looked mortally offended. 'And it was doctor's orders.'

Yet more of Marcus' friends arrived as the morning wore on, and something curious started happening. They mostly brought wedding gifts, only small but usually considerate.

The *braai*, coming so soon after her arrival, had turned into some kind of celebration of their "marriage". Sophie began feeling really guilty: they wouldn't understand the

113

subterfuge and accepting something felt so wrong. After an hour, as the drinking began, the meat cooked, and the men gathered around to offer cooking tips, she escaped upstairs for a few minutes, to recharge her batteries.

Marcus must have been up and left the windows open to dispel the smell of sex. The bed linen had also been straightened. As it was cooling down outside, Sophie went to pull the window closed.

As she grabbed the handle, she heard voices from below. She glanced down to see Bridget standing with Gert, and was about to say something when Gert swore.

'I've told you, it's none of your business!'

'You have a responsibility –'

'You leave us alone, and you leave your brother's relationship alone.'

Gert ranted something further in Afrikaans, threw his hands up in frustration, and stormed off.

Bridget shook her head and sighed, 'Stupid, stupid man.'

Sophie edged back from the window, not wishing to be seen eavesdropping. She thought that Gert would be flirting with Bridget considering last night, not arguing. Then she recalled their reactions. When a couple of the others had looked intrigued. Gert and Jan had been more alarmed than lecherous.

Strange. Sophie shrugged her shoulders; it was none of her business. Bridget hadn't interfered with her and Marcus, so Gert must have been mistaken there. She lay down on the bed, had a relaxing half hour break, then returned downstairs.

Loads of people were in the pool, playing a boisterous game of water polo, and others were cheering them on from the sides. She wound her way around to the cooking area, where most of his close friends had gathered together again.

'Hey, *cherry*, I missed you.' Marcus smiled at her

114

return, and dropped his arm around her shoulder. 'Want some meat?' In his other hand, he held tongs with a captured sausage.

'Why not?' she answered with a saucy wink and a pinch of his rear, which quickly turned into a fondle. 'You can give me a sausage any time.'

His whole body stiffened for a moment and colour rose on his cheeks. Sophie's body began to warm.

'You two, stop it,' scolded Kara, handing Sophie a plate with salad on. 'Otherwise you'll be disappearing upstairs again and we won't see you for the rest of the afternoon.'

'Do you need a hand with anything?' asked Sophie as her plate was piled high with different types of meat.

Kara shook her head. 'Nah, Piet is the *braaier*, the head chef. Marcus and Gert are permitted to help him, but all the rest of the boys stand around drinking and critiquing.'

'And the women?'

The dark beauty rolled her eyes. 'You know we mentioned the sexism last night? We're only allowed to make the salads and desserts. The one time I tried to pick up a set of pincers, Piet spanked me!'

'Spanked you?' exclaimed Sophie.

Gert chuckled and leant over, examining the meat on Sophie's plate and taking it out of her hands. '*Ja, dit was fokken snaaks.*'

'English, Gert,' scolded Kara.

'It was very funny, except he was so distracted he burnt the steaks.' He gave the plate back to Sophie. 'Hey, Piet, ease off the sausages, they're a bit overdone.'

Piet responded to Gert with a rude sign, and a flurry of Afrikaans which made Kara gasp and blush. 'I won't ask him to translate that.'

Sophie laughed, and began eating the food on her plate as she listened to the banter tossed back and forth. Despite what Gert had said, the meat was cooked perfectly.

Marcus leant over and gave her a kiss, which rekindled the heat from earlier in the day. She ran a hand over his buttocks and squeezed them.

He lightly bit her ear and whispered, 'Please, not now. Otherwise I'll pop an erection right here.'

Sophie snickered – at least she had a chance of hiding her arousal. If she pretended she was really married to him, she couldn't be happier. His friends were good fun, if a little arrogant and boisterous at times. Kara did introduce her to a lot of the others at the *braai*, but many names passed her by as she kept glancing at Marcus, and he at her. Despite his request, she kept allowing trailing hands to brush over him, even braving the odd grope.

Todd popped in briefly, complete with a crowd of kids who bombed into the pool and hoovered up the leftovers – or what turned out to be just the end of that round of eating. New dishes magically appeared after the rabble had left.

Bridget had come over and spoken to her for a while. Sophie had profusely thanked her for helping Tandy. She felt vaguely uncomfortable about the scene she had witnessed with Gert, while Bridget continued to ask some probing questions about their marriage that Sophie had to pretend she didn't know the answer to. To her relief, Bridget had departed shortly afterwards.

Finally, after the sun had gone down, they sat and sprawled around a campfire and drank and ate yet more meat. Most people had only come for a few hours, so it was reduced to a similar group to the previous night, with six of them drinking and chatting, sitting separately from the rest of the debauchery.

Marcus sat beside her on her bench and pulled her to him. Unlike the previous night, he'd had a lot less to drink. 'You OK, my frisky little *bokkie*?

She smiled at him, enjoying the warmth of his body

116

next to hers. When the sun went down, it had turned quite chilly and she'd added more layers, including a pair of leggings under her skirt. 'I'm great, thanks. It's been a good day. Your friends are very entertaining.'

'They like you too. I knew you had nothing to worry about.'

She lowered her voice, 'Bridget was asking questions earlier.'

Marcus shrugged. 'Don't worry about it, she's just nosey.'

'I'd say she was more of a protective older sister, for good reason too. I'd be very suspicious if someone I was close to magicked a wife out of thin air.'

'We're not that close any more, not since I left here five years ago. Your presence is working, though – no strange women turned up at the game yesterday at the behest of my parents, and the only woman feeling me up today was you!'

She sniggered. 'You weren't complaining.' He didn't laugh along with her so she sobered. 'Was it really that bad?'

'The previous home game, two "eligible ladies" turned up with my parents, sisters of a family friend. After my parents left, they proceeded to charge their drinks for the whole night to my tab, swore at my friends, then insisted I drive them back to their hotel.'

Sophie snorted.

'I poured them into a taxi. My mother didn't believe me, she thinks they were "nice girls" as she knew the family from Ireland. What's worse is that they somehow got my number and were texting me about coming again this week. Even to the *braai*.'

'Oh dear.'

'Every time there's a home or away game, certain women turn up. Some of them get the message, others remind me of that bitch Andrea from Harford – thick-skinned and fake.' He sighed, 'This weekend was heaven in comparison.'

'Really?'

'Yeah, having you here was like having an invisible force field repelling them.'

She turned her head to stare at him. 'Seriously, the women chasing you were that bad?'

Gert overheard her incredulous query. 'Hey, Sophie doesn't think Marcus is that much of a catch.'

There were hoots of laughter.

'He's going to own a world-renowned vineyard, he's good-looking, fit, and his family are practically Cape royalty.'

Sophie blushed, 'I never knew ...'

'That's probably what attracted him to you, you had no idea about him. Why do you think he spends so much time in the UK? He can keep under the radar there much better than here.'

Sophie knew that he didn't even have his own flat, he shared a place in Harford with another couple of players. His car was inexpensive, and he was careful with money.

'He came out of the Army, started playing rugby professionally, then headed to the UK as soon as he could get away, like the Hounds of Hell were chasing him.'

'There were a few bitches and dogs after him,' laughed Jan as he got up and wobbled towards the house, clapping others in other groups on their backs as he passed.

Kara inserted, 'The biggest problem was that they all thought he was looking for a wife, because his parents were, so he couldn't just ...'

'Just have fun, fuck around,' filled Gert. 'They either held back the goods waiting for a ring, or thought sleeping with him would lead to one.'

Kara sighed. 'Some days, I'm ashamed of my own sex. It was only a few, rapacious women, but they scared the normal ones away.'

Piet cuddled his girlfriend. 'That's what brought us together. Kara overheard some women planning to spike Marcus' drink one night in a club.'

'I don't know if they were serious or joking,' interjected Kara. 'But someone had tried to roofie me a few weeks earlier. Things were weird here at that time. I went to warn him, but Piet was the only one sober enough to listen to me.'

'We got talking, she helped me get everyone out of the club, and we've been together since.'

'And I headed to the UK a couple of weeks later,' finished Marcus. 'Though I do miss you guys.'

There was a chorus of "awwws".

'Hey, we could be coming to join you in the UK once the season ends here,' Gert suddenly added to Marcus.

'For sure?'

'*Ja*, we have an agent finding us a club in Europe, in England or France. Hopefully will be near enough to catch up, have a *braai*.'

'I'll keep my ears open. We could end up playing against each other.'

'I promise I won't smash your pretty face in if we do. Or smash anything else in.'

The group all sniggered, though Sophie noticed some nudging going on. Jan returned, plonking down another case of beers.

'Score us a *dop*, Jan,' asked Gert from his position lying on the ground.

Jan passed out fresh beers to everyone, then joined Gert near the fire as they exchanged a few hushed words. It was quiet for a while.

Kara nudged Piet to speak. 'So, Sophie, how did you meet Marcus? Did you have to seduce him?'

She snorted. 'The first time, he got me drunk then had to take me home and nurse me while I puked.' There were a couple of laughing gasps at this. 'The second, he gave

119

me a lift home, I tripped over him, and we came this close to shagging before he fought me off.' She held her fingers a cock's length apart while the sniggering increased. She shrugged wryly. 'The next time, he was topless and he didn't even recognise me!'

Marcus groaned, 'To be fair, you used to have that horrible hair, pancake make-up and tacky clothes, and I hadn't seen you in decent light.

Kara laughed, '*Sooo* smooth with the ladies, Marcus.'

'He's right though, it wasn't the most flattering of looks. Some good friends helped me with a "make-under".' Sophie stroked Marcus reassuringly, feeling the simmering heat still present.

'So, what happened after that?' asked Gert.

Sophie shrugged. 'We started to get to know each other, doing the match analysis, then a month or so ago, he proposed at a friend's wedding.' That was close enough to the truth. 'Everything's a little blurred and rushed after that.' She left the rest to the man next to her.

His friends all stared, their gazes switching between them both. Sophie got uncomfortable. These were his best friends, and he was going to lie to them.

Kara groaned and asked quietly, 'What happened, Marcus? Spill it.'

Sophie held his hand and hoped he would come clean, for his sake.

'Look, we can understand the subterfuge. Your relationship's too new. It's clear you two feel something for each other, but you don't act like a married couple. Not yet. You can tell us,' cajoled Kara.

Marcus looked around to check there wasn't anyone close to their small group, then let out a massive deep breath, 'I knew you'd figure it out, you're too perceptive, Kara. It's true, we haven't tied the knot.'

Sophie felt a rush of relief at his honesty, as it looked like he did too. She kept her hands on his reassuringly as his friends shook their heads and profuse swearing under breath occurred.

'Thank you for your honesty.' Kara's words were echoed. 'We can all understand why you did it, can't we?' She nudged Piet and stared pointedly at Gert and Jan.

'*Ja*, completely.' Gert and Jan both looked away to stare into the fire.

Piet nodded. 'And your secret is safe with us.' His friends concurred. 'I was surprised you came back this year, I didn't think you would want to live here again. I know how the roofie thing ...'

'Yeah, let's not talk about that.' Marcus embraced Sophie and whispered thanks in her ear. The vibrations ran through her body and she struggled to concentrate on what he said next. 'While we're on the subject of marriage ...'

Piet hugged his girlfriend. 'What can I say? She wants us to wait until I've finished playing at the top level. Gert and Jan aren't the only ones thinking about going to Europe. I won't go without her, but Kara can't get a work visa.'

'I'm not skilled enough,' she grumbled. 'Teachers aren't generally wanted.'

The conversation moved on to nights out when they were younger and their group slowly expanded in size, with others joining the storytelling. Sophie leant back into Marcus, their bodies comfortably melding together. She was happy he'd told the truth to his close friends at least – she could feel the stress draining away. She could also feel something else.

Gert and Jan were regaling them with tales of threesomes. Wild tales, which always finished with the women bow-legged and soaked in bodily fluids.

All the talk of fucking was too much for her. She couldn't keep her body away from Marcus. Whatever they had done that morning had set off something inside her, making her even more unbearably horny. All she could think about was how he felt plunging into her. She twitched inside. Her hips kept moving slightly, searching for something.

He noticed her light shiver. 'Want a blanket?'

She nodded, and was shrouded in another layer. Others had blankets wrapped around them, but Sophie wouldn't like to say what was going on under some. Which gave her an idea as Marcus took the wool across his lap.

When he pulled her closer, she leant back against him, straddling a leg and surreptitiously, rhythmically driving her hips into him.

'Please stop that,' he hissed into her ear, even though he was pressing back at her. She could feel a bulge which must have been his cock. Inching over, she got it where she wanted it.

She turned her face into his neck as she shivered with pleasure. Under the blanket, his fingers began stroking her thigh, moving over and gently cupping her mound. Seconds later, his other hand sneaked up under her jumper to cup a breast. Both hands squeezed and twisted slightly. Despite the layers of fabric, she swallowed a moan as bolts of electricity shot through her.

'We'll be off for a walk now,' declared Kara with a smirk at the entwined couple. 'I really don't want to see my friends having sex in front of me, and you two are on the verge of it.'

Piet added, 'We'll be about an hour, and no one else will need to enter the house in that time, will they?'

His edict was greeted with a chorus of negative responses. It occurred to Sophie that she should feel embarrassed, but her body was driving her beyond distraction.

'We'll walk you to the door,' offered Marcus.

His idea of walking was holding a wobbly Sophie in front of him as they skirted the house, and standing at the entrance with her body plastered against his while they both waved Kara and Piet off for their "walk". Two paces backwards into the house and he slammed the door, yanked her skirt up, leggings down, pulled her knickers to one side, and thrust inside her, plastering them both against the door. Barely a couple of thrusts and she was on the verge of coming.

The restriction and friction of the clothes they both still wore made it even hotter. One of his hands moved from her hips to between her legs, ruthlessly scissoring around her and forcing them closer.

Somehow they made it to the floor. He kneed her legs wider open and thrust harder. The hand squeezing her mound hit something even deeper inside and she wailed as she came, sinking onto the polished floor.

A few more thrusts and he was coming too, yelling a curse as he pulsed inside her. His hands stayed on her hips and between her legs as they collapsed on their sides.

After a few minutes, he took a breath. 'I thought I was suffering with a rock-hard cock, but I can't believe how wet you are.' His hands began smoothing a mixture of her juice and his come over her skin, around her thighs. 'Do you like these knickers?' he asked.

'Yeah, they match the bra.'

'Shame. I was going to rip them off.' With her help, he stripped them and her leggings off, disposing with her top layers too, and digging her breasts out of the bra. His hands kept returning to between her legs, finding more fluid for him to smooth over her.

Where it dried, it felt tight on her skin but Sophie enjoyed the feeling, especially across her breasts. He seemed to enjoy licking her there too, and other places where his hands had been.

'We're going to go upstairs, and we're not leaving until we've done this a few more times. Through the night.' Another squeeze of her breasts and he was helping a dazed Sophie, naked apart from her misshapen bra, to her feet.

Chapter Nine

'Don't you have training today?'

After waving his friends off the next morning, they lay in bed recovering from another exhaustingly pleasurable bout of fucking. Sophie throbbed in a good way and she idly touched herself. Marcus stared at what she was doing.

'Hello, Marcus?' She realised she was distracting him and pulled a sheet up.

He tore his eyes away. 'This afternoon, we're doing the match debriefing. Although I won't need much of it after your efforts this week. You'll do some analysis for the games you're here for, won't you?'

'Yeah, get me a copy of yesterday's and any others and I'll see what I can do. I'm still under orders to take it easy this coming week, so it'll keep me busy.'

'I'll fit some small trips in around training, and the away game this weekend isn't too far.'

'Great.' She started playing with her nipples.

'May I help?' A male hand came up to join hers.

'Of course.'

She waved a brief "hello" to the other partners in the hospitality section, grabbed some food and drink, and went to sit in her favourite area of the stand, with the best view for analysis. It had become more like a working day than a holiday for her, but it felt good that she was being helpful and productive in exchange for Marcus helping her out.

He'd obtained a few videos of previous matches, and helped her set up some shaded screens on the *stoep* to complete the analyses. Going through the tapes reminded her how much she loved watching him play, how graceful he was with the ball. On his return from training, they would discuss what she had identified, and how best to resolve it for the next game.

The away match the previous week had been up the coast and they had spent a couple of nights christening every surface of the hotel room. She had managed to squeeze in the smallest amount of sightseeing, including a wander round a nature reserve and a boat trip with Marcus on the Sunday.

He'd had another decent game too, his confidence was improving in leaps and bounds and he was starting to try out more moves, some of which he had walked through during their analysis sessions. He couldn't seem to get enough of her mind or her body.

Her body reminded her of this as she gingerly sat down. It didn't take long before a crowd of kids surrounded her. She waved at Todd, who was in one of the hospitality boxes. He gave her a thumbs-up, mouthing was she OK, and she nodded and smiled.

'Hi, Sophie.' Kara managed to make her way through the kids, and took a seat next to her.

'Hey, Kara, late as always?' teased Sophie. Marcus had told her it was normal for Kara to miss at least part, if not all, of a game.

'At least I made kick-off today.' The referee blew the whistle to start the game. 'Just.' She reached into her handbag and brought out a bottle of wine and two plastic goblets.

Sophie accepted a glass. 'You would get on so well with Sarah, she's always turning up a minute before the match starts. Ouch, I bet that hurt.' On the pitch, Piet had been slammed to the ground by an exceedingly ferocious opposition tackle.

Kara took a large swig of her wine, and with her other

hand, gestured towards her prostrate boyfriend. 'That's the reason I don't come to many matches, I'm having to quell the urge to run down there to check he's OK. I did that once, he's never forgiven me.'

Sophie half laughed, half gasped, 'Oh no! Really?'

Kara peered over her glass at Sophie. 'Hmmm, Marcus hasn't been badly injured yet, has he?'

Sophie frowned. 'No, just the odd knock and twinge. His shoulder's finally settled down too, he didn't play much for Harford in the last year.'

'You just wait,' Kara threatened morosely. 'Not that I'm wishing it on him, but can we agree to sit on the other to prevent any pitch invading? Oh my God,' she gasped as Piet was mashed to the ground again. 'I need more alcohol. Top up?'

Sophie waved the bottle away as her glass was still mostly full. 'Thanks but I can't drink too much, I'm supposed to be analysing to help Marcus.'

'Plus doing a bit of babysitting,' chuckled Kara as the kids started calling things out to Sophie. 'Isn't this supposed to be a holiday for you?'

Sophie shrugged, 'I don't mind, it's nice to feel useful.'

At half time they continued chatting, as they popped to the ladies together and returned to their seats, with a detour to brief Marcus on anything Sophie had noticed. There was much less this time: he was alert to the defensive positioning. When the match restarted, she was relieved to see Kara had slowed down her drinking and wasn't cringing so much every time Piet was anywhere near the action.

'So, how has the last fortnight since the *braai* gone?' asked Kara during a break in play when Sophie wasn't fielding questions from her followers.

Lots and lots of shagging, but little ears didn't need to overhear that. 'Good. I've seen a bit of your country so far, looking forward to seeing more. My head's fine and the bruising's all but gone so I'll be going a bit further afield, as far as having no passport can take me.'

'And where Marcus' away trips take you both.'

'Yeah, he's made loads of plans so I don't miss any of his games, bearing in mind he doesn't want me travelling by myself. He's pulled in a few favours from friends in different towns and cities to give me guided tours and somewhere to stay.'

'I bet many of them are downright intrigued to meet the woman who caught him.'

Sophie coughed, 'That's been my experience so far.' Her attention was caught by Marcus making a break. 'C'mon, Coetzee!'

In one swift move, the opposition were floundering and Marcus and his team were camped yards from the line. The ball spun out from a ruck. Marcus caught it, dummied to pass outside but fed inside, and the rampaging player ran in under the posts.

'Nice work,' applauded Kara. 'That was one of those bits of info you talked over with your man, and he used it well. That dummy was outrageous.'

Sophie chuckled. 'Wasn't it just? Their defence was drifting out slightly for most of the first half, leaving a small gap around the breakdown with the slower hooker covering.'

'You're really good at this, aren't you?'

'I've always liked puzzles and working out how things work.'

'Logic.'

'Rugby's not always logical, though. It's about technique too, and getting things right mentally as well as physically. The heavier pack won't necessarily win the battle at the scrum.'

'And the most talented team may not win if the opposition are hungry enough to fight every step of the way.'

'Yeah, I like the oddities. I like the patterns. I like to see what's out of place and what should be improved or exploited. Never thought I'd be doing this, though, even this time last year.'

'You were working in the City?'

'Yeah, stock market data analysis. It pays better than the rugby work, but isn't as much fun. Tom, the assistant coach at Harford, has said he'll employ me in one of his companies in the City if I want to go back to it, either full or part time, but I'm undecided. I'd like to do something enjoyable for a few years.'

'Is the analyst role at Harford not full time?'

'It could be, but I need a lot more training. Ooh, go Marcus!'

They focused as his team had five minutes of defending their try line.

'Watch how the opposition are pulling our backs in, they're trying to create a mismatch – their faster back against a slower forward – to open up the wings. Someone needs to spot that.'

A certain blond-haired someone did, the ball was turned over, and his team were back on the attack.

Kara sipped her wine. 'Is Marcus likely to stay at Harford?'

Sophie hadn't thought about that. 'Not if he continues to play like this, the Premiership teams will be after him. I reckon it's only due to injury that he's not been spotted before.'

'He wasn't playing like this before, you know. Well, he was solid, but Piet says he's lifted his game immensely in the last couple of weeks, since you arrived. If Marcus continues like this, Piet wouldn't be surprised if the national side started sniffing around.'

'Really? He's a bit older than the current incumbents, definitely older than your average first cap.'

'If he's good enough, he may get into the setup. How do you think he'd feel about that?'

'I don't know, we've never discussed anything like that.' Marcus had always just said he wanted a decent run of games, he'd never voiced any further aspirations in her hearing. If he had the chance, would he stay in South Africa? Her heart twanged.

'And how would you feel?'

Sophie didn't answer. Kara patted her on the shoulder.

They lay on the bed after another torrid session. Sophie felt like she was getting addicted to sex, to the glorious feeling of him inside her. His body moving on hers, the sighs, gasps and groans that she teased out of him. She had never realised how good it could be, despite getting carried away during their first intimate contact.

She frowned as she thought back to that event, 'I wondered … why did you ignore me after we kissed?'

Marcus lifted his head and stared at her. 'Didn't I tell you before – I didn't recognise you.'

'You were telling the truth?'

'Of course! I had never seen your face in decent light, without heavy make-up, that dreadful haircut, and the horrible clothes, plus you walked differently in those stupid shoes. I looked for you for a few weeks, and assumed you'd stopped coming to the games.'

'That's why you blanked me?' She began laughing.

'Yep. I wasn't embarrassed about the groping, I just didn't recognise you after you cut your hair and returned to your natural colour. I couldn't even remember your name.' He made it all sound so simple. 'And your eyes? I didn't even know what colour they were, that horrible heavy fringe obscured them completely.'

'I hated that fringe.'

'Your mouth however, I should have recognised this …' He rubbed her lips with his thumb and Sophie

130

playfully nipped and laved it with her tongue. He groaned. 'When Sarah and Clare were so intent on setting us both up, I was confused about being attracted to another woman in such a short space of time. And the way your big eyes were looking at me.'

Sophie had her own confession to make. 'I didn't know it was you who took me home that time. I only realised recently.'

Marcus laughed. 'You were in such a state, and I wasn't totally sober myself, otherwise I'd have realised I wasn't to blame for you being that legless. You knew how to get home, I just made sure you got there, in between bouts of puking. You started pulling your clothes off and I didn't know what to do with myself. Then you puked again and nothing more came up, but I left you propped up with a basin anyway.

Sophie groaned with embarrassment. 'I didn't feel right for days. Whatever was in the drinks Andrea gave me, I've no idea. I'm not great at drinking, but I've never had that sort of reaction, with a near-total loss of memory.'

Marcus ruffled her hair. 'Probably just alcohol, but a lot of it. There's nothing of you, it makes you a cheap drunk.'

'Thanks,' spluttered Sophie with laughter.

'Seriously though, you've no idea how attractive you are. I know exactly what that bitch was doing when she had you fuck your hair up.'

'What?'

'You were too much competition. You've got this fresh and innocent thing going on which brings out a mixture of a protective instinct and overwhelming desire to debauch you. Your eyes widen at the slightest thing and you nibble your lips and make me so fucking hard, and then you take so much joy in the slightest, smallest detail, I feel evil for even thinking of how many times I want to fuck you.'

Sophie gulped.

'You haven't got a nasty bone in your body, you seem

so naive and unworldly, yet when I get inside you, you're so hot and responsive. You drive me wild.'

She couldn't look away from his blue eyes. She could feel her nipples knotting, her hands wandered up to rub the sides of her breasts for relief.

He groaned on seeing her hands. 'That's what I mean, I'm hard for you already. Again. Most of the time, you don't even realise you're doing it.' He nodded at her chest.

She glanced down, somewhat surprised to see her hands presenting her breasts towards him.

'You're going to fucking kill me; I've never been so randy so often. Come here. Keep your hands on your breasts.'

He pulled her over him, her legs parting naturally and his erect cock teased her.

'I don't know how …' she began. Then he began slipping up into her. 'Oh. Ooh, that's nice.' Her eyes crossed as she felt him harden further.

His laugh was cut short when she began trying out different hip movements, to find out which one she liked best and what he liked too. Her sporadic gasps were joined by almost-continuous groans of pleasure.

She loved the intimacy when she bent forward, the naughtiness when she leant back. Swirling her hips touched places inside her, bringing her legs inside his rubbed others and made him feel even more like he was invading her, but in a good way. Not just good, incredible.

His fists were clenched on the sheets as he watched her move around from under shuttered eyes, and listened to her vocal enjoyment. Most of the time, apart from when she was using them for balance, her hands were on her breasts, squeezing them, teasing and pinching the nipples.

After trying a reverse cowgirl, when he complained he couldn't see much apart from her back and feel her squeezing him, she returned to facing him and he lost his restraint. His back arched as his hands clamped on her hips. 'Fuck, Sophie.'

She whined as he was forced further up into her. 'Wow.' She fell forward, her breasts rubbing against his firm chest.

He groaned, his hands moving to cover her breasts. After watching her, he seemed to have learnt exactly what she liked, what gave her pleasure, and how far to push her. With his feet flattened on the bed, he began a rhythmic jolt upwards to meet her writhing hips.

With her hands freed from holding her breasts, one of Sophie's hands slithered between his thighs. Gentle fingers on his bollocks made him tremble and she could sense he was close. She was close too, her other hand was playing between her legs and she began clamping down even tighter on him.

Their matching shouts came within seconds as Marcus pumped inside her. His hands tightened on her nipples and she shook in bliss with him.

She subsided over him, tremors still running through their bodies, and they dozed, his arms around her.

'Hot tub?'

'Hot tub.'

The hot churning water had become addictive for them every evening, and the warmth helped loosen Marcus off after a game. They would fill a basket with drinks and snacks to enjoy while they wallowed in the water. Grabbing towels, they made their way down outside. As Marcus lifted the lid off, Sophie headed to the kitchen.

She discarded the towel to free her arms as she selected what to take outside, chucking packets into the basket. Bending over, she rummaged in the fridge and pulled out a couple of bottles of water. Placing one in the basket, she unscrewed the other, drinking the refreshing water straight down.

'Save some for me?'

She looked over her shoulder to see Marcus leaning against the kitchen doorway, as naked as her. Despite their recent tussles, the break was long enough that he was fully erect again.

'I don't know about that,' she purred. 'Unless you have something that'll interest me?'

As she went to close the fridge door, she could hear him approaching. His hands clamped down on her thighs, pulling her up and her legs apart. He thrust inside her, giving way to him easily. She grabbed the nearby counter as he hammered inside, gasping in pleasure.

'Nice,' muttered Marcus, withdrawing from her body, grabbing the half-empty bottle, and swigging the rest down. 'Was that interesting enough?'

Sophie couldn't even speak, and her legs were like warmed Plasticine. With her head on her arms, she hung on to the counter, the only thing keeping her upright. Her eyes refused to focus, she tried to voice words, but only moaned. The incessant throbbing between her legs took all her effort in mastering. She twitched her hips, rubbing her thighs together.

'Want more?' asked Marcus smugly, stroking his cock. He took one hand off and licked it, 'Mmmm, delicious Sophie. Want to try?'

Without waiting for her response, he stuck two slick fingers in her mouth. She automatically sucked and licked them, taking in both of their fluids.

'Good girl,' praised Marcus as her eyes fluttered closed. Without removing his fingers, he grabbed her hips again with his other hand, thrusting back inside her. 'I would love to be in two places at once, with a hard cock between both sets of lips, on either side. Wouldn't you like that?'

Sophie sucked faster on his fingers and thrust her hips towards his, barely hearing his inflammatory words. Just as she was about to come, he withdrew, slapped her buttocks, and continued to gulp water down as he watched her.

She keened, one hand going to between her legs. Even without him, she was desperate to come.

'Nuh-uh,' he scolded, grabbing the wrist of the guilty hand and turning her towards him.

She hissed at him, and he laughed back, hoisting her over his shoulder, grabbing the basket of supplies, and carrying her to the hot tub.

En route, she tried to touch herself, but despite wriggling, couldn't get near. He however kept stroking her softly between her legs and squeezing her buttocks. Frustrated, she managed to get her face near his back and bit his upper buttock. Hard.

Marcus gasped. 'Ouch! You're so going to regret that.'

He slapped her arse. Hard.

'Ow! You bully!'

He laughed and rubbed at her skin, soothing the sting.

Sophie couldn't believe the softly spoken, gentlemanly Marcus had disappeared and she was left with this tyrant, a despot who insisted on teasing her unmercifully. 'You're being mean,' she sulked.

'Mean?' He spanked her again. 'You're constantly teasing me, and you think I'm being mean?'

Oops. He'd spotted that. Bollocks. Sophie squirmed. Despite the discomfort, what he was doing to her made her hotter and hotter.

He carried her along the side of the pool, towards the steaming tub. Placing the snacks to one side, he unloaded her until her legs were wrapped around his waist, with her facing him. His cock rubbed her mound and with a push of the hips, almost entered. He grinned mischievously at her. 'Comfortable?'

What was he up to? She distractedly stared at the hot tub behind him as he stepped away from it, towards …

The pool!

135

'You bast –' The cold water rushing up muffled the rest of her cursing and his laughter.

As they were drying off after a soak in warmer water, his phone rang. He glanced at it and passed it over. 'I think this is for you?'

On seeing her friend's name, she pressed the answer button. 'Hi, Sarah.'

'Sophie! I've been trying your mobile for days but there was no answer. You OK?'

A naked and damp Marcus pressed against her and his interest lodged partly inside. 'Ohhhh, yesss.'

'Oh?'

'Oh, I had an accident and it was stolen. I'm fine.' He kissed her neck and thrust deeper, she had to concentrate to not drop the phone. 'Oof.'

'Are you OK? Soph?' Sarah was beginning to sound worried. 'Are you still staying with Marcus?'

'Yeessss, I'm with him.' She squirmed away from the hot body behind her just for a few moments. 'I had a bang on the head but I'm fine now.'

'A bang?'

Marcus evilly punctuated this with a bang of his own.

'Just a little one.'

He whispered in her other ear, 'This isn't a little one,' and covered her mouth as he thrust quickly inside her a few times.

The tinny voice spoke again, 'That would explain why you're not sounding yourself.'

'Sorry, I'm in the middle of so-omething.' The middle of getting fucked again by a rampant man. 'Can I call you back la-ater?'

'Sure, and you can tell me about all the romantic things you're getting up to with Marcus.'

Sophie gulp-laughed, 'No, no romance here. No romance at all.' Just plain, hard fucking.

136

'That's a shame. Talk later?'

'Yeeeeahhh, will speak to you later. Ta-raaahhh.' Sophie only just disconnected the call before Marcus lifted her off the ground, bent her over the side of the hot tub, and began fucking her in earnest.

They settled into a pattern over the weeks it took for her new passport to be processed. During the week, either he would show her around or she would take a tour, finishing wherever his next match was, and sharing at least half of his travel. If he could get away from training, they would venture somewhere for a couple of days together. Two away games in a row in the north east of the country meant she saw a great deal of the Kruger Park, including the infamous Big Five. Marcus shared a safari lodge with her in the middle of the wilderness, and between trips out, they gorged themselves on each other's bodies. The days without him only served to sharpen her need for him, and all either of them needed was a look or a touch to be ready.

Finally, with mixed feelings, she received her new passport.

Chapter Ten

'I still haven't organised any travelling.' Sophie lay on his bed after another marathon sex session. Her loins throbbed pleasantly from semi-rough use, and her nipples were nearly as dark a red as the cover of her new passport. Marcus enjoyed pulling, sucking, and nibbling them, calling them his cherries while she writhed in pleasure.

'I mentioned it before, didn't I? You can go on Klaus' overland truck safari. It's about three weeks, through Namibia and Botswana, into Zimbabwe and up to Victoria Falls, sleeping in tents. It's rough, but you see loads of wildlife and scenery. I've already asked Klaus if there's room for a small one,' Marcus grinned wickedly at her, 'and he says you're welcome.'

Sophie couldn't decide whether she thought it was insulting or gratifying that he had already sorted it out. His parents were due to return within the week, so it meant that she would miss them. Perhaps that was for the best? She would feel rather dishonest pretending they were married all the time.

Sophie stared at the passport in her hand, and the truck she was about to board. Well, they were calling it a truck, but it looked like some kind of bus on steroids. Crates of food were being loaded into the kitchen area at the back, and other travellers were milling around with their bags, gradually disappearing inside.

She was the only person there actually being seen off. Everyone else had been dropped off by impatient taxis and minibuses, or staggered up the street rucksack-laden from unknown origins. There was a real assortment of nationalities; so far she had picked up German, Australian, Japanese-sounding, and maybe an American accent as well as a couple of Brits. Like her, they were all wearing what appeared to be ubiquitous travelling gear: flip-flops, loose long shorts or trousers, and T-shirts with the odd jumper or jacket to ward off the early morning cold.

'I'm gonna miss you.' Marcus almost sounded surprised.

Sophie smirked. 'No sex on tap for three weeks?' The previous night had been another gluttony of sensation, as if they were trying to make up for her absence in advance.

He reddened. 'It's not just the sex. I like your company, too. And the rugby chats we have. I'll miss you at the game tomorrow. I won't know how to rip open the defence!'

He sounded so uncertain and Sophie experienced a moment of disquiet. 'You'll be fine. I have faith in you and we've studied the tapes. You know what to do.'

'Thank you.' He hugged her fiercely, and she luxuriated in the contact, not wanting it to end.

'Hey, my *bra*, Marcus! You have to let your woman go now, we'll look after her for you.' The shout came from a tanned, blond guy climbing into the driver's seat.

'Klaus, late as always I see.' Marcus gave her one last squeeze and carried her bag over to the truck towards his friend.

When he paused at the door, she smiled a "hello" at Klaus, and copied the other travellers in carrying her bag into the vehicle. There were six rows of seats, and it was already half-full of curious faces. She gave another brief smile, slung her bag on the floor by a couple of free seats, and started back towards the front. Just in time, as Marcus dashed up the couple of steps and gave her a peck on her lips and dashed back out, slamming the door behind him.

'I'll see you soon!' he yelled, waving goodbye.

She started waving, but glimpsed the rings still on her fingers. She pulled them off, yanked the window open, and yelled, 'Here! Look after them – I don't want to lose them.'

He jogged back up to the window and caught them, giving her the thumbs up. 'I'll put them with your handbag.' She had left the gorgeous item behind, along with a few pieces of clothing she didn't really need while roughing it.

'Good luck tomorrow!' she called back, waving until he was out of sight.

Sophie could hear Klaus and the other guide chuckling in the cab as they pulled out of the street and to the west. 'Hey, Sophie, *isit*? My boy is real *bossies* for you.'

She hummed, not knowing how to react, and went to take her seat.

A few days later the truck had arrived at a campsite near the Orange River, on the border between South Africa and Namibia. They would be canoeing down the river the next day.

Sophie had been dismayed to discover she was the odd one out on the trip. The others were friendly enough towards her, but were either couples or friends travelling together. She had her own two-man tent to erect every night, and felt embarrassed when Klaus had to come over to help her. Nevertheless, apart from missing Marcus with a chest-deep ache, she was really enjoying herself. The country was so beautiful, and there was so much desolate, open space that she felt free.

Klaus seemed permanently amused by her – by her lack of coordination, her bravery when faced with creepy-crawlies, and the way she squared her shoulders and lifted her chin when daunted. Unlike some of the other travellers who were moaning about sleeping on hard ground, or the lack of variety in the food, she didn't complain about anything, preferring to just dig in and get on with it.

In the evenings when they sat around chatting, he and sometimes the other guide would often seek her out, hand her a beer, and chat about nothing in particular. She couldn't tell, as the odd-person-out, if they were just keeping her company or really were interested in her.

At the centre of their latest destination was a sprawling house with a large *stoep*. While the travellers disembarked, Klaus joined the mixed group of men hanging there and began a complicated set of greetings.

Sophie had just grabbed her tent when she heard a buzzing and a small white aircraft overhead. Everyone stopped to watch it land alongside the campsite, and taxi towards the house. Once the engines shut off, a familiar figure jumped out and jogged towards the group of locals on the *stoep*.

'Hey, my *bra*, howzit?' shouted Klaus. There followed a convoluted set of handshakes. '*Yoh*, you're here to see the *bokkie*? She is fii-iine, *nè*?'

'*Ja*, Klaus, I don't trust your *laaities*.' The boys around him cackled and playfully punched each other. 'We'll *doss* in the bush tonight, I'll return her tomorrow.'

Marcus glanced over and saw Sophie nearby. He grinned at her and she grinned back. 'Grab an overnight bag, cherry, we're going bush. Just the two of us.'

'Really?' she continued to grin. So did he. It seemed an age since she had seen him, and he looked so good.

There were groans from the *stoep*. 'Have some dignity, *bra*.'

'Huh?' Marcus broke their gaze and looked around.

While he engaged in some horseplay, Sophie returned to the truck for enough gear to camp overnight, just her toiletries bag and a change of clothing. No nightwear, she was already looking forward to sleeping skin-to-skin with Marcus, amongst other things. Between her legs was already starting to throb.

'Ready?'

Sophie nodded and blushed. He must have read her mind, as his gaze went to her lips. She remembered how much he liked her mouth around him, and licked her lips, 'Very ready.'

He groaned, and pulled his shirt out to cover his groin, before picking up a large water container.

To catcalls from the *stoep*, they departed, heading for the small plane. Sophie took a moment to look it over as Marcus did some pre-flight checks. The plane was mainly white with some red stripes running the length of the body. Several seats were visible inside the cabin

'It's a Cessna 210. It belongs to the family, we all fly it. It's relatively simple to pilot,' Marcus called. 'I've brought kit to camp out, although you'll have to do without a proper loo.' He grinned apologetically as he pulled a door open for her to clamber in.

Sophie giggled at the array of controls in front of her. Marcus slid onto the seat next to her, and within moments they were taxiing down the runway and lifting off into the air.

She amused herself for a few minutes by looking out of the windows and examining the controls. She loved watching Marcus fly, it reminded her of when he drove her home, his confidence and mastery of the machine was rather hot. Sexy.

'Have we … far to go?' she asked, running her hand up his thigh.

'Not far, it's minutes, really.' Her hand ventured further to find him hard and ready. 'Fuck, Sophie, let me get this plane down.'

As the plane dived towards a strip levelled out of the surrounding scrub and plateau, Sophie divested herself of her clothes. The wheels touched down, the plane braked to a stop, the engine cut out, and Marcus hauled a naked

Sophie towards him, unzipped his fly, and pushed inside her.

They both groaned in pleasure at her tightness. She writhed on top of him, and he held her as close as the cockpit allowed and rolled his hips.

She didn't care about knocking against the sides or roof of the plane, she just wallowed in the pleasure of his solid cock inside her, something she'd missed in the last few days.

The slight rocking of the plane added to the illicit interaction, but Marcus wasn't quite satisfied. 'As I flew here, I fantasised about having you in the cockpit.'

'Cockpit?' Sophie sniggered, and gasped with him.

'I wondered if you were small enough to fit over me like this.'

'It's a tight squeeze.' She added a squeeze of her own, and felt him flex inside her.

'Fucking hell, Sophie!' He grabbed her breasts, leant forward and nipped a nipple.

The small pain tipped her over, she braced her hands against the roof and thrust onto him as hard as possible while he licked the excruciatingly sensitive teat. He copied on the other side, and she felt like she peaked again, clenching around him.

He shouted something as he came, his head dropping back against the headrest and veins cording in his neck. The plane rocked violently a few more times as he hammered into her, then the plane and their bodies gradually stilled.

Marcus pulled a couple of bags out of the rear of the plane, then took some wire netting from behind the back seats and wrapped it around the landing gear.

She watched with interest as she pulled her outer layers back on. 'What's that for?'

'To stop wild dogs nibbling at the rubber. We'll camp

close enough, but they're cheeky buggers.

Half an hour later, the basic camp was set up, and he was hooking a bag over a nearby tree. 'It's a solar shower, the water's heated by the sun.' He nodded to the setting sun. 'We'll give it a chance to heat up a bit, then I'll help you soap up first to save water.'

'Really? Out of the goodness of your heart?'

He grinned and walked back towards her. 'Of course. You'll have to strip off again though.'

'Of course.' She smiled happily at him, and he pulled her in for a snog, his hands sneaking under her clothes. She had enjoyed watching and helping him capably create the campsite for the night.

'Before all that, we'll have to put the tent up and get a fire going for dinner.' He rested his forehead against hers as one hand squeezed a tender breast.

She gasped, 'You've already restarted one here.'

'It cools quickly up here once the sun goes down.'

Freshly showered and sprawled on a blanket by a hearty camp fire, they demolished plates of *bredie*, a spicy tomato and mutton stew Marcus had brought to heat up over the fire. Marcus twisted around so Sophie was cradled between his legs, and she could feel his arousal poking into her.

'Hmmm, what do we have here?' His trousers came easily undone for her to stroke his shaft.

Marcus groaned, helped her pull off her trousers, and pulled her over him for the second time that day.

She laughed joyously as he speared inside her. 'Feels so good, hot and thick.'

'You love that, don't you?' he murmured, and let her stay on top of him for a while. His eyes glinted in the firelight as he watched her use his body with abandon.

When she seized around him, he turned them over and pounded inside until he exploded too. They lay on the blanket, catching their breath and watching the stars.

Marcus pulled a spare covering over her bare skin. 'Can't have you getting cold.' The temperature had dropped a great deal since the sun went down.

'Thanks, the nights are slightly warmer here than down south but not by much. How did you manage to get away?' she asked, stroking his thigh.

'I left after training and tomorrow's my day off. I'll join you for the canoeing trip in the morning, and afterwards I was thinking I could fly you up into Namibia. We can traverse the canyon, and I'll drop you off at the camp before making tracks for the Cape the next morning,' proposed Marcus.

'Wow, that sounds great.'

'The canyon's best seen from the air, you can't get an idea of it by walking to the side and peering down.'

'That sounds fabulous. It's incredible out here,' sighed Sophie. 'You can see further than anywhere I've ever been. No light pollution, only the stars.'

There was a sudden electronic beep.

'What …?'

'Ummm, I was hoping, if you have a spare moment, you could look at the match from the weekend and tell me what you think?'

Sophie felt a moment of unspecified disquiet, of unease. 'You brought your laptop?' It seemed improper in the middle of the wilderness.

'Yeah, fully charged. It would be great if you could do some analysis. I have some clips of the opposition if you have a chance also?'

She sighed and started pulling her trousers back on. 'Hand it over.'

It took the best part of three hours to do a brief analysis on the match and the opposition, far less than she would normally take, but she was concentrating on Marcus. There weren't many new points to make; he was stepping up and attacking more decisively, spotting gaps, and repairing the defensive line so ably that it felt so wrong that he was hanging on to her every word.

She also had a chance to watch the opposition clips, but it was mostly Marcus checking points with her. By the time they finished with the battery beeping warningly, her eyes stung from squinting at the dim screen and her neck and back ached. It was a relief to close the lid and watch him pack it away.

She yawned, rubbing her sore parts. 'Bed now?'

'Yep, go get comfy, I'll be there in a minute.'

As he doused the remaining embers, she sleepily climbed into the double sleeping bag. Instead of a mat underneath, he'd brought a proper blow-up mattress. After nights with only a couple of inches of foam between her and the ground, it was luxurious in comparison, and her eyes shut in seconds.

Several times during the night, she woke to find him restless. Body contact seemed to soothe him, which led to more intimate acts. The urgency gone, they hazily moved together, breaths quickening and slowing after the waves of pleasure had washed on through.

She didn't know what had roused her.

All she could hear at first was her own breathing. In. Out. In. Out. After a while, other desert noises intruded. Crickets. A thump and pant of an animal which wasn't necessarily friendly. 'Marcus?' she whispered tremulously.

No answer. Only thin fabric separated her from whatever was outside. It must have been near dawn, the nascent light penetrating the dark fabric.

Where the hell was Marcus? She pulled on her clothes and shoes, and cautiously exited the tent. It was cold, so she ducked back into the tent for a jumper. The fire had been kindled, although it was starting to burn out. She dropped more fuel on before beginning to wander into the

147

bush, keeping the plane and campsite in sight at all times. She wasn't stupid enough to get lost.

Half an hour later, she was still puzzled and still hadn't found Marcus. There was the odd noise she would guess was animal-made, but no one answered to her calls. She shrugged her shoulders, returned to the camp, and began cooking breakfast.

Bacon and eggs. Yum. She couldn't find milk so had her coffee black. It still tasted great.

As she was about to tuck in to her fry up, a hand sneaked over her shoulder and nabbed a rasher. She squealed in fright.

'Sophie, it's only me.'

'For fuck's sake, Marcus, don't do that! Where have you been?' She turned to see him sweaty, dressed in clothes from the night before, and holding a milk carton.

'I hiked back to pick up some milk.'

'You could've left a note.'

He opened his mouth to respond, then stilled, listening to something. '*Voetsek*, Klaus, I can hear you trampling through the bush.'

'*Ag man*, you get me every time.' Klaus emerged from the surrounding scrub. 'I come bearing gifts.' From his pocket he brought out a bulky wrapped pack of what Sophie recognised as *boerewors*, a spicy sausage.

'Ooh, lovely.' She clapped her hands in glee and gestured to the pan. 'Stick them on, I'll get more eggs.'

Marcus actually dared to look upset. 'But I wanted coffee! And you to myself.'

Klaus laughed and tweaked his eyebrows suggestively, 'Sophie likes her sausage in more ways than one.'

Sophie giggled. 'Don't tell him everything!'

'So, can I get a lift back to the camp please? And a shower? And a clean tee?' Klaus decided to delay his request until the other two were humming with delight over his sausage gift.

'If you must. Fuck me, your friend makes good sausage.'

'I'd rather not *fok* you again, that one time was enough.'

Sophie nearly choked on her sausage. 'How *do* you two know each other?'

Klaus grinned. 'We were in the same army regiment. They called us twins because we were so similar. We used to go out drinking and pulling *stukkie* together. One time, we shared.'

'Klaus!' Marcus made a throat-slitting gesture.

'*Vergewe my bra, maar jy moet saamstem, dit was fokken jags.* It was fucking horny. Don't worry, Sophie, she was *lekker*, not some *fokken loskind*. A nice girl who was just horny. Those were the days.' He sighed dramatically.

Marcus wouldn't meet Sophie's eyes, but she wasn't critical of what they had got up to – she was rather intrigued, and slightly envious.

'Anyway, about that shower? I stink, but you two *fokken ruik*. Perhaps we could share?'

That was enough for Marcus. '*Hou jou bek,* Klaus, otherwise I will close it for you, tie you up, and leave you here. Let's pack up what we can then shower.'

They set about clearing the camp, the remaining heat from the fire was used to warm up the shower water, and everything non-essential packed away in the plane.

Sophie wrapped the towel around her as she left the stripped-down tent and walked towards the shower. 'Marcus, I can't find the biodegradable … soap.' Her voice petered out.

Instead of Marcus, it was Klaus under the spray. She swallowed a gasp; he was built as well as Marcus, even between his legs. His eyes were closed as he vigorously rinsed soap off his face and ears, which accounted for him not hearing or seeing her. Then he turned so his back was to her and the view was as good as the front. Despite the night of slow sex, the earlier conversation had made her frisky again.

'Naughty *bokkie*,' Marcus whispered in her ear.

She felt his naked body press against hers and gulped. 'I was just looking for you.'

'You found me, and Klaus. He took the first shower. Did I do this to you?'

He was running his fingers over the faint bruises on her hips, arms, and legs, from where he'd clasped her or she'd hit sides of the plane. 'Yes, and I loved every second of it,' she purred, 'I want more.'

He backed her away, to the part shelter from the tent and plane, then put her on hands and knees and thrust inside her. She could still see the torso and legs of Klaus, soaping his genitals under the meagre spray. As he rinsed and lifted himself up, his shaft thickening, Marcus thrust harder.

As a hand ventured between her legs, he whispered to her again. 'I think Sophie likes to watch.'

She came seconds later with a yell, her eyes fixed on the other naked man until her eyelids blinked closed and she felt Marcus come in her. When she opened them again, seconds later, Klaus had disappeared.

'Time for a wash. Come on.' Marcus slapped her arse.

Suspiciously, she looked around as she stumbled to her feet and picked up her discarded towel. Marcus guided her to the shower, took her towel from her, and soaped them both up before turning the water on and rinsing. Drying off and pulling on her bikini, shorts, and T-shirt took barely seconds, and Klaus reappeared as they finished packing the plane.

Chapter Eleven

They took off for the short hop back to the campsite a short time later. Sophie opted to sit behind Marcus and Klaus and enjoy the view, both inside and outside the plane. They really did look similar from behind, although Marcus had marginally more muscle and Klaus a darker tan. The way they joshed and elbowed each other, it was plain that they had known each other for years.

The canoes were already packed on a trailer behind a small minibus, which took them upriver. Marcus helped them offload, stripping his shirt off in the heat, and Sophie stood back and enjoyed the view again. With her record of clumsiness, she was banned from helping out for fear of her tripping over and falling into the swift-flowing river.

A couple of the other travellers wandered up to watch too. 'That is a bloody unreal sight!' remarked one of the Australian girls. She pointed at Marcus. 'He ya bloke?'

Sophie nodded the affirmative. He was a bit, anyway.

'Aww, I thought you and Klaus had a thing going on? That means he's free, I'll have to tell Charlene.' She hissed not-so-quietly to another girl a few yards away, 'Oi, Charls, Klaus isn't taken after all.'

Klaus overheard, and the look of alarm on his face made Sophie quell giggles. Within seconds, the Australians were asking him to help fasten the perfectly easy zips on their lifejackets, and apply sunscreen to their shoulders.

'Here, put this on.' Marcus handed her a lifejacket. 'It's the smallest they had, a youth size.'

It fitted perfectly, and she certainly didn't need any help with the zip. She grinned at Marcus in triumph.

'Shame.' He shook his head as he pulled his own on. 'I was looking forward to a sneaky grope. Let's get going.'

The canoes were lined up neatly along the riverbank. While Klaus briefed the others, Sophie was handed a paddle and they set off.

The dusty, orange-tinged flow carried them along for hours, past the green banks fringing the massive, grey-brown plateaus. Marcus kept pointing out birds to her, but she preferred to look at him. There was the odd squeal and splash from the rest of the group upriver.

'Fancy a dip? Take your shorts and shoes off, then tumble out.'

They were both warm and sweating from the paddling so the idea was very tempting. 'OK.'

Purposefully falling out of a boat was odd for her, and accomplished with her usual lack of grace. The water was cool but not cold, and quite refreshing. Marcus wrapped his arms around her and they floated for a while next to the boat. Their legs entwined and he began kissing her.

A few minutes later, she felt her bikini bottoms being pushed to one side and him entering her. She gasped, 'Marcus!'

'Shhh, no one can see. You're so warm and tight. We'll just float like this for a while.'

They were still a way ahead of the others. She wrapped her legs around him as he surged deeper. It was different in the water; she could feel her excitement but there was more friction. It was good friction, great friction, as there was nothing else for them to push against so she couldn't get sore.

As they kissed, the other boats floated by, with a certain amount of envious commenting flying from the occupants, all unaware of what was happening under the opaque flow. Then they were alone. She tightened on him as much as she could and he groaned. It felt good, so she kept tightening and releasing. The flotation effect of the lifejackets kept their upper bodies high in the water and limited their movement. She leant back for a different angle, he squeezed a hand in, and she broke, coming in waves around him. He pulled her tighter and came too and the water splashed.

Sophie let the swells of pleasure die before commenting with a grin, 'That was interesting.'

'Mmmm.' He kissed her neck. 'A bit frustrating without anything to push against. Thank you for doing the work.'

'I could feel you twitching inside me too, that felt really good.' Just talking about it was revving her up again. Then she shivered.

He groaned, 'Come on, let's get back to the canoe, we don't want to overshoot the stop, and we're both getting cold.'

It was floating with them a few yards away. Marcus hoisted himself in, then easily heaved her out of the water. Ten minutes later, they were pulling in at a bank near the campsite and Marcus took the paddles back to the storage area while Sophie gathered herself and dried off.

Klaus came over. 'Enjoy that, then? Do you two ever stop? You can tell you're *bladdy* newlyweds!'

She blushed fiercely.

He laughed, keeping his voice low, 'Don't worry, no one else knew for certain what you were up to, and I owed you one for setting the Aussies on me. Thought you were going to keep me safe on this trip, we don't get many single women.'

'Sorry about that.' The penny dropped. 'You wanted me to protect you from them?'

'*Ja*, it's better to leave the paying guests alone – some of them get strange ideas – but the temptation is often too great.'

'And I've blown your cover, whoops.'

'*Geen problem*. I'll just tell them I'm obliged to keep an eye on you so you don't go off with any strange men.'

'Strange men?' Marcus rejoined them.

'You forgot to brief Soph on her mission. Operation: Ladydodge.'

'I thought you were joking! You've never been shy with the ladies before.'

Klaus sighed, '*Aweh*, you get to an age when the thought of settling down is more tempting than fo –' He glanced at Sophie. 'Umm, affairs. My *bra*, you didn't hang around putting a ring on the *bokkie*.'

Marcus looked awkward, clearly not comfortable continuing the lie with a friend as close as Klaus. He started fussing with the canoe by his feet. 'Help me with this please, Klaus. Soph, go have a shower to warm up, I'll see you by the house.'

It was odd for Sophie to be told to go away like that. She felt like she had been reprimanded. Head down, she picked up her things and made her way to the reed-walled shower block.

Within minutes of entering the cubicle, Marcus joined her. 'Want me to soap your back again?'

Nodding, she turned around, the back wall closer than she thought.

Massive. Spider.

'Eek!' She squeaked and threw herself back against Marcus. Their arms windmilled to find a grip on something. He slipped and fell against the door, and they landed inelegantly in a pile.

'You OK?' he asked.

She shuddered as she stared at the hand-sized creature. 'I'm so sorry, it just gave me a shock. I'm not usually that squeamish.'

'You are that clumsy, though.' He rubbed his shoulder. The bad shoulder, the one which had given him problems for years.

Sophie's heart dropped, 'Oh no, are you OK?'

He laughed, 'Fine, not even bruised. I'm not that easy to break. Let's get up, finish this shower, minus Mr Spider, and get flying.'

After he had filed a flight plan, they took off, and instead of following the road, Marcus followed the river. After Sophie had seen the spectacular falls, he flew the plane north. They raced the truck to the next campsite by the side of a massive canyon.

En route, he pointed some of the various landmarks out to her, and Sophie felt like a kid, squealing and gasping at the magnificent sights, clapping her hands in glee. Marcus chuckled at her, but seemed to take pleasure in her wide-eyed excitement. They cleared customs in Namibia, once across the border, before continuing to the overnight camp and barely beat the truck labouring its way along the rough road with a trail of dust in its wake.

Marcus alighted, removed their bags from the plane, and tied it down for the night, while Sophie stood by, feeling a little ineffective. 'Anything I can do?'

Marcus shook his head. 'Nope. Although you can treat me to a back massage later?'

'You're on!'

A battered Land Rover drew up beside them and Klaus jumped out, grabbed their bags, and gestured for them to get in. 'Come on, we need to be at the edge of the canyon for sundown.'

They met up with the truck as the sun began to set, painting the sky in oranges, pinks, and finally purples, casting silver the long-distant river at the bottom of the canyon. The wind seemed to be strengthening, whistling eerily around the rocky outcrops.

'We flew along there, but it's still incredible to see how massive the rocks are,' marvelled Sophie, and shivered.

The temperature had started to plummet and they were exposed.

Marcus wrapped his arms around her. 'That better?'

She luxuriated in his body heat. 'Yes, thanks.'

Klaus draped a blanket around both of them. 'Here, share this. I'm off for a run.' He loped away along another path.

They sat on the ground, Sophie between Marcus' legs, to watch the day's end and the sky dramatically darken. The rest of the travellers watched and wandered along paths, needing exercise after a few hours of being cooped up, but Sophie didn't feel the same restlessness.

'You two camping with us tonight?' asked a returning, sweaty Klaus. He began stretching his leg muscles.

'Yeah, I need to be off at first light,' confirmed Marcus. 'Got training later.'

'Any more unexpected visits planned?'

'Unfortunately not, next week the truck will be too far north for the Cessna to fly in one go.' Marcus was quiet for a moment. 'You'll be in Swakopmund for my game this weekend, it's being televised live. You'll be able to help Sophie find a place to watch it, won't you, so she can call me at half time?'

'*Ja*, if possible. I can't promise anything though; it depends on what activities the group wants to do.'

'What activities are there?' asked Sophie with interest.

'Sand-boarding, quad-biking, skydiving …'

'None of which I'd be safe doing with my lack of coordination.'

'And … err, dolphin watching.'

Sophie could feel Marcus stiffening around her, waiting for her response. 'I'd probably fall off the boat.' She felt him subtly relax. 'I may go for a massage though. I have the feeling that after a few more days of sleeping rough, I'll need one.'

'Is that a hint?' Marcus murmured in her ear. His hands

started caressing her.

Klaus laughed and diplomatically turned away. 'Do you two ever stop?'

The wind picked up during the night, buffeting the tents, whipping the canvas loud enough to wake Sophie from an exhausted sleep. The sound was eerie in the darkness. She lifted her hand in front of her eyes to see its vague outline. Only faint moonlight provided illumination that far from the main buildings. Their tent was also as far away from the others as possible, but she had still had to muffle her gasps of pleasure with a mouthful of pillow.

As she lay there in the near pitch-black, she could feel Marcus restless beside her. The more the wind wailed, the more agitated he seemed to become. 'No!' he muttered, followed by something in a guttural language Sophie didn't understand.

She didn't know what to do until his mutterings became pleadings. 'Ssshhh,' she soothed. 'Everything's OK, you're safe.' Sophie carefully felt around to place a hand on his shoulder.

Marcus shot up, rolling over and pinning her under him, his arm around her throat.

'Eek!' she squeaked. 'It's me, Marcus, it's Sophie! Everything's fine, you're safe.'

'Sophie?' He rolled off her. 'Oh shit, are you OK? Did I hurt you?'

She coughed. 'I'm fine, I'm more worried about you.' The wind took that moment to whistle sharply and she felt him cringe and take a gasping breath. 'Is it the wind?'

'I don't ...' He gulped. 'Yeah, yeah it is.'

'Want to talk about it? You don't have to.'

All she could hear was his breathing.

'Or, I could ... distract you?' She slowly ran a hand down his taut stomach, towards ...

He seemed to decide something, and wriggled down,

splitting her legs apart. 'Nope, it's my turn on you.'

'Oh? Ooohhh!' She grabbed for the pillow again.

As the sun stretched over the horizon, they walked towards the plane. She watched while Marcus completed pre-flight checks, going around the whole plane with a fine toothcomb.

Finally, he returned to her, hands in pockets. 'You will catch the match, won't you? Klaus says you'll be in a town.'

'I'll do my best, but I'm sure you will too.'

He glanced at his watch.

'You do really have to go, you've got a long way to fly.'

'Are you sure you don't want to come back with me?' He smiled temptingly.

A part of her wanted to, but she knew she had to continue her journey. 'I'll be back before you know it.'

'Good.' He enveloped her in a fierce hug.

She wallowed in the physical contact. It took all her strength to let him go. It was worse than saying goodbye to him in Cape Town.

She watched the plane take off, waved as it turned into a little dot, and headed back towards the camp, swallowing the lump in her throat.

The camp was being packed up so she gave them a hand, while contemplating the time she'd spent with Marcus. As she chucked a tent in the storage compartment under the truck, she was still in a world of her own.

'You OK, Soph?'

She gave a concerned Klaus a smile. 'I'm fine, just thinking about things.'

The other guide leered at her. 'I've never seen him chase after *stukkie* before now. You must make him *mal jags, nè?*'

As Klaus clouted his colleague over the head, Sophie

158

smiled as if she knew what the effusive guy was on about, carefully climbed into the truck, and sat down, hiding her wince. Marcus had been insatiable after his nightmares had woken him. She'd hardly had any sleep and felt bowlegged. The other passengers gave her curious and envious stares, but she was in no state to socialise and quickly dozed off.

Every night she missed his comforting presence, and despite the mosquitoes whining around some locations, she would sit outside to look at the stars. It reminded her of lying there together, chatting about nothing in particular.

She noticed a few nights later that Klaus never camped with the rest of them. Shortly after lights out, he would disappear off with his pack and reappear the next morning. One night, when they were camped in the middle of the desert, she decided to follow him out of curiosity. The moon was full so she could see him as he hiked about half a mile, following a path around a massive boulder, then his outline vanished.

She glanced behind to reassure herself that the path back was obvious, and crept on.

'Boo!'

'Eek!' she squeaked.

'What are you up to, little *bokkie*? Your clothes are too noisy to move silently.'

'Ummm, I was wondering where you went every night.'

Klaus was quiet for a moment. 'I snore very loudly, so I camp further away.'

'Oh.' She felt foolish. 'I suppose I'd better be getting back.'

'Want a beer first?' There was some clinking and a hiss.

'Ummm, OK.' She took the bottle he offered.

'And a seat?' He briefly turned his head torch on to check the area for any undesirables, then set his bed roll, blanket, and sleeping bag down so they could lean against the rock. He patted the area next to him.

'OK.'

They sat looking up at the stars in silence, letting the minutes slide past, and sipping from their bottles.

'It's so massive, isn't it?'

'Incredible. It's one of the things I miss when I am home. Speaking of which, how are you missing your man?'

'Dreadfully. I keep expecting ... wanting him to be there.'

'I know what you mean,' Klaus added quietly.

'Oh, do you have anyone at home, back in Cape Town?'

Klaus swigged deeply from his beer. 'Not now, no.'

'Wanna talk about it?'

He sighed heavily. 'We were supposed to be in love. We had burglars. I fought them. We got injured. It was my fault. She left me.' He finished his bottle and cracked open another.

'Oh, Klaus. I'm so sorry.' She laid a hand and head on his shoulder for comfort.

'Completely my fault, we should have hidden. Instead, I thought with my army training that I could fight them. They had guns and knives. I killed one, the police got the other two, but we were both shot and I was stabbed.'

Sophie gasped, 'That scar on your ribcage.'

'One of them. She didn't want to be with someone who had no remorse about killing.' He was silent for a few minutes. 'I don't really snore. Well, I probably do a little. I sleep further away as I have nightmares still. I was bad out of the Army, I had PTSD. Now, it is worse. When we go bush in the Delta, I can't sleep on my own as I would be lion food, so I stay awake.' He shrugged.

She shivered slightly.

'Here, get in this with me to keep warm.' Klaus shook out his sleeping bag. 'I have an extra-large bag as I feel too restricted in a normal one.' It was his time to shudder.

'Restricted?'

'I was once caught by some rebels. They wrapped me in sacks, as they had no rope, while they discussed how they would kill me. Since then, I can't bear it.' He lifted an arm, tucking it around her and drawing her to his side.

Sophie felt comforted, even though she was trying to comfort him.

'I see his face ... the burglar ... he was so young. I see all their faces. In Rwanda, the Congo, the innocents everywhere ... Marcus and I, we're like brothers. He was with me in the Army, he saw the same things. We both left on the same day, he got me out before I went totally *bossies* – mad. I owe him so much.'

'Marcus didn't sleep so well last night. He was restless when we weren't touching.'

'The wind. One of the rebels used to make this whistling noise before they ...' He took another gulp of his beer.

She couldn't imagine what they had both gone through. Marcus had some scars on his body, but she had assumed they were the results of rugby studs, not bullets.

Klaus took a steadying breath. 'Camping outside probably brought memories back. We spent months living under canvas.'

'Of course,' sighed Sophie. 'I feel so guilty now, I wish I'd known. I saw lodges at both sites we could have stayed in. I didn't mean to distress him, he just never told me about it. I appreciate your honesty.'

'Oh Sophie. If he was not my *broer*, my brother in all but name, I would be making a move on you. You are perfect for him. I am envious.'

In the silence that followed, Sophie thought about the

161

different perspective his words had put on their situation, and the mistruths. 'Did he tell you we're not really married?'

'Huh? For sure?'

'We're not married. There was a mix-up when I banged my head, and he asked me to continue the pretence as he was getting less hassle.'

'Oh my *liefie*, no wonder you took the rings off.' He groaned. 'I knew something didn't make sense but we didn't have time to score a *dop* and chat.'

She shrugged. 'We weren't even sleeping together right away, that happened by accident. But it seems there's something between us, some chemistry, so we didn't fight it.'

'*Fokken doos.*'

'What?'

'He's an idiot. I knew his family would force him to do something *dof* – dumb ... rash ... stupid, even. When I first heard, I was surprised: he's much too sensible to get married so abruptly. And he would never have left you alone in the UK.' There was quiet for a few minutes until Klaus chuckled unexpectedly. 'By the way, I'm not going to ask you how you know about my scars.'

Sophie squeaked in embarrassment. 'This isn't going to be awkward for the next few weeks at all, is it?'

Klaus just hugged her. '*Nooit* – no way, we're going to have a great time.'

'That's a relief.'

He laughed again. 'You should know that I had an eyeful when I went to dress after my shower. The plane and tent didn't disguise much, and there's no mistaking the sound of a woman coming.'

'Oh, hell,' she groaned.

'Don't be embarrassed, it was beautiful.'

They fell into silence again, staring at the stars. Before she knew it, Sophie's eyes drifted closed. She sleepily felt herself being lowered lengthways onto the bedroll, with a blanket for a pillow.

During the night, Klaus' restlessness woke her. In a muddle of somnolence, she calmed him with a few soothing words as she had done with Marcus, and that seemed to be enough.

It was strange waking in a real bedroom with solid walls, in a real bed with sheets. Even stranger being on her own. She had kept him company at night since their chat, but Klaus did not think it would have looked right for them to share a room, so she had a room to herself for a couple of nights. They had arrived late the previous evening, an awkward puncture delaying their truck, and a very dirty Klaus had needed to scrub the road filth off before meeting with them in a nearby restaurant.

On their walk back to the lodge, Klaus had pointed out a sports bar to watch the match in. They were advertising rugby, so she wasn't worried about catching the game. Having a lie-in and a wander around the town before kick-off was her plan.

Just as she was contemplating getting dressed, there was a loud bang on the door. 'Soph! I have a surprise for you.'

She opened the door to see Klaus standing there, holding two dusty helmets.

'Still in your PJs, *bokkie*? Get dressed – the other night, you said you weren't so dangerous on two wheels, so I've hired us some mountain bikes!'

Sophie grinned in delight. 'Excellent! Give me a few minutes.' She excitedly pulled on a suitable outfit and applied some sunblock to any exposed parts. After not riding a bike since leaving the UK, she really missed it.

As they shot down a trail an hour or so later, Sophie was laughing as Klaus tried to keep up with her. 'C'mon K, get those legs pedalling!'

'It's not my fault, my wheels are digging into the sand. You're so light, you just float over the top.'

'Excuses, excuses,' she teased. They came to a fork in the road. 'Which way?'

'*Yoh*, it's back into town that way …'

She pouted.

'Or it's a few more miles the other.' It was his turn to laugh. 'OK, OK, stop pleading at me with those *bokkie* eyes. We can't be out too long as the hire guys said *berg winds* are likely later. Hey, wait up!'

Sophie was already setting off on the longer trail.

Time flew so fast that it was barely five minutes before kick-off that they tumbled into the sports bar Klaus had pointed out. The wind had strengthened, blowing them back towards town, lifting sand to obscure the path and work its way into their clothing. There had been no time for a shower, so they just had to put up with the gritty feeling.

The bar was half full, with many of the occupants turned towards a couple of screens. With relief, Sophie recognised the strip of Marcus' team – they were showing the game. 'Woohoo, it's on.'

'You grab that table, it's got the best view. I'll go to the bar. What do you want to drink?'

'A pint of OJ and soda, please, I'm parched.' Sophie's attention concentrated on the pixelated images as she brought out her phone to take notes. The camera focused on the rain-soaked players warming up, and on a familiar blond passing a ball. Despite the fun she'd had that day, Sophie felt a pang in the chest when she saw him. He looked so gorgeously serious, so masculine. His name popped up on the bottom of the screen, *Marcus Coetzee, Centre*, plus his height, weight, and match statistics of averaging a try per match. She vaguely heard the commentators talking about his recent streak of incredible form, about the promise he'd shown when he was younger that was interrupted by his army career and injury, and his chances for the national side. As the team ran back down the tunnel and out of the rain, a montage of clips from recent matches illustrated his deft handling, committed tackling and support work. Then, they cut to show some of the South African coaches in the stand.

'*Jislaaik*, that's my *bra* they're focused on?' Klaus placed a large glass in front of her. 'They're saying the national coaches are watching him?'

'It appears so.' What had seemed like pie in the sky now appeared incredibly real. She busied herself with drinking the refreshing juice.

Minutes later, the players were taking the field and the cameras showed a wide shot of his team. Marcus fiddled with his socks, then took two bouncing jumps, knees reaching his chest. The ball was kicked in the air, the picture flickered, and … nothing.

There was assorted swearing around them and groans, then most of the patrons turned away from the screens, shook their heads, and started talking to their neighbours.

Sophie was bewildered. 'What's happened?'

'Sand storm, it sometimes takes out the satellite signal.'

'How long for?' Panic began to rise. What would she tell Marcus when he called at half time?

'I'll check.' Klaus wandered off and spoke to the barman for a few minutes, receiving shrugs in response. He returned unsmiling. 'He says it could be a few minutes, or the whole match. Beer?' He nodded at her empty glass.

'Maybe later.'

For the next forty minutes, Sophie chewed her lip and paced back and forth, scowling at the intermittent pictures, at the tempting glimpses of the action. It was with trepidation that she answered the phone. 'Hi, Marcus.'

'Hey, I said I'd call.' The line was poor, she could hardly hear him. 'So, what have you seen?'

Think, Sophie, think. 'How do you feel after that?'

'Good. Loads in my legs despite being soaked. Did you see their scrum? I don't think they're going to … much of the second half. What did you think?'

Blag it, Sophie, blag it. 'Just keep it tight while the ball's damp. Make them think that, then throw in some longer passes.'

'Like we've been doing?'

'That's it. If you keep the upper hand in the scrum, you needn't worry about the odd knock-on.'

'But they have one more player than us after that yellow card.'

Shit. 'Err, I missed that, the signal's not very clear up here.' Try virtually non-existent. 'Get off this phone and go listen to the coach. You're playing well; just keep looking for those mismatches.'

'I don't know what I'd do without you, Soph. Thanks for not mentioning the tackles I missed. See you in two weeks!'

She disconnected and exhaled. Despite the stress, his voice had given her shivers down her spine, and reminded her body of how much she was missing the regular intimacy, and how she missed his company.

'You OK, *bokkie*?' Klaus had stayed quiet while she stressed. 'You did the best you could, and I'm sure he'll be fine.'

Sophie laughed. 'I was talking absolute crap, I know. He'll be fine, though. I'll have that beer now, please.' Ironically, the picture cleared in time for her to see Marcus running in a try, and stayed more or less clear for the remainder of the match.

As they walked away from the bar at the end of the match, Klaus slung an arm over her shoulder to help her against the wind. 'What does he expect you to do next week? We'll be in the middle of the Delta, definitely no match coverage there.'

'I've done some analysis of the opposition already, and

166

he's calling later to chat about today.'

The wind took that moment to gust strongly. 'I doubt he'll get a signal, the wind is worsening.'

Sophie shrugged. 'I'll email him then.'

'Hmmm.' They crossed the street. 'Soph, I know you enjoy doing this, but please don't let this affect your trip, hey?'

'I won't. Honest.'

'Good. Now let's get back to the lodge and make the most of those hot showers before we go bush.'

Chapter Twelve

Sophie finally arrived back in Cape Town late one morning, on a southbound truck. The previous couple of weeks had been brilliant, and Sophie had seen more than she thought was possible, including more Big Fives and lots of other wildlife and sights. She had drifted in a boat past clumps of hippos, held her breath as crocodiles snapped feet away, snuggled in her sleeping bag as she heard herds of elephants tramp past, and in Victoria Falls, had rafted down the wild Zambezi.

Although there was still a touch of attraction between her and Klaus, they had managed to build a fraternal relationship. She kept him company at night, talking with him and continuing to share a tent with him, which seemed to help with his nightmares. In the early hours, he told her more about his background, about school and the Army with Marcus, and she told him about her lackadaisical parents and how she'd met Marcus. Improved nights of sleep meant he looked several years younger by the time they parted, with Klaus taking the truck further north while she jumped on a truck going south, back down to the Cape.

Sophie had texted Marcus to say she was on her way, but told him not to worry about picking her up as he wouldn't be able get away from training. She had tentative plans to stash her bags and head up Table Mountain again. A full twenty-four hours cooped up in the truck was enough for her.

Despite that, she did look for him on stepping off the bus, stretching up on tiptoes to futilely scan the meagre welcome party. Instead of his blond head, she saw someone else she recognised approaching her. 'Joseph!'

'Hallo, Sophie, welcome back to the Cape.' He nodded at her, pleased about something. 'You are looking very well.'

She laughed. 'I feel dreadful; I didn't sleep on the truck.' It was partly due to the noise, but mostly the anticipation of being reunited with a certain blond rugby player. She lifted her bag on to her shoulder, and waved a farewell arm towards the guides as she walked away with Joseph. 'Did Marcus send you?'

'The vineyard were sending someone, but I thought you would appreciate a friendly face. Here is the car.' Joseph seemed embarrassed. 'We do not usually drive this out of the vineyard, but Tandy has borrowed my *bakkie* to go to work.'

An excuse for a car sat on the sloping road in front of them. It looked like layers of dirt, rust, and paint held it together.

'That's OK, it's nice to have a lift,' Sophie said cheerfully as they got in the vehicle and a rolling start coaxed it into life. 'Anyway, tell me about how you and Tandy are getting on.'

A huge smile split Joseph's face as he manoeuvred into traffic. 'Everything is very good.'

They chatted on the way out of town, eventually arriving back at the vineyard. The car coughed and wheezed its way up the drive, and Joseph drove it straight around to join the other vehicles just before the engine cut out.

'I am sorry, I could not risk stopping by the house in case it would not start again,' he apologised.

'No problem, a little walk is fine for me. I'll probably come by later, I need the exercise.' She hoisted her bag on her back and headed to the large, imposing residence.

The house was ominously quiet when she opened the

170

door and made her way to Marcus' room. About to unpack a few things, she pulled open a drawer to find the items she'd left behind missing. So, too, were the spare items of clothing she'd left neatly in the wardrobe, apart from the handbag. Inside the handbag, in a side pocket, were the rings.

Shrugging, she took a shower, grateful to wash off the discomfort of travel, and pulled on some walking gear.

Making her way back to the main door, a throat was cleared, 'May I ask where you are going?'

Sophie jumped and turned to see Marcus' mother standing in the doorway to the lounge. 'Oh, I thought everyone was out.' She plastered a smile on her face and held out a hand. 'I'm sorry I didn't get time to introduce myself before, I wasn't feeling well after the accident. I'm Sophie.'

Her hand was ignored by the scowling woman. 'If you are going outside, we do not allow anyone who doesn't work here to enter the vineyard unless they are part of an escorted party.' Her tone was icy.

'I'm sure ...' Sophie trailed off – she didn't want to get Joseph or any others in trouble. 'I'll just walk along the drive then.'

'Dinner will be served in half an hour. Don't be late.'

The atmosphere in the dining room was tense when Sophie entered, and Bridget avoided her eyes. Sophie had a sinking feeling something was up. The chicken course stuck in her throat and the fruit pudding was sickly sweet. She kept glancing towards the main door, wishing that Marcus would return. He should have been back by then. What was keeping him?

She had been looking forward to seeing him so much. However, with the disapproving looks directed her way by his mother, she wasn't sure if a reunion under that roof was such a good plan. She felt like she had regressed years, to the poisonous atmosphere of blame that always hung like a stench around her family's table. She shrank into her body, the comfort of being herself as she had for the last few weeks disappearing.

Bridget tried to make stilted conversation throughout, asking her parents and Sophie about their separate trips. Sophie answered a couple of times, tried to give more than one word answers, but throat-clearing and condemnatory glares shrivelled the words up.

Once the dishes had been cleared, she summoned the courage to flee. 'Please excuse me, I'll wait for Marcus upstairs.'

His mother threw down her napkin. 'Hah! You may as well. If you open your legs at least Marcus will get something out of the relationship.'

'Mother!' exclaimed Bridget.

'It had to be said. As far as I'm concerned, she's been acting the whore and he's been running around waiting on her hand and foot. He missed training when he chased her around Namibia! He could've been dropped!'

Sophie's heart sank even further. Marcus had told her he had the day off!

The vitriol continued. 'He's been chauffeuring her around South Africa when he's supposed to have been training. Buying her expensive gifts and paying for her treatment when he's not even going out with her!'

But I've been helping him with his rugby, and he's been playing well, Sophie wanted to scream.

'She's been milking him. And while she's been away, she's been fucking another man!' His mother turned accusatory eyes on her. 'Well? What do you have to say for yourself?'

She couldn't say anything. She was so unprepared for the accusations that her mind went blank. Years of conditioning overruled the tentative progress she had made in the last few months. Sophie turned and ran to her room.

172

Well, the room she'd originally been allocated. The bland guest room. His mother wouldn't like it if she went to Marcus' room. She huddled in the corner, arms wrapped around herself.

There were footsteps outside. 'Sophie?'

She stayed hunched in the corner, hidden behind the bed, hoping Bridget would give up.

Doors in the adjacent room opened and closed, the door to her shelter also opened and closed. It went quiet.

She wasn't welcome there. She had to leave.

She waited a while longer, then slowly stood up. Beside her was a black bin bag, looking out of place in the bland quarters. Out of curiosity, she peeked inside to see the items she'd left behind in Marcus' room, piled and crumpled haphazardly.

What did this mean? Who had put it there? Had Marcus had enough, but not told her? Had he come clean to his family? Had he ... blamed *her*?

She picked the bag up, cradling it in her arms, and crept to the door. She cringed as it squeaked open, and scampered across into Marcus' room. Her rucksack was still mostly packed, and it didn't take long to stuff the black bag inside, and grab her handbag, throwing her smaller pack inside.

Her handbag. Not her handbag.

She gazed at the unknown designer, at the beautiful leather which had apparently cost Marcus a fortune, and put it back down. Gently, she removed her pack and stuck the contents in the front compartment of her rucksack. Perhaps Bridget could use the handbag?

She quickly searched her rucksack, removing anything else Marcus had given her. The only thing she kept was the SIM card from the phone – it had valuable numbers on it and she could buy a cheap handset to use with it. Sophie left some rand to cover it next to the phone. Her last task was to remove the sham rings, placing them on the bedside table.

As she crept down the stairs, there were raised voices coming from one of the rooms. The imposing main door opened soundlessly, and she ducked out into the light from the setting sun.

What could she do? Where could she go? Thoughts cannonballed through her mind as she skittered down the drive and towards the main gates, her rucksack heavy on her back.

'Sophie?'

The familiar voice came from the vines, not the house. 'Joseph!'

'Are you OK? You do not look so well.'

She was about to say everything was OK, but she couldn't. The unexpected sympathy broke what remained of her composure. Holding back sobs, she managed to gasp, 'Could you ... would you take me to a bus or train station please? I have to go. If you can. If you're not working. Please.'

'I am just finished. Where are you going?'

Where could she go? The only people she knew were also Marcus' friends, and that would be awkward. 'Back to the city, to a hotel. I have outstayed my welcome here.' She smiled tremulously at him.

'I will take you there. You would not be safe at the bus station.' He nodded decisively. 'My *bakkie* is by the gate, Tandy dropped it off earlier.'

Only a few yards away was a battered and dusty white pick-up truck, half hidden by the growing vines.

'Thank you.' Sophie clambered in to sit on the bench seat, her bag in her lap. The engine purred into life, belying the vehicle's tatty appearance, and he drove out of the drive and onto the smooth tarmac road. She was so grateful Joseph did not ask her anything, only the hotel name, and let her sit in shell-shocked silence as they approached the lights of the city.

They drew up at the hotel where Sophie had originally stayed. 'Joseph, thank you … for the lift and for not asking about … this.'

He stared forward through the window. 'When I lost my family, it was worse when people asked. It was like they wanted to feel my pain too. I could already feel your pain. I felt your pain when I first met you.'

Sophie nodded and climbed out.

'You must keep in touch,' he called. 'Tandy is very happy in her new job, and we are doing well.'

She gulped. 'Good. Please give her my love.'

'I will.'

With a chug, he pulled away, and Sophie waved goodbye.

The concierge on the door was different from her earlier stay. She nodded at him and refused the offer of assistance with her bag. At the front desk, she enquired about a room, and gave her details.

'Have you stayed here before?' asked the receptionist, frowning at the screen.

'Yes, but only briefly.'

'You had an accident, *nè*? You are recovered now?' He looked her up and down, as if puzzled she wasn't physically damaged.

'Yes, well recovered, thank you.'

'We have something of yours, it was handed in afterwards. There was no answer on your contact phone number, so we have sent a letter to your home address in England. I will find it.'

The receptionist disappeared into a back office, and emerged minutes later carrying a white polythene sack.

'It has been sealed since you were taken to hospital, in case the police needed it.' He ripped open the polythene to show a familiar handbag. 'This is yours?'

Sophie squeaked, 'Yes!'

She barely restrained herself from ripping the bag out of his hands, impatiently waiting for him to pass it over. Inside were all the things she remembered, even her passport, purse, and dead phone in the hidden pockets.

He looked surprised when she drew the items out. 'We didn't find those, or we would have tried harder to contact you.'

The bag had done its job a little too well. Thanking the receptionist profusely, she made her way to her assigned room. Luckily, the charger for her tablet fit the phone, so she set the handset to charge. The SIM card would be useless as it had been cancelled, but she could insert the one Marcus had given her.

At the thought of Marcus and the horrible event, her control finally broke and she began to sob, tears pouring out. All her hopefulness from the morning had gone, leaving only a shell adrift.

It was strange turning the phone on and seeing her welcome screen. All of her address book, messages – it felt like a lifetime ago. New messages began to arrive as soon as it connected to the network and wireless internet, and several beeps heralded missed calls, emails, and texts as she got ready for bed.

Bridget. *Where have you disappeared to? Mum is sorry. She didn't know you had been helping him train.*

Bridget again. *Really worried now. Please let me know you're safe. Marcus is back and he's not happy.*

Marcus. *Bridget and my mother have told me they confronted you. Where have you gone? Come back, it'll be fine. I'm so looking forward to seeing you. Mx*

Marcus again. *Why did you leave the things I bought you behind? I can't contact you now. I don't know if you're even receiving this! I'll email. Mx*

And an email. *I have the full story now. I appreciate how you must have felt. My mother is very embarrassed,*

176

she misunderstood completely. I admitted that I took advantage of your confusion, and she walloped me over the head. Please get in touch to let me know you're OK. I miss you. Mx

Sophie's finger hovered over the email reply button, eventually composing a bland response. *I'm fine, I am in a hotel in Cape Town. I'm sorry I caused all this, please apologise to your family. Sx*

She stared at the message, finger hovering over the send button. Then she deleted the initial and kiss and just signed it with her full name, *Sophie Edwards.*

Writing it out made her feel better, and the lack of sleep finally caught up with her. She turned the ringer off, and extinguished the bedside light.

In the morning, she woke early feeling restless, needing the exercise she had craved the previous day. With a few items chucked into a small day bag, she headed up Table Mountain as the sun came up.

Climbing the face, she focussed on her steps, on the path in front of her, rather than the various thoughts trying to buzz around her head. The view from the top was as spectacular as she remembered, the new day's light washing over the city below.

Seeing the few other people taking photos, she pulled out her phone to take her own. The first thing she saw was the message to Marcus – it had failed to send. She tried again, and the envelope assured her it had gone.

There were yet more missed calls from all kinds of numbers. She turned the ringer on, and the phone rang straight away, Sophie got ready to reject the call, but saw Sarah's name flashing up.

'Hey.'

'Soph, are you OK? Marcus has been in touch. He says you've disappeared, he's really worried about you.'

The tears started before she could compose a reply.

177

'Oh, S-s-Sarah.'

The truth came out as she perched on a nearby rock and sobbed: the friends-with-benefits relationship she'd been wallowing in with Marcus, the pretence of being further involved, and the eventual denouement by his family.

Sarah sighed. 'I had a feeling something was going on. You're usually the most open person I know, and I could tell you were holding back. Have you thought what you're going to do now?'

'Apart from lick my wounds?' hiccupped Sophie. 'I don't know yet. I don't need to be back for another month, I don't want to return early. M-Marcus has shown me so much of South Africa. I've been on safari and up as far as Victoria Falls. I need to be here for a match on Saturday, I promised the kids I'd be there and I can't let them down no matter what else is going on. I don't know.'

'What about going further north, or heading to Europe if you're not comfortable travelling by yourself? Hang on.' There was a brief pause with whispering in the background. 'If you're running low on funds, Tom can sort out an advance.'

'Money's not a problem, thanks. I saved a fortune staying with Marcus, and the trip to Vic Falls was discounted.'

'It sounds like you worked for it, though, being his own personal performance analyst. For a nice guy, he's really done you up like a kipper.'

'I didn't mind doing it, I love watching him play. I love him.' Sophie realised what she had just said. 'Oh. Hell.'

'I was wondering when that penny would finally drop.'

'But he … he loves Clare!' blurted Sophie.

Sarah was quiet for a moment before responding. 'Does he really? How do you know?'

'He was really unhappy at the wedding, he gets upset whenever her name is mentioned.'

'I did notice he liked her, but I suspected it was just a

crush. Recently, he spent more time focused on you than her.'

Sophie had to ignore the jolt of hope from her heart. 'Really? He's attracted to me, he's admitted that.'

Sarah hummed, neither agreeing nor disagreeing. 'I wish I could give you a hug. It sounds like you need it.'

What she wouldn't give for a hug. 'Yep, I do. Thanks.' The phone beeped in warning. 'I have to go now, the phone's struggling for battery. All the calls I've missed have killed it.'

'OK, but promise to stay in touch,' coaxed Sarah.

'I will, I promise.'

They said their goodbyes and Sophie reluctantly hung up. She stared down at the phone in her hand and saw more notifications flashing on the top of the screen. The social media ones she ignored, but one belonged to the app she used for her checklists. Remembering her puzzlement over the travel insurance, she opened it.

Yep, the insurance box was definitely ticked. Out of curiosity, she clicked on it, her hands shaking as she hoped the phone battery would last. Further details flashed up.

GoTraveller plcy no. C898565EDW

Under that were emergency contact numbers. Sophie stared at the screen in incomprehension. Then the penny dropped – the celebratory drinks she'd had with Clare and Sarah. She'd purchased a rucksack online when she got home that night, but could only vaguely remember it. She must have bought the travel insurance policy at the same time.

So she did have cover all along! Sophie groaned in frustration. A few clicks confirmed the policy number was valid – the original confirmation email must have ended up in her junk mail and been deleted.

Once back at the hotel, she fired off an email to the contact address, explaining her situation, and supplying details of her stay in hospital. At least Marcus could be

179

paid back.

The phone rang again, it was a strange number so she ignored it. Minutes later, her phone beeped an email alert.

Hi Sophie, it's Todd Duncan. Joseph gave me your details, hope you don't mind. Heard about the "non-marriage". Hope you're doing OK. The kids are really looking forward to seeing you on Saturday, although I'll understand if you can't make it. Call if you want a chat. Todd.

P.S. kids suggested you come to stay, let me know where you are & I'll arrange a pick up. You'd be very welcome.

Todd's "ranch" wasn't as sterile and neat as the Coetzee spread. Disorganised chaos would have been a better way to describe it – there were kids and adults everywhere. A track ran through the grounds and people were zooming up and down it on battered-looking bikes, a ball was being kicked around a yard, and some vine poles had been consigned for use as volleyball net posts.

'It's not usually this chaotic,' laughed Todd as he came out to greet her, helping her out of the truck he'd sent to collect her. 'Yesterday, we received some donated sports equipment so I gave them this morning off work and school.'

'That's nice of you.'

'Not really, we're a bit overstaffed at the moment, so we're up to date on the seasonal work, plus the kids need a break.'

'Soph-ee! You're here!' A couple of kids ran their way, wrapping themselves around her legs in welcoming hugs. 'We missed you at the games. Come play with us!'

Sophie felt a smile breaking out, overcoming her natural reticence. 'OK, but I warn you I'm no good at any of this, except maybe the cycling.'

'It doesn't matter at all as long as you enjoy yourself,'

soothed Todd. 'I'll take your bags inside, we'll see you at lunch. I've arranged for you to go for a walk with a friend, to have a chat.' He patted her on the arm, just before she was dragged off by the kids.

Mosa was a counsellor Todd had on call, who lived in the sprawling mess of buildings behind his house. Some of the children and adults arrived at his ranch highly traumatised, and Mosa helped them settle in. She also taught in the school. Her beaming, welcoming face reminded Sophie of Tandy and she immediately felt comfortable, despite her problems not seeming as severe as the counsellor's usual patients.

As they walked up and down the vines, Mosa prised her life story out. Her parents' arguments, their emotional distance from her, growing up isolated as an only child, and what had happened over the previous few months and twenty-four hours.

As they talked, Sophie could feel a weight lifting off her. She hadn't done anything to be embarrassed about and Mosa stopped her every time she started to castigate herself. Sophie eventually sighed, 'I just can't stand up for myself. I get emotional, I can't speak, and I just want to run away.'

'You are a strong woman, you just don't realise how strong you are. But your parents' actions have conditioned you into escaping any taxing situation. They could always out-argue you, and disparaged you for it rather than encouraging you to make a case for what you believed in. Then they sent you away.' Mosa shook her head. 'So, in awkward situations, you have learnt to give up fighting and disappear. Flight rather than fight.'

Sophie nodded. She had suspected as much herself, but it helped for someone else to voice it.

'You have done well to recover your confidence, but it was only a thin veneer and didn't hold when things

181

became turbulent. We need to teach you to break your conditioning, so you can stick up for yourself. That will begin by recognising the situation. You'll get plenty of practice here, there's always some bickering going on.' Mosa gestured towards the buildings, where people were milling around. 'Next, you have to face unpleasant situations, meet with people who have intimidated you to run away in the past. Perhaps even counter an argument?'

Sophie's heart dropped. 'It's possible that the Coetzees will be at the game on the weekend.'

'Then we don't have much time to lose. Let's find a quarrel!'

Sophie laughed at Mosa's exuberance, but remembered one more thing, 'There's also Marcus. What am I going to do about that?'

'What do you want to do?' Mosa asked gently.

'I miss him. I've missed him while I've been away, but it feels like all he wants from me is sex and my ability to analyse his game, which …' Sophie trailed off, 'I suspect that he doesn't really need me for that any more.'

Match day came sooner than Sophie expected. She longed to see Marcus – he had sent messages asking if she was all right, where she was, and who she was with, but all she had said was that she was with friends and she would see him after the game. He wasn't happy with that, wanting to meet up beforehand, but she didn't feel she would be strong enough to cope yet. She sent him some analysis information using clips he had provided. Shortly after, he went ominously quiet.

She arrived at the teeming ground with Todd and his troop, who, on escaping from the vehicle, dispersed in all different directions. Todd gave her arm a reassuring pat before heading to the bar.

Sophie decided to wander around the busy concourse, soaking up the atmosphere. It was a warm day, probably too warm for the jeans and jacket she was wearing. She was grateful for the sandals on her feet, although the small heel didn't give enough height to see much. She stepped out of the way as she took off her jacket and looked around, biting her lip in indecision.

'Sophie!' There was the sound of running feet, and arms wrapped around her, lifting her off her feet. 'I've missed you, my *bokkie*-Soph.'

Her heart leapt until she realised it was Klaus holding her, beaming down at her. 'You're back?'

'This morning, I came straight here. We didn't need so many drivers for that route, so I took a truck back. Hoped I'd see you before you leave again. Marcus around?'

She shrugged, 'I've no idea where he is.'

'Haven't you –' He groaned. '*Ag, sies man,* what happened? He's not been at our place.'

'His family found out we weren't married. They weren't happy.'

Klaus let loose a profuse chain of what she guessed were Afrikaans swear words. 'And what happened with Marcus?'

'I don't know – he wasn't there when they confronted me. I did the cowardly thing and ran away. I've been staying elsewhere.'

'You haven't seen him?'

She shook her head. 'I've been working through some issues. I needed to. The confrontation set off emotions I needed to deal with. My parents and all that.'

'*Ag,* Soph.' He hugged her again. 'But you're OK now?'

She nodded, 'Better.'

'He must be going mental.'

'You could say that.' The wary and weary voice came from a couple of yards away. They turned to see a wrecked-looking Marcus with his kit bag thrown over his shoulder. 'Looks like you two got on well. I didn't want to believe it when I heard you were fucking each other …'

'What?' Sophie's mouth dropped open in disbelief. 'What the hell, Marcus? How dare you think that of your friend?'

'And of Sophie,' added Klaus, shaking his head in dismay. 'She missed you every day. We comforted each other as friends, that was it.'

Their outraged reactions must have pacified Marcus. He stared at his feet. 'I'm sorry, I heard …' His name was called. 'Oh, fuck, I have to go. I've never felt less like playing a game of rugby.'

'Wait!' His name was called again, and an irate Sophie yelled back, 'For fuck's sake, he'll be there in five minutes! Keep your *bladdy broekies* on!'

There was a glimmer of a smile on Marcus' face. 'I've never heard you shout and swear like that before.'

She gasped and covered her mouth in shock. 'That's because I never have. Oh my. Oh, gosh. *I shouted at someone!*' For a moment, the awkwardness was forgotten as she did a happy little jig.

A throat was cleared. 'Umm, Sophie? I will need to go soon.'

She stopped dancing and flushed. 'Sorry. Actually, I'm not sorry, that was just a reflex. I'm learning not to be sorry all the time.' Her hands went to her cheeks as she chattered. 'And I shouldn't be blushing either. Damn body.'

Both of the blond men were grinning broadly at her.

'What? Oh, good grief. Klaus – go get me a drink. I think I need a pint of something alcoholic.'

Klaus obediently headed towards a bar, leaving her with a more cheerful-looking Marcus. His shoulders had straightened and he didn't look quite so jaded.

'I am really sorry, I should've known better.'

'Yes, you should.' She couldn't be angry with him. He looked like hell.

He sighed. 'I've really missed you, Soph.' He tried to smile at her, then his name was called again, this time by someone else. He glanced over his shoulder, and back at her. 'I need to tell you something.'

Another yell.

'Marcus, you'd better be going before someone has a coronary. We'll talk about this after the match. Go kick some *gats*.' She fluttered her hands at him. 'Go.'

He laughed at her attempt at Afrikaans. 'Just one moment, something for later.' Marcus lunged forward, picked her up, and as she gasped, planted his mouth on hers.

Oh, he felt good. Oh, he smelled good. Oh, he *tasted* good.

Before she knew it, her arms and legs were wrapped around him, and she was giving as good as she got, meeting his lips, groaning as they tasted each other for the first time in weeks. Thrilled, she rubbed her chest against him as she pulled up his jacket. His hands squeezed her buttocks, and one started to make its way to her breasts.

'MARCUS!'

'SOPHIE!'

The twin roars from either side of them halted the fast-escalating clinch.

'*Bladdy hell*, you two, you're in the middle of the concourse and there are children around!' hissed Gert.

'And sponsors,' added Jan.

'And children of sponsors.' Gert rolled his eyes.

Marcus slowly let Sophie back to her feet. Her legs nearly gave way as she felt the hump in his jeans before they separated. Her body protested, and she opened her mouth to suggest they go somewhere private.

Marcus' hot eyes looked like they wanted the same thing. They stared, heat rebuilding, until two bodies sliding between them broke their gaze: Gert and Jan, tutting.

Gert faced her, blocking her view, Jan faced Marcus,

taking his shoulder. 'C'mon Marcus, we're late. The TV people want to interview you.

Gert nodded at her. 'Sophie, we'll see *you* later. Fix your lips, he's made one hell of a mess of your gloss. And your hair. And you need to straighten your clothes.

'Huh?' Sophie's attention was on the man being coaxed to walk away from her.

'Sophie?' Fingers were clicked in front of her face. '*Ag sies*, girl.' Gert pulled her to one side and down a quiet walkway, away from curious eyes. Her clothing was tugged back into place and a tissue wiped around her mouth. 'Comb and lip gloss?'

Distractedly, she rummaged in her handbag and handed over a small tube and comb. What did Marcus want to tell her? Why had he grabbed her like that?

Gert whisked the comb through her hair then delicately applied the gloss to her swollen lips. He looked proud of his efforts. 'OK, good to go. Ready?'

'Thanks.' Sophie pulled herself mentally back together. 'Sorry about that.'

He led her back out to the concourse. 'I have to go now, I'm not playing due to a niggle, but I still need to be there. You look after yourself.' He kissed her forehead, ruffled her hair, smoothed it down again, and jogged away.

She gazed in the direction Marcus had been shepherded, a part of her wishing he'd reappear. Instead, she saw another face.

'Sophie!'

'Kara, hi!' Sophie smiled at Kara, not knowing what to expect. A brief hug wasn't it.

'Hey, how are you?' Kara stood back and gazed searchingly at her. 'We heard word was out.'

'Confused. I didn't know how anyone would react. I've just seen Marcus, he wasn't very happy but we ended up snogging. Gert and Jan broke us up. Gert was almost protective of me rather than flirting. It was weird.'

186

Kara nodded. 'That's because you're not attached any more, they don't want you to get the wrong idea.'

'Huh? I don't understand.'

Kara dropped her voice lower. 'I was hoping someone would tell you first but, Gert and Jan, are, well, together. They're bisexual. They fuck each other as much as women.'

Sophie's mouth dropped open, 'But ... they're such flirts?'

'They are both in the closet. Very much so. It can be dangerous here to be openly anything-but-straight, and their families would never, ever speak to them again. Only a few close friends know, and we respect their need to keep it quiet.'

Sophie remembered what she'd witnessed at the *braai*. 'I saw Bridget and Gert arguing ...'

'Bridget can be rather ... idealistic. Just because she lives openly as a lesbian, with the protection her wealth and status brings, she doesn't always understand that for others, it's more difficult. Like how Piet and I are estranged from our families – even in this day and age, they did not want a white man going out with a mixed race girl. Bridget doesn't understand why we are not angry at our families. We know why Marcus did what he did; we saw the pressure he was under before you arrived.'

'He mentioned he was teased, some boys called him gay?'

'Some of the younger idiots did, yes. No one in our group. I don't think that really bothered him, it was the women turning up here and elsewhere.' Kara sighed.

'I still don't understand how his family could treat me like that, yet they are OK with Bridget's sexuality.'

Kara spluttered. '*Jislaaik!* Whatever gave you that idea? They're not OK with it, not really.'

Sophie was confused. 'But she can live openly?'

'I shouldn't tell you this but Bridget can't have

187

children, she's infertile. Which means Marcus is their one hope of continuing the Coetzee dynasty. They need him to make a suitable marriage. It doesn't have to last, as long as it bears children.'

'And I'm not suitable?'

'Marcus told them that you weren't interested in having children for another few years. You're only young, no one could really blame you. His parents are panicking as Bridget's partner will be inseminated soon, and if Marcus doesn't have children, they would need to disown the child to ensure the vineyard and entails are passed to his offspring. They don't approve, but they don't want to hurt her.'

'I see.'

'You were just unlucky to be caught in the crossfire.' Kara shrugged.

'Sophie!' Klaus returned holding a couple of plastic pint glasses and handed one over. 'Sorry for being so long – the queue was massive.'

Sophie took a sip of the beer. She needed it. 'Klaus, have you met Kara, Piet's girlfriend?'

Kara oohed and smiled softly, her hands going to her cheeks. 'Not just a girlfriend any more.'

Sophie caught a glimpse of something sparkling on her left hand. 'Really? Congratulations!'

Kara's smile blossomed into a beatific grin. 'Piet proposed while you were away. He saw what Marcus was going through and decided he didn't want me to get away. Here he is. He's going to join us as he's not in the squad for these matches.'

Piet wrapped his arms around his fiancée and smooched her briefly. '*Howzit*, Sophie. Hey, Klaus.' He did some handshake thing with the other guy. 'We going to watch this game then or what?'

Chapter Thirteen

After a quick bite to eat, they settled in the packed stands, in the section reserved for friends and family of players. The army of kids weren't allowed in, so Sophie arranged to chat with them the next day.

'It's playoff time, some of the last games of the season. It always gets a lot busier,' shouted Piet from his seat on the other side of Kara. 'Marcus has done really well to be first-choice for these games: he was supposed to be backup support, but he's been one of the players of the season.'

When the game started, it was certainly up a few levels from the matches a few weeks ago. Marcus seemed to be everywhere, involved in everything, rocketing around the pitch with daring intent and commanding his teammates. He looked self-assured, decisive, completely in control, and a different player to a few months earlier. At half time, when he searched for her, Sophie popped down the stairs with Piet to chat to him briefly, but in truth, she didn't have much to add.

After a quick conversation with the children, they returned to their seats to find Klaus had gone to the bar with Kara. Piet sat next to her and took a deep breath. 'I've been meaning to have a word. I wanted to speak with you about Marcus.'

Sophie nodded. 'Go on.'

'He's just such a nice guy. He never thinks of himself; he's always been so considerate to others, even if it means he misses out. We've been frustrated for years that he just wouldn't stand up for himself. Until your accident and it appeared he'd left his wife, you, in the UK. We finally thought he'd grown a backbone at some stage. You turned up, not what we were expecting, and then he confessed you weren't married.'

'Not the best of ideas.'

'No, it wasn't. Though it's clear you do have feelings for each other. But he's still been all overprotective and at your beck and call.'

'Beck and call?'

'*Ja.* He didn't stop wondering if you were OK the whole time you were away. Got a bit boring after a while.'

'My apologies,' Sophie commented dryly.

Piet barked a laugh. 'It's not a bad thing. Plus, with your influence, he's turned into one of the best players in the country.'

Sophie sighed unhappily. 'That wasn't me though, please don't think that. He was always a good player, he was just rusty from not having a decent run of games. I didn't exactly tell him anything he wasn't aware of, did I?'

Piet hummed thoughtfully.

'And I'm concerned he's relying too much on me and not listening to his coaches here.' She'd caught a few frowns when he'd deserted their huddle to speak with her. 'This is a different level to Harford Park, to anything I've watched except for internationals. And I have a feeling he won't be returning to Harford.'

'He'll be returning to the UK. Trust me. He won't stay here.'

There was something in Piet's melancholic voice that made Sophie turn to stare at him. 'Why not? His family's here, his friends.'

'Do you remember how I met Kara? It was worse than it sounded. After I spoke with her, I found Marcus with some women. He didn't seem drunk, it was something else. He was ... malleable. We got him away from the women, took him home, and the next day he didn't

190

remember a thing after arriving at the bar.'

Sophie shook her head in horror.

'I mean, we're men, we're South African. We should be able to look after ourselves. We're not supposed to get taken advantage of. He used to drink a lot more, but he cut right down after that. Then he went to the UK.'

'That's why he only ever drinks a lot when his friends are around?'

'*Ja*, and why he'll be returning to the UK. He feels safer there.'

While a small part of her was thrilled at the thought of him returning, another felt guilt for feeling that way, and compassion for the man she loved not being able to stay where he loved, with his friends and family.

It was a hard-fought win, both sides battered and bloody by the time they came off the pitch.

For a change, Marcus hadn't crossed the whitewash, but, instead, had supported other scorers. He had been pulled off with fifteen minutes to go after developing a slight limp. Piet had nodded in approval, stating that it was a sign of how much the coaching team valued him, before trotting down the stairs to join his teammates.

Marcus beckoned for Sophie to go down as well, but she shook her head. That wasn't the place for her. So, icepack strapped to his knee, and boot bag in hand, he had vaulted the barriers and clattered up the stairs to join them, receiving pats and handshakes on the way up

Sophie moved over for him to sit down between her and Klaus, discreetly taking a lungful of Marcus-fragranced air. Her eyes fluttered in pleasure and her mouth watered. She licked her lips instead of the tempting skin close to her.

Kara laughed beside her. 'I saw that!'

'Huh?' The men turned their heads while Sophie blushed.

'Sophie likes her man when he's sweaty,' giggled Kara.

'Good,' murmured Marcus with an intimate grin at Sophie, before leaning over and replacing his boots with a pair of flip-flops from his bag. 'I can't say my feet will smell as good though.'

He dropped a damp sock on her lap and she squealed. Kara and Klaus both chuckled.

To disguise her embarrassment, Sophie concentrated on the last few minutes of action. Some time in that period, Marcus' hand graduated to her thigh, and hers to his. The embers of the earlier conflagration were still smouldering inside, and having him temptingly beside her, rippling muscles under her hand, reignited the blaze. The distraction of analysing and commenting on the game held her together, just. Marcus' insights were a massive jump in comparison with earlier in the year, she hardly contributed anything new. For some reason, instead of feeling surplus to requirements, it reassured her. She found this masterful Marcus even more attractive.

At the final whistle, they stood, and Piet rejoined them. 'Players' bar *isit*?'

'Sophie will see you there, we're going for a chat.'

Sophie wasn't given much time to object as Marcus grabbed her hand and tugged her away in front of others who were departing. Following a tunnel inside the stand, they took a few turns and mounted some stairs which took them higher and higher. They encountered the odd steward, but Marcus was let through, his team kit acting like a magic pass.

Marcus pushed open the last door at the end of a hospitality corridor, checked there was no one inside, and pulled her in. It was one of the boxes overlooking the pitch, thankfully unlit so no one could see inside.

'Strip,' ordered Marcus as he locked the door and jammed a chair under the handle for good measure. He started pulling his jersey off. 'Strip now. Otherwise your clothes will tell everyone what you've been doing.'

Her body flushing with heat, Sophie kicked off her sandals and wiggled out of her jeans and knickers. Whatever happened, she needed this. Her body was crying out for it.

She had help in whisking her top over her head, then his hands lifted her, split her legs and he breached her, started entering her.

She gulp-laughed at his speed. 'What about ... foreplay?' Her arms and legs wrapped around him, pulling him closer. She breathed him in, licked his neck as she had earlier craved.

He panted. 'Sophie, you're soaking, you don't need any more foreplay.'

He was right. Despite being tight, she was ready, as gravity and his hands eased him into her. 'I still have my bra on,' she gasped.

He walked backwards, giving her glorious sensations of him shifting deeper and deeper inside. A ledge pressed against her backside, held her up as he unfastened her bra. 'Now you don't.' His hands squeezed her, and his hips picked up speed.

A burst of muffled laughter echoed through the room. 'What was that?' she squeaked.

'The ... box ... next ... door.' Marcus punctuated each word with a thrust. 'We need to keep ... noise down. Fuck, you feel good.'

He didn't just feel good, her body was singing with delight.

A hand wormed between them. 'I can't hold on for much longer, I want you to come with me. Come. Come.'

She came, gripping him tightly, muffling her yell into his chest. He thrust harder, several times, and let out his own bellow into her neck. They eased to the floor, Sophie splayed on top of him, as their bodies calmed. It was quietening around them as the stand below emptied. The people in the box next door left, taking long minutes to get out of there.

Sophie lifted her head to look through the tinted glass at the rest of his team finishing their warm-down on the pitch. 'Will anyone be missing you?'

Marcus laughed. 'I don't care, I needed that more than I needed a warm down.' He twitched slightly. 'I may need it again quite soon too.'

'You'll be recovered that quickly? Mmmm.' She'd only just come, but wouldn't say no to another round.

'I haven't seen you for a few weeks.' He began running his hands up her body. 'I've missed your pretty breasts.' He moved her so he could squeeze them, play with, tug, and suck the nipples.

Yep, the warmth was definitely returning. Sophie gasped as he shuffled along the floor, so his face was between her legs.

'I've missed this too.' He licked her and her back arched. 'I think I've found something I'll enjoy doing until my cock is hard again.'

She could only groan.

As Sophie pulled her jeans back on, she realised her knees were a little sore from their second encounter – riding him until he'd turned her onto her back and hammered into her. A bottle of water and a few napkins had cleaned her up enough to re-dress, but Marcus was in dire need of something more.

He sniffed his armpits and pulled a face, 'I *really* reek now. I need a shower. And we still haven't had that chat. Will you meet me in the bar downstairs?'

'I don't know when Todd's heading back to the ranch, but I'll stay as long as I can.'

'That's where you've been staying? I'll come to pick you up from there tomorrow.'

'Will you? What if I don't want to go anywhere?'

194

He seemed to realise what he'd done wrong and groaned. 'Sorry. Look, I'll have a shower and we'll discuss it in the bar. I've got to meet … well, my family … They'll be wondering where I am.'

Her heart sank. She'd forgotten about them, about the confrontation to come. Her head ducked down and she checked she hadn't left anything behind, then unblocked and unlocked the door. 'How did you know this room was empty?'

'I could see it was dark from the pitch, though it's often unused.'

The corridor was empty apart from a cleaner hoovering at the far end. 'I'll see you later,' she threw over her shoulder.

'One moment.' He caught her wrist, cupped her cheek, and smooched her deeply. 'OK?'

She half-smiled back.

There were a few smirks when she appeared in the heaving bar after popping to the ladies to check she was presentable. 'Had a good chat?' asked Kara.

Sophie felt like she'd spent half the day blushing. 'Well …'

Kara noticed her swollen lips. 'I'm guessing not. Where on earth did he take you … and take you?' she whispered.

Sophie glanced around to check no one was close enough to overhear. 'An unoccupied hospitality box.'

The dark beauty chuckled. 'The one at the end on the top level? I've been there. Do you need any cream for the carpet burns?'

Sophie wiggled, the tender skin was hardly noticeable amongst the pleasurable soreness she felt elsewhere. 'He did most of the work.'

'Good boy.' Kara's cheerfulness dimmed slightly. 'Just to let you know, Marcus' family are here. They have a hospitality room near the far end of the bar, with their cronies.'

'Oh.' Sophie took a cautious glance towards the area Kara had indicated.

'Don't worry, if you decide to approach them, we're here to back you up.'

'Thanks for the support.' Sophie felt surprisingly undaunted. 'I think I'll be fine, though.' After the initial concern, she didn't feel like running away – she felt calm and composed.

It wasn't long until Marcus appeared, his hair hastily dried. He gave her a kiss on her cheek and whispered in her ear, 'Thank you. Sorry we didn't manage that chat.'

He smelled as good clean as he did freshly sweaty. 'It's OK, here probably isn't the best place or time. How is the knee?'

'Hardly twinging, it'll be fine for training on Monday. Are you OK for a drink?'

Sophie held up a full glass of wine, courtesy of Todd. 'I'm fine, thanks.'

'Good. Umm, I have to find my family now, they're in one of the boxes down here. Come over when you can.' He laid a gentle kiss on her lips, and disappeared.

'Marcus gone already?' Kara was drinking the same wine. She was more sober than usual, not having had to gulp the wine down as she watched her man being smashed into the ground.

Sophie had decided to pace herself slowly too, not knowing what to expect. 'He's finding his family. I don't think we're going to manage a chat today.'

A short while later, Todd wandered over. 'We'll be off in about an hour, will you be OK with that?'

'Yes, thanks. I'll just say goodbye to people.'

She meandered through the still-busy bar looking for Marcus, saying hellos and goodbyes to some of his friends she recognised from the *braai* and elsewhere. Some of the other hospitality rooms were discharging their inebriated occupants, so she stood out of the way to let them pass. Finally, she came to the room Kara had pointed out, which was also emptying. However, the door shut without any of the Coetzees exiting.

She waited for a few minutes before softly knocking. No answer. She pushed the door open.

The entire Coetzee clan stared over at her.

Sophie girded her loins. After the welcome embrace of Marcus' friends, it felt like an ice-cold wave had washed over her. She gave a careful nod at his family. 'Sorry to disturb you. Marcus, I'm leaving soon.'

Bridget was the first to break the silence. 'Hi Sophie, we're glad to see you're OK. I wish you'd stayed around to sort out our misunderstanding.'

Time to stand up for herself. She straightened her shoulders. 'I didn't exactly feel welcome.'

'The least you could have done was let us know you were leaving,' snapped Maureen. 'Marcus was very worried about you, you put him through a lot of stress.'

So, nothing had changed there then, despite what Marcus had said about her feeling sorry and embarrassed. She looked to the man in question.

Marcus shrugged embarrassedly. 'When I couldn't find you, I called the UK – Sarah and … er, your parents.'

Sophie sighed in exasperation. 'Didn't you learn that wasn't a good idea last time?'

'I thought I'd caught them on a bad day.' He shrugged again. 'But they were no different, couldn't give a damn. What …' His voice trailed off.

'What? What were you about to ask me?'

'What happened –'

Maureen interrupted, 'What did you do for them to virtually disown you?'

Sophie couldn't believe what she was hearing. 'What did *I* do? How can you automatically blame *me*? I existed, is that enough for you?'

'I didn't mean –'

'Well, what did you mean?' Sophie's voice had risen in fury. 'Listen to me, I'm arguing with you and I *hate arguments*. My parents argued all the time, and they didn't give a damn if I was there or not. They would make up, then five minutes later they would be yelling again. It was their way of showing they loved each other, but they never loved me, I was just in the way. When they weren't screaming at each other, they were screaming at me. I was brought up being told I wasn't wanted, that I was a nuisance. I used to hide away in my room. Did I deserve that?'

Maureen looked somewhat abashed.

'The only time I was wanted was when I stayed with my aunt.' Her voice broke. 'Until Sarah and Clare came along, she was the only one who had ever hugged me and supported me. She was the only real mother I've ever had. I was hoping that I would get on with my future mother-in-law. Then I met you.'

Maureen opened her mouth to speak, 'I'm sor –'

'Don't even dare to say it! I can't forgive you yet, if ever. I can't even understand you. How could you treat a stranger like you treated me? You had never even exchanged a word before you saw fit to judge.'

'Sophie,' interjected Marcus, 'it's my fault.'

'No, it's not all your fault.' Sophie shook her head in vehement disagreement. 'You acted wrongly by resorting to a lie, but your family should have had faith in your decisions. You're a grown man.'

'We didn't mean any harm!' It was Bridget this time.

'You asked me not to hurt your brother, yet you didn't give a damn about hurting me! She spoke to me like I was dirt and you and your father let her! She treated my belongings worse, throwing them into a bin bag. How do you think *that* felt?'

198

Marcus' gasp and the frown he threw at his mother meant that particular titbit was news to him.

'Oh, they didn't tell you *everything* then? I had to wash my clothes before I could even wear them. They were trying to get rid of me and they succeeded. I bet they tried to persuade you to let me go, that it was my fault or that I had been rude? Even the lie that I had been fucking Klaus?'

Another direct hit.

'I've learnt I have friends, I don't need any of you and life's too short to go where you're not wanted.' She glared at the four of them. 'I am so bloody relieved that I was never actually married to Marcus, that I saw what you were really like – shallow and judgmental. Now, I'm off to join my real friends, those who were there for me and never judged me. Have a nice life.'

'Sophie?' pleaded Marcus.

'Marcus.' She gently cupped his chin. 'You need to tell your family to stay the hell out of your love life, and to treat other people with respect. No woman is going to want a man who can't protect her from his own family.' She tiptoed and brushed a light kiss to his lips.

His arms went to catch her, but she refused to be pulled closer despite the comforting familiarity of his touch, laying a hand across his heart and meeting his confused and hurt eyes.

'You have a father who doesn't exactly stand up for himself, that doesn't mean you have to follow in his footsteps. You're a good man, you're a great friend, you're an excellent rugby player, and a superb lover. You're not far off perfect.' *And I love you.* 'You just need to have the confidence in yourself to realise all these things.' *I can't do it for you, no matter how much I love you.*

Before his anguished eyes made her break, she turned and stepped away, holding back tears.

Bare yards away were Klaus, Kara, Todd, and Marcus'

rugby friends.

'You heard?'

'We didn't want to leave you on your own. Well done,' congratulated Todd softly.

Piet nodded in agreement. 'You said what we've been dying to say for years.'

'I want to clap my hands in glee, but it would be really twinky and I'm more of a bear,' added Gert.

Jan nudged him playfully. 'I thought I was the bear?'

'We can both be musclebears, if we want. Or otters. But we'll need to stop trimming our body hair.'

'*Ek sê*!'

'*Ja*, that's what I thought.'

'You two!' scolded Kara. 'Let us deal with one emotional upheaval at a time.'

'It's OK, I'm ready to go now.' Sophie gave a nod to Todd. 'The Coetzees need to sort themselves out, and someone needs to be here for Marcus. You are all his friends foremost.' She gazed at Klaus, and an age of understanding passed between them.

Klaus nodded, lifted a hand, and gently squeezed her shoulder, 'I'll look after him.'

'Good.' She smiled brightly as he turned to join his friend, before she was hugged by the others. She followed Todd out, taking one last glance at Marcus before she left.

He stood tall, over his sister and mother, and he finally looked like the man she knew he could be, the man she'd seen earlier on the rugby pitch. Klaus said something to him, he looked up, and saw Sophie leaving. He mimed "I'll phone you," to her and she nodded. That was enough for now.

Chapter Fourteen

'I've said I'm really proud of you, haven't I?' Todd was driving the minibus full of tired kids back to the ranch.

Sophie was enjoying the dimming landscape from the passenger seat. 'I'm really proud of myself too, for once.'

'You were calm, cool, and rational, with just enough emotion. Magnificent.'

'I didn't want to run away, I said what I needed.' She rubbed her chest. She missed Marcus so much. Whenever she saw him, she just wanted to throw herself into his arms. 'I just hope I haven't hurt him.'

'It needed saying. I'm no psychologist, but he should've stood up to them way before now. Resorting to subterfuge wasn't the answer, just a symptom.'

'It seems so stupid now, we were never going to get away with it.'

'You looked like a couple though, at that second game. At the first, you were too awkward.'

'We hadn't – oops!' She glanced back to check the children were out for the count, and whispered, 'We didn't sleep together until after the first game.'

'That explains it.' They were quiet for several minutes. 'So, do you think he'll be in contact?'

'He mimed he'd call me as we left. I don't know how soon that'll be.'

'You only have a few days before you were planning to depart.'

'Yeah, I haven't made any firm plans yet though. I don't know where we'll go from here.'

Her phone rang early the next day, just as she was helping Mosa with laying out materials for that morning's class. Marcus had texted her to apologise again for his family's behaviour, and said he would call.

However, the name displayed wasn't the one she was expecting. 'Good morning, dear Klaus,' she answered with a smile.

'*Bokkie*-Soph, how are you today? Still feeling like conquering the world?'

She snorted, and wandered outside amongst the vines while they caught up. The early morning was tranquil, the sun rising over the rows of growing plants. Beautiful.

Eventually, she asked the pregnant question. 'How's Marcus?'

'I've never seen him like that. He gave his family a bollocking for how they treated you, told them he was disgusted with them. I don't blame him – Maureen was out of order with her outrageous behaviour. And the other two just let her dictate.'

'They took their lead from her. We did behave wrongly at the beginning.'

'As you said yesterday, he would never have done that if he hadn't felt pressurised in the first place. He's at our place in Cape Town for a few days while he calms down.'

'Urgh, they'll hate me even more for this. They've hardly seen him while he's been here as it is.'

'Soph, his parents chose to go away on holiday to Ireland when they knew he was returning to South Africa, and their behaviour is also their responsibility.'

She sighed. 'I know that, I'm not blaming myself. But will they?'

Klaus grunted. 'Good point. Maureen can be rather *bladdy* minded. It'll take a while for her to come around.'

'It doesn't actually matter that she can't stand me, does it?' Sophie's voice was hollow. 'Even if he returns to the UK, he won't be coming back to Harford. As soon as I leave, it's over between us. If it isn't already.'

'Is that what you want?'

She didn't answer, but her chest hurt.

Klaus cleared his throat. 'Listen, you said you hadn't any plans – there's a trip up north that needs a couple of guides, you fancy giving me a hand for a few weeks?'

'Me? Why me?'

'You're great company, you never moan, and you help me sleep better.'

'I can sleep with you again, but I don't know anything about guiding.'

'You'll pick it up. I'll forward the trip info when I have more details. You know the basics of overland camping, you were super-fast by the end of last week, plus your wide-eyed enjoyment is infectious. The guests will love you. And you'll get to see more of Africa.'

'How could I refuse such a tempting offer?'

'Plus, I'll arrange a couple of mountain bikes to be on the truck, so we'll do some exploring on two wheels.

'You're always great for a ride, honey.'

He chuckled at her innuendo. 'Brilliant. Love you, Soph. Look after yourself.'

'Love you too, Klaus.' Sophie smiled as she hung up, feeling much better.

'Sophie.'

She whipped around to see Marcus standing behind her.

'Is it over then? Between us?' He watched her searchingly, his hands restless until he tucked them into his jeans pockets.

'What?'

'You said when you leave, it's over.' His shoulders shrugged defensively.

How much had he overheard? 'I don't really know where we go from here.' All she wanted was to be enfolded in his arms. She folded her own arms across her chest to keep from reaching out to him. 'It was only supposed to be a temporary thing, wasn't it, while I'm here?'

'You're still here, I thought …' He shrugged. 'Have you fallen in love with Klaus?'

'What? No. No, Klaus is like the brother I never had. I love him as a brother.'

'You've been sleeping with him though?' He gulped, looking sick.

'No!' Sophie ran her fingers through her short hair in frustration. 'It's not like that. He suffers from nightmares, like you. We fell asleep under the stars one night and he sleeps better with company. He goes days without doing more than napping when he's travelling, it stopped him being totally exhausted.'

Marcus recovered some of his colour, his stance straightening. 'I never realised, though he's always exhausted and sleeps like the dead whenever he returns. And the riding?'

'Bikes. We did some mountain bike riding in Namibia. Just before we watched you play that game, in fact.'

'Oh. That makes sense.' The gorgeous blond man, the holder of her heart, sighed.

They really did need to have that chat. 'Look, Marcus, there seem to be so many misunderstandings, we really do need to sit down and talk about everything.'

'OK. How do we do that? Would you … would you come back to stay with me at the flat? Klaus will be there, and it's a bit poky, not as nice as the house in the vineyards.'

Sophie harrumphed. 'I'm certainly not going to be welcome at your homestead for some time.'

'I'm so sorry about my mother, about all my family. I told them I didn't want to see them for a while. I can't forgive them for doing that to you.' He shrugged with a combination of anger and resignation. 'I picked up my stuff from the house first thing this morning, decided to come here on my way back to the city. On the off-chance that you'd see me.'

'Why wouldn't I see you?'

'I thought you'd be angrier about how they treated you.'

'I'm not angry now, there's no point in being angry. Just frustrated for you. And,' she threw her hands up, 'I don't know how I feel. I'm confused.'

'Oh.' He spent a few minutes in deep thought, contemplating the ground. 'What are your plans for today?'

'Today? Helping Mosa with the kids.

'On a Sunday morning?'

'Yep, before they head off to church, like a rugby-themed Sunday school. I promised I'd go through the match with them again.'

'Would you mind if I watched?'

Sophie laughed dryly. 'You'll be taking part! The kids will go wild for you – you're one of their heroes.'

Marcus *had* changed. Despite his earlier indecision, the self-assuredness she'd spotted on the pitch yesterday returned when he talked about playing. He was more comfortable in his skin than she'd ever seen him before. That confidence she'd first observed when he had driven her home, the commanding air when he'd coached the women, and which she had seen when he'd flown the plane, had flourished into life elsewhere.

He was great with the children, demonstrating some skills and even helping out with drills before they played a hectic match of touch rugby which left them sprawled and panting on the wiry grass after the energetic kids were called in for a scrubbing.

Marcus chuckled. 'You *have* improved – you're not the klutz you once were.'

'Really?' Sophie thought back, it was true she hadn't

felt as ungainly as normal.

'Yeah, you look more comfortable in your body.'

Sophie lifted her head up and stared at Marcus. 'You know, I was just thinking the same about you.'

'Really?'

Before either could elucidate, Sophie's name was called and she rolled to her feet to see what Todd needed.

The American exile looked satisfied with himself as he pulled his tie straight. 'I take it you'll be heading off today?' He nodded at Marcus, who had gone to pick up the equipment.

'This afternoon, probably. Do you mind?'

'Not at all, go be with your fella. There's always a place for you here if you need it.'

Sophie smiled, stood on tiptoes, and planted a kiss on his cheek. 'You're an angel. I didn't think you were much of a churchgoer though?'

Todd pulled at his tie again. 'Well, I've gotta help Mosa ...'

Sophie thought she detected a faint blush. 'Thanks for everything.'

'It sure was a pleasure.'

'We need to start talking. Properly.'

Marcus hummed in agreement. 'OK. When do we start?'

'How about now? Can I ask you something a bit personal please?'

They lay together, limbs intertwined and relaxed in the bed in Marcus' flat. After his warnings, Sophie had been prepared for a poky bachelor pad, but it was surprisingly light, clean, and welcoming, in a nice-looking apartment complex not far from the rugby ground.

As soon as a brief tour was completed, he'd picked her up, deposited her on the sheets, and stripped his clothes off. She had followed with his willing help. They had both sighed in bliss once they were skin to skin, and Marcus was pushing inside her. As they caught their breath afterwards, they agreed it was better in bed. They had fallen into a comfortable silence until Sophie initiated conversation.

'Personal? What do you want to know?' He sounded slightly wary.

She turned to face him fully and placed a hand on his face. 'I want you to be honest. Will you promise me that?'

He cupped her hand. 'I'll do my best.'

'Clare Prince.' She felt him stiffen and his hand dropped away from hers. 'What happened between you, and how do you feel about her now?'

He tried to escape her hand, but she kept a firm but gentle pressure on his cheek. He looked away, focusing his gaze over her shoulder. 'I don't want to talk about it.'

'I think you need to. I see how you react whenever her name is mentioned. I know something happened between you.'

He laughed harshly. 'Nothing happened between us, it was all me.'

Sophie stayed patiently silent.

Eventually, he exhaled heavily. 'At Tom and Sarah's wedding, I danced with her, and we kissed just before I left. Only a light kiss, but it was good, so sweet and magical.'

She had to ignore the stab of jealousy in her stomach.

'I said I'd call her. I came back here for a couple of months, spent a lot of time thinking about her. When I returned to Harford, she was already married to Alex.'

Sophie winced.

'That night she saw you with Alex and I took you home? I returned to the bar to find her inconsolable. Her pain was so raw.' He took a deep breath. 'I've never seen anyone hurt like that; it was like her heart was bleeding. I could've killed Alex for doing that to her, and I was

207

jealous that he could make her feel so strongly.'

'Jealous?' She was only just realising how much Marcus hid behind his easy-going facade.

'I suppose it was nice to be the knight in shining armour, and a part of me hoped that I could sweep her off her feet, that I would be enough of a man for her to forget him, that I could seduce her instead. That I could make her feel that way about me.'

Sophie felt for him, her hand squeezed his shoulder. 'She likes you, she values you as a friend. I call her an incorrigible romantic, but you can't dictate who to love, it just happens.' *And it's happened to you*, a wicked voice inside of her whispered. Her heart dropped and she almost missed what he next confessed.

Marcus sighed and rolled on to his back, 'That's about right. A part of me didn't want Clare getting back with Alex, I now know that was for the best. What could have been between me and her was sweet and there was an attraction, but you've taught me that attraction, even white hot, isn't what it's all about. There needs to be more than that.'

Ouch.

She didn't want to ask any more. She had been firmly put in her place. It took some effort to clamp down on her feelings, squeeze them into a little box, remember that it was supposed to be a fun, exploratory, light fling. She couldn't reveal that she'd fallen in love with him.

That vague sense of panic she felt for the approaching end of her holiday turned into relief. She needed to get away, sooner rather than later. Try to forget him.

'Do you know what your plans are for the next month or so?'

'The final match next month will be here, in Cape Town. I'll stay for that, then head back to…' Marcus trailed off. 'Actually, I don't know where I'll be going yet. My agent has had several offers, some Prem clubs in

England, a few from France. And ...'

'And?'

'Here. They want me here.'

Just as she had feared. She didn't respond for a few seconds, tamping down her feelings. 'Do you want to stay?'

'I don't know. When it's the two of us, travelling together, going to all the games, that's the most I've enjoyed playing rugby and living here for years.'

She let out a choked laugh. 'You'll enjoy going out with your boys without having me to worry about.'

He groaned. 'That's where you're wrong. I'm dreading it.'

'Why so bad?'

He didn't answer.

'C'mon, it can't be that bad, getting legless and pulling gorgeous women.'

'I don't want to lose control ... or forget.'

He didn't seem drunk ... He was ... malleable ... the next day he didn't remember a thing. Piet's words echoed in her head. 'It was only one time, wasn't it?' He didn't answer, and she felt her heart sink. *Oh hell, no.* She placed a soothing hand on his arm.

He grasped the hand, measured her fingers against his, folded them together. 'I've never said this before, but ... I'm not sure if it was the first time. We were drinking heavily most weekends. There were a couple of times that I woke up and couldn't remember what had happened the previous night. I just assumed drink was to blame, and it probably was. But ...'

'It made you doubt yourself.'

'Yeah. I didn't want to wake up with an unfamiliar woman and not remember how I got there. Never mind the risk of forgetting to use protection. I only drink around friends that I trust now, if at all. Even in Harford, I don't drink that much. And I haven't been to the bars around

209

here for ages, not since I've been back.'

Hence his low tolerance for alcohol. 'We should go out, visit your old haunts while I'm still here.' Now she had come to think about it, they hadn't done any bar-hopping at all.

'Ummm. OK.'

'Tomorrow night? Klaus too.'

'Hang on, while you're still here? I'd hoped you would stay a bit longer, there's only a few matches left.'

This was a conversation they needed to have while dressed. 'I haven't decided for definite. We can talk about this tomorrow.' Her hand slid under the sheets and down his chest, to gauge his interest. Which was substantial. And increasing.

Surfacing from a deep sleep, Sophie didn't know what had woken her up. Then she saw a shadow by the door.

'Marcus!' came the soundless whisper. 'We have trouble.'

In seconds, Marcus was out of the bed, joining Klaus by the door and speaking in hushed tones.

'What's happening?' croaked Sophie.

'Shush. Stay there, please. Don't turn a light on. We'll be back.' A rustle as he pulled on some trousers.

Some metallic clicks, and the two of them ghosted out of the room. Sophie was wide awake, and wondering where the hell the two of them were going.

It was silent for a while, and Sophie stayed in the bed as ordered. Then she heard shouts and a couple of popping noises from outside. An approaching siren.

She moved out of the bed and over to the window, stepping to one side and cautiously peering through a gap in the curtains. There was a group of people outside, some flashes, and chatter. A vehicle with blue flashing lights drew up.

She pulled her pyjamas on just in time for the door of

the flat to open.

'Sophie? You OK?' It was Klaus. He turned some lights on as she hurried out of the bedroom. He was dressed only in pyjama bottoms, and he was pale, except for the blood on his arms and face.

'What's happened?' she gasped. 'Are you OK?' She looked closer, it didn't appear to be much of his blood. 'Is Marcus OK?'

Klaus nodded. 'Just some grazes and cuts. We had to scale a fence.'

'What the hell happened?'

'I was on the balcony, couldn't sleep. I spotted some burglars trying to get into the house next door.'

'So you decided you'd be the hero and take Marcus along too?' She whacked him across the head. 'What the hell were you thinking?' she yelled. 'Were you trying to kill yourself again? You stupid bastard!'

Klaus' face crumpled. 'Oh.'

She hugged him as his legs gave way. His skin was icy cold. Then she recognised the arms of a bare-chested Marcus coming around the both of them, guiding them to the sofa.

'We were sensible. Honest,' Marcus saw fit to add. 'We stayed protected the whole time, until security arrived.'

'I'm sorry for overreacting.' She lifted her head and saw blood oozing sullenly out of cut on his forearm. 'I reserve the right to call you stupid idiots though.'

'Noted.'

'You two stay there. Where's your first aid box?'

'Under the sink in the kitchen.' Marcus stayed on the sofa with his shaken friend.

Sophie pulled out the massive box from under the sink and took it into the living area. Under Marcus' direction, she rummaged for saline wash, plasters, and bandages and left them cleaning up while she made some hot drinks.

Fortunately, it appeared none of the cuts or grazes was particularly deep.

A knock came on the half-open door just as Sophie was handing over the mugs. The police officer took in the skimpily clad Sophie and her two half-dressed companions, and his eyebrows raised. 'Mr Coetzee and Mr Kotze? The captain has arrived.'

Marcus stood and placed himself between the officer and Sophie. 'We'll be down in a couple of minutes, once we've dressed.'

The officer nodded, and backed out.

'Coetzee and Kotze?' asked Sophie bemusedly.

Klaus nodded. 'That's how we were paired together in the Army, along with our physical resemblance.' He had recovered a normal colour. 'Thanks for the hot chocolate. We'd better get dressed and down there.'

Minutes later, she was heading to bed while they reported back downstairs. She didn't sleep though, tossing and turning until the room began to lighten and she heard the flat door open and the shower run.

She opened her eyes when she felt someone in the room. Marcus was naked and rummaging in his wardrobe. She watched him pull fresh clothes on. 'You're not coming back to bed?'

'Can't, I have training. I'll be back mid-afternoon. Klaus is having a nap, then he said he'd take you somewhere, for lunch, shopping, anything. You have a fan.'

She yawned. 'He's like the brother I never had.'

'Little brother or big brother?'

'A combination,' she muttered sleepily.

After Marcus had left, she could still hear noises in the flat. Drowsily rubbing her eyes, she wandered out of the bedroom to find Klaus sitting out on the balcony, gazing at the winter-sun-drenched Table Mountain.

'I thought you were having a nap.' He turned towards

her and she swallowed a gasp at how haggard he looked.

'Sorry. I didn't want to sleep. Where do you want to go? If you're not sleeping either, we could go for a walk along the beach?'

'The beach at Simon's Town?' She grinned as he nodded back. The penguins and seals were so cute, they would cheer up anyone, and the fresh air may help him sleep. 'OK, gimme ten minutes to get dressed.'

It was a relatively still day, akin to a mild British summer. They took jackets, expecting the coastline to be more exposed, but were delightfully surprised when it appeared unseasonably warm. Sophie laughed and oohed and aahed at the little creatures waddling around them, and Klaus even cracked a few smiles. The crisp sea air also triggered some stifled yawning.

After a couple of hours wandering around, she noted Klaus' eyelids were drooping with fatigue and manufactured more of her own yawns. 'Wanna pop back? I think I need a nap.'

If she was expecting an argument, she didn't get one. They returned to his car and she chattered all the way back, forcing him into conversation. On entering the flat, she was surprised to see him head to the kitchen and pull a jar out of the cupboard.

'Coffee? Won't that keep you up?'

He didn't look at her. 'I'm not going to sleep.'

She strode up to the kettle, slapped it off, took the jar out of his hand, and pulled him towards his bedroom. 'You look like death, you haven't slept all night, and you won't be fit to come out with us tonight if you don't get some sleep.' She drew the curtains closed.

'Tonight?' His legs gave way and he sat on the bed.

'We're going bar hopping. You need some sleep so you don't look like death warmed up for the ladies. I'll give you five minutes to put something comfortable on, then we're going to sleep.'

What little had been holding him together seemed to dissolve and he hunched further. 'But … Soph, I'm … I'm scared. The nightmares. Last night brought back so many memories, it triggered the flashbacks.'

'Shhh. I'll stay with you.'

'But Marcus?'

'He knows, it's fine.' She resolved to text him as she changed into comfy clothes. 'Now, five minutes.'

When she returned to his room, Klaus was huddled under the sheets, fighting sleep like a child determined to stay up, his eyes red-rimmed. She lay next to him, pulled a light blanket over herself, and placed a comforting hand on his shoulder.

'Soph?'

'Yes, sweetie?'

'You've really changed. You're much more confident now compared to when I first met you. Every day you seem to get stronger and stronger.'

Was she that much different from the woman who'd run from the vineyard in tears barely a week ago? 'Not this time last week.'

'That was a relapse,' he yawned, 'a temporary blip. On the whole, you're so much more assertive. It's strange, 'cos so is Marcus.'

With that, he mumbled to himself, his body relaxed, and his breathing deepened. Sophie let the encroaching sleep take her too.

A short time later, she felt the bed dip, and another body join them on her other side, placing an arm around her waist.

Chapter Fifteen

A flash of setting sun through a crack in the curtains woke her. Sophie glanced at her watch. Despite his fears, Klaus had slept well for several hours. So had Marcus. However, she had had enough, and nature was calling. Slowly, carefully, she wriggled out from between them and stood, looking down at her blond-haired lover and her almost-brother. She really was going to miss them. Sophie bit her lip to stop her eyes tearing up.

Once her loo visit was complete, she rummaged in the fridge and put together a massive pot of chilli. As it cooked, she sat on the sofa and caught up on her emails. Sarah had messaged saying she had some exciting news for when she returned. Sophie quirked a brow and grinned.

'What's so amusing?' Marcus carefully shut the door to Klaus' room and wandered towards her.

She took a moment to appreciate his naked torso and thin cotton bottoms, which didn't disguise a hefty bulge. 'Sarah has news she won't tell me yet. I bet she's pregnant.' She kept her voice low.

'Really? Brilliant, I was expecting that. Tom will be delighted. And very amusing to watch – he's protective enough of her as it is.'

Would Marcus be there to see it? The tears threatened again, so she looked down at her tablet while he went to the kitchen.

'*Kiff*, chilli. Have I told you how much I love you? I'm starving.'

What? Sophie's head shot up, but Marcus was busying

himself by pulling plates out. She dismissed his affectation as hyperbole. 'It won't be ready for another half an hour or so. Is Klaus awake?'

'Not yet.'

'Do you want to tell me about last night? He was rather shaken up and I didn't want to pry for details.'

'Come.' Marcus led her out to the balcony. 'You see that house there, with the pool? Klaus saw some figures climbing over the external wall. We went down, scaled the wall, and set up there,' he pointed to a couple of ornamental sections of wall by the pool, 'and there, just as they were breaking in. One of us covering each intruder. We shouted a warning, let off a couple of warning shots, and they surrendered. The police arrived and took them away.'

'Warning shots?'

'Many households here have guns. I'm not a fan, but Klaus and I are both highly trained from our army days.'

'Why didn't you put more clothes on?'

'Partly not having time, partly to distinguish us from the bad guys for when the police arrived. They were only young, armed just with knives. Desperate.'

'Young ... of course, they reminded him of ...'

'*Ja*. He was fine at the time, it was only when he got back here that it hit.'

'Oh hell. He wasn't sleeping terribly well before. He needs counselling – this may only make his PTSD worse.'

'We both had some counselling after we left the Army, but that was a while ago.'

She went back inside, grabbed her tablet. 'He'll come with me to see Mosa tomorrow. I'd like you to see someone too, he's not the only one who has trouble sleeping.'

'Sleeping?' Klaus stood in the doorway of his room, looking rumpled but much better. 'I think I've done enough sleeping for today.' He sniffed. 'Do I smell

216

something cooking? I'm *bladdy* starving.'

'Chilli. Sophie made it while we were both in the land of nod. Ready in thirty.'

'*Lekker*. Just enough time for a quick workout first. Big ups to you. If Marcus doesn't marry you for real, I will.'

Silence.

Sophie busied herself with finishing the email she was sending Todd regarding Klaus, while Marcus made himself a protein shake.

He took a gulp. 'Hey, Soph, do you want a shower before dinner? I'll take care of the rice and stuff.'

She hummed in agreement, and escaped from the room.

'What do you want to drink?' yelled Marcus. The sports bar was playing deafening music and crowded for a weekday night. It was the third they had visited. The first two had been much quieter.

'A beer is fine,' she called back.

Klaus echoed the same as he looked around at the occupants. Sophie was bemused by the amount of interested stares the two men were getting from an intimidating number of absolutely stunning women. It had been the same in the previous venues.

Marcus and Klaus were worth staring at: their height, the collared shirts they wore clinging lovingly to their torsos, jeans cupping where they should and hugging their thighs. Absolute knockouts. When Marcus had walked out of the bedroom, she had wanted to pull him back inside, to run her hands all over him. If it had been the two of them, they wouldn't have left the flat. Fortunately, Klaus had joined them, so all she could do was wolf whistle.

In comparison, she felt rather underdressed, despite wearing a small top, skirt, heels, and make-up. And short, she felt very short. It was even worse than at the stadium, as many of the women were so leggy *and* wearing skyscraper heels.

She was the shortest in the place.

She didn't care.

'Beer.'

A cold bottle was pressed into her hand and she took a grateful gulp.

'Slow down. Tequila first.'

Salt. Shot. Lemon. Beer. 'Whew,' she giggled, 'here's to being short!'

'What?'

'Dance?

'Why not?'

There was a small dance floor which was thankfully quieter than the rest of the bar. She was spun between the two of them until the beers made themselves known to her bladder. 'Loo!' she yelled and wobbled off, somehow skirting around the mass of bodies, with others parting for her.

Luckily there was no queue, for the cubicles or the sinks. Sophie took a moment to look in the mirror as she washed her hands. She was hit by a strange sense, not of déjà vu, but of progress. By the time she returned to the UK, it would be almost a year since that fateful night in Jester's when Marcus had handed her a shot.

She was in the loo by herself again, but she felt good and looked good and, outside, real friends were waiting for her. She wouldn't let anyone intimidate her. She was short and slight but she was a good person, a worthy person. She beamed at the mirror. It was time to celebrate!

She made her way back to the main room with confidence to find in the time she had spent away from them, Marcus and Klaus had been surrounded by women. She bit back a slash of jealousy as one stunner placed a hand on Marcus' arm, and was gratified to see him subtly shrug the contact off.

Klaus had his own admirers and was looking more cheerful. A few yards away, she changed course – if she

218

did interrupt, she may possibly scare away the crowd around Klaus. Sophie determined to hit the bar instead for more beers, so headed for a slightly quieter area.

'You're a cute little one, aren't you?' The comment came from a young, British-sounding guy with dark hair queuing next to her. She glanced over as he apologised. 'Oh, sorry. You must have heard that so many times. Well, not so many times, you're not that short. But you're cute. Oh, why don't I just shoot myself now?'

She laughed. 'Little is fine, it's a fact. Cute, I'm not sure about.'

'Oh, you're British also. What a relief. I'm Jeremy. Are you as intimidated as I am?'

'Intimidated?'

'By all this gorgeousness. Not that you aren't ...' He groaned. 'Seriously, shoot me now.'

Her order of beers arrived, but she asked for an extra and handed one over to Jeremy. 'Here, sounds like you need it more than me. I'm Sophie.'

'Thank you so much, Sophie. I'm so clueless, I didn't even know what to order. I thought I'd ordered beer my first round, but it turned out to be cider.'

'Here by yourself?'

'Meeting someone from work, but they've texted to say they're going to be late. I only arrived this week, I'm on a temporary secondment.' Something in his hand flashed and he looked down. 'Oh, shit, they're not coming at all. I am totally by myself now. That sounds like a line, doesn't it?' He showed her his phone and she saw a succession of recent messages. 'See, it's true.'

'Don't worry so much, I'm sure you'll be fine. Everyone's really friendly.'

'These Cape women? They're stunning. I'm scared to approach any of them. And the fellas are mostly muscle, like that hunk approaching us.'

Sophie looked around to see Marcus scything through

the crowd towards them. It was strange, she'd forgotten how big he was, and hadn't even realised how tall he was, as many of his friends were taller. Compared to others in the bar, he dominated. 'Hello, hunk,' she purred. 'Meet Jeremy, he's new in town. Jeremy, this is Marcus, my lo … friend.'

Marcus folded her protectively into his side. 'Hey, Jeremy, what's up?'

Jeremy visibly blanched. 'Nice to meet you.'

'I got the beers in,' added Sophie to break the awkward moment, and took several gulps of her own. Had she really been about to call Marcus her lover in front of a complete stranger?

'Good girl. This is my last one though, I've got training tomorrow.'

'Oh, you're Marcus Coetzee! I saw you play last week. No wonder you're built like a brick sh –'Jeremy cut himself off.

Sophie giggled as Klaus joined them, grabbing the remaining bottle. She ended up perched on a bar stool with Marcus' strong arm wrapped around her waist while the three men chatted. She was happy enough to watch as Jeremy relaxed and more women drifted over to chat with him and Klaus. The way Marcus was holding her deterred any from being too forward with him.

In a short time, she realised she was getting distracted. His arm felt so good, so solid around her. Her free hand covered it, stroked it. His fingers somehow buried between her top and skirt and began caressing her bare skin. She bit her lip to restrain a gasp.

'Sophie,' he spoke in her ear, 'are you turned on?'

She squeaked as his voice rumbled through her, increasing the arousal.

'I can always tell. Your lovely eyes grow bigger and lose focus, and you begin chewing your lips. Biting and licking. Your chest heaves, I sometimes see the outline of your nipples through your clothes. Your hands flutter, you want to pinch and caress yourself.'

She gulped, turning herself towards him. He pressed his hips into her thigh, she could feel he was becoming aroused too.

He continued murmuring in her ear. 'It's like you really can't restrain yourself, your need for sex takes over. Nothing matters except getting a hard cock in you. That sharp, analytical brain is overpowered by your hungry body.'

She grabbed his collar, pulling him towards her so she could hiss in his ear. 'Stop talking and get us out of here, so we can start fucking.'

'I thought you wanted us to be out bar hopping for longer?' He laughed at Sophie's petulant scowl. 'Well as Klaus is getting on well with Jeremy, I'll make our excuses.'

That he did, citing training the next day. She had the feeling no one was fooled by that, but she didn't give a damn.

As she was switching the kettle on the next morning and stretching out a few pleasantly sore muscles, the flat door quietly opened. Klaus entered, and began tiptoeing to his room.

'Dirty stop-out!'

He jumped. '*Jislaaik!* Shush, my head hurts.'

'Your hair looks like you've been dragged through a hedge backwards. Have a good night?' She smirked.

He groaned and sank down on the sofa. 'Great night. That Jeremy is a decent guy, the women loved his shyness, and we ended up at a house party. Marcus at training?'

'Yep, you just missed him. Coffee? Bacon sandwich?'

'Please. Have I mentioned how much I love you, *bokkie*-Sophie?'

Klaus related some of the events from the previous

night as he rested on the sofa and Sophie busied herself in the kitchen. He declared his love for her again when she presented the hangover relievers to him, and fell silent as he cleared the plate in minutes.

He watched her as she consumed hers at a more moderate pace. 'You know, Marcus really likes you. I've never seen him with anyone like he is with you.'

Sophie laughed dryly. 'That may be the case. We're attracted to each other, no doubt.'

'He was over like a shot when he saw you talking to Jeremy. He's possessive of you. I really do think he loves you. He didn't look at any other women last night, despite them throwing themselves at him.'

'He …' She didn't know what to say to that.

'I love you too. Not like I think Marcus does, I don't fancy you. Well, I did, but you were first like a little sister, then big. I've never had a sister before.'

'I've never had a brother or a sister. I'm an only child. I like having a sibling, little or big.' Sophie could feel her eyes getting teary.

'Me too.' Klaus noticed her lower lip wobbling, and changed the subject. 'So, what are the plans for today?'

'I've been meaning to speak to you about that. In my official Big Sister capacity, there's someone I want you to see.'

She explained who Mosa was, what she did, and how she could help. Todd had warned her that she may encounter some reluctance, but Klaus was remarkably acquiescent. She knew how weary he was of the insomnia, the flashbacks, and nightmares when he did sleep, and of not dealing well with stressful situations.

'What about Marcus? He's a bit different to me, you think he's fine, then his self-confidence goes AWOL and he gets paralysed with indecision, starts pulling in on himself. He needs to see someone again too.'

'Again?'

'Has no one …' Klaus trailed off, looking guilty.

'No one, what?'

He visibly thought as he drank his coffee. 'Have you ever googled Marcus?'

'Why should I have done that?'

Klaus muttered something in Afrikaans and brought his tablet out. He typed in a few words, and handed it over. 'These first.'

A succession of headlines. *Coetzee shines again. Is he the best talent South Africa has ever seen? Coetzee continues to impress. U18 star Coetzee called up by Boks.*

'There's clips of him when he was younger, of him playing age-grade rugby, and he's so *bladdy* good. World class at eighteen.'

'What happened?' Sophie had the feeling it wouldn't be good.

Klaus typed again. This time, Sophie gasped in horror.

Goosen paralysis fears. Coetzee cleared of foul play in youth match. Former rugby player commits suicide after tackle results in paralysis.

A picture of a much-younger Marcus, head in his hands.

More headlines. *Coetzee quits! Distraught Coetzee loses appetite for rugby.*

'I couldn't believe it when he rocked up next to me that first day of training. The blue-eyed boy, the great hope of South African rugby, chucking it all in to join the Army?'

'It explains so much,' murmured Sophie. 'Marcus blamed himself.'

'*Ja.* It was such an innocuous tackle, just solid. After the autopsy, it emerged that Goosen had been taking a shitload of drugs, which weakened his body. He should not have even been on the pitch. Marcus took it hard. When we left the Army, his family got him some counselling, and he decided to play rugby again.'

'He's so happy on the pitch.'

223

'He is now. His first game back, he was sick the night before, and sick in the morning. I had to drive him to the game as his nerves were so bad. He was shaking, green. As soon as the game started, he was fine. Rusty, but fine. For a while, there were a lot of people interested in him, but he never showed his earlier talent. Until now. Somehow, you've brought it out of him.'

They sat in companionable silence for a while until Klaus yawned. 'I need some sleep before heading out to Todd's place.'

Sophie yawned too. 'That reminds me, Todd said you can stay with them overnight, whenever you want. The ranch is relaxed about that sort of thing. In return, all he asks of is help with the odd few practical jobs in between your trips.'

'Speaking of trips … you know the one I mentioned? I had a text this morning, they need us to fly out this Saturday.'

'That soon?'

'One of the guy's wives is pregnant, she's been having warning contractions.'

'What time on Saturday?'

'The flight's mid-afternoon. We'll be able to catch the first half of the game, if that.'

'Marcus won't be too happy.'

That was an understatement. Marcus wasn't too chuffed at their plans to go somewhere without him. 'I can fly you places on my days off.'

They were having a quiet evening in the flat, a simple pasta meal and glass of wine followed by a film on the sofa. Klaus had gone to see Mosa, leaving Sophie a chance to speak with Marcus. 'I've seen as much of Africa as I can manage from here. I'm going to head north with Klaus.'

'But I only have a few games left, you could wait a

224

week or three for me. I'll sort an itinerary out for you.'

Uh-oh. Sophie had the sinking feeling events were spiralling out of her control.

'Give me a couple of hours and I'll plan it out for you.' He grabbed his tablet and started typing.

But it's my *holiday!* He was so determined, she really didn't want to say anything, but she had to. 'Marcus, it's already arranged.'

He wasn't listening. Selective deafness. Very male but unusual for him. Hmmm.

She laid a hand over the tablet. 'Marcus, stop it. I'm going.'

He looked up at her with panic in his eyes. 'But you won't be able to watch me play and help me know what to do.'

'Marcus, I've been meaning to speak with you about this.' She held his hands. 'You don't need me.'

'But ... the last three years, I've hardly played any rugby, I've been injured all the time. This is the best run of games I've had in my life. And it's all thanks to you. I don't want you to leave. Let's get married for real.'

She had to ignore what he said on the spur of the moment. 'Marcus, you don't need me. Even that first match, you picked your game up and did all the hard work yourself. It was confidence you needed.'

'But –'

'You've become reliant on me, but you shouldn't be. You're good. You're great. You don't need me. That first game, yeah, I told you about that first gap, but the rest was you. You.'

'What ...?' he trailed off, her words obviously hitting a note.

'I need to go strike out by myself, then I need to go home, to the UK. I need to decide whether this, this analysis, is going to be my whole life, or whether there's something else out there for me.'

'But you're brilliant at it!'

Sophie sighed. 'Not really. I've had several flukes, I've spotted things others really should have had they not been distracted. I've had great support from people around me and I've pushed myself to make them happy, to keep them being impressed with me, and it's exhausting. I need to please myself. I need to learn when to draw the line, when to walk away. Starting now. I've helped you all I can, you need to realise your own strengths. You need to realise what you really want to do.'

This time he was paying her attention.

'You have coaches that you need to listen to, people who know one hell of a lot more than me about the technical side of things. Try approaching them.' She could tell it was slowly sinking in, that he was thinking about her words. 'You also need to think about more counselling.'

'More …?'

'Klaus told me about what happened when you were younger. About Goosen and quitting rugby to join the Army.'

He visibly cringed. 'I was hoping no one would mention that.'

'I'm glad he did. You were never going to. You really need to talk about it.'

Bit by bit, as they sat on the sofa, Marcus finally revealed things about his earlier years, about his time in the Army and returning to rugby. 'Klaus says I saved his life, but I owe him mine. He was there for me, in the Army. He held me together, he was always cheerful, and wouldn't let me withdraw. After we left, he cajoled me into playing again, I was ready to run out of there.'

Sophie half-laughed. 'You know, you've done the same thing as me a few times, in escaping or avoiding awkward situations. Like when you went to the UK.'

He thought about that. 'That's true. I've never seen it that way before.'

226

'It also reminds me – you need to make up with your family. What they did was hurtful, to me and to you, but they're your family. They'll be here when I'm not.'

He exhaled heavily. 'I know, once they've had some time to realise their mistakes. Bridget has already contacted me to apologise, profusely, several times. I'll see them next week. After you … you've gone.'

Sophie had to hold back the urge to apologise herself for leaving.

'We don't really have time to organise a leaving party for you, but Piet and Kara are having a *braai* on Thursday night to celebrate their engagement – there should be a chance to raise a glass then.

Piet and Kara's house was comfortably compact, with a garden just big enough for Piet to be able to wield tongs like the master *braaier* he purported to be, and room for their friends as they sat and stood around to chat, eat, and drink.

Not that those who had a game on Saturday were drinking much. There was a tension in the air whenever the daunting match was mentioned, Sophie even thought she caught someone wincing. Those who didn't have a game were more than making up for it. Klaus was topping Sophie's glass up with bubbly whenever she wasn't looking.

Hence, when she stood to go to the loo, she was rather wobbly, and trod on a couple of the men's feet. 'Oops.'

They just laughed at her, as she was so light it was like a butterfly landing on an elephant. She harrumphed, and stomped through the kitchen.

Piet was in there, fussing with a tray of meat. He laughed at her too.

'It's not funny being the smallest person all the time,' she muttered.

He continued to grin, 'You are absolutely bladdered,

dear *bokkie*, you are very funny.'

She grumbled, 'You,' she flayed a hand in his direction, 'are not allowed to call me that. Only Klaus. And Marcus. He calls me lots of lovely names. Which is nice, but he's never told me he loves me. Well, he did the once but that was hyper – hyp … rubbish. Glad you think I'm so amusing. Now, where's your loo?'

Piet, amused, pointed down the hall. Sophie lurched that way. On her return, he was waiting with a large glass of water. 'Here.'

'Thank you.' She had recovered slightly, and sipped. 'Look after him when I'm gone, won't you? Don't let him pull away. He needs his friends, and you're all great. Weird and cocky fuckers sometimes, but great.'

'We'll try.'

'I only found out about Boosen the other day.'

'Boosen? *Ag*, you mean Goosen? That *fokken moegoe*. He was a liar and a coward.'

'You knew him?'

'*Ja*, I was at that game, playing against Marcus. We were losing badly. Goosen was on some shit, looking for a fight. I told the coach to get him off the pitch. Afterwards, I reported him and the coach. I wanted to tell Marcus, but he ran away to the Army.' Piet looked up, and stopped talking.

'What are you two gossiping about?' Marcus entered, carrying some empty bottles.

'I was sobering Sophie up.'

In more ways than one. 'I think I overdid the fizz.' She held up the water glass.

'Glad to see this trip hasn't turned you into an alcoholic.' Marcus held out his hand.

Sophie went into his arms, snuggling up to him. 'You always smell so good, and feel so good,' she mumbled. 'Gonna miss you so much.'

'Gonna miss you too.' She felt him kiss the top of her

228

head and hug her back. Turning her head to one side, she caught a worried frown from Piet.

Her last night in Cape Town. Sophie couldn't believe the time had flown so fast. Over three months of learning more about herself – how she was a lot stronger than she had thought. What she hadn't discovered was what would happen with Marcus.

Klaus had gone to Todd's to give them some "alone time". He had already had a couple of sessions with Mosa and seemed to be feeling a bit more positive. Marcus and Sophie had gone out for an early meal, but headed back to the flat for one final night together.

There should have been urgency, with the time dwindling quickly, but it was the longest, most drawn-out seduction she had ever experienced. He must have caressed every part of her body, and she returned the favour. The way he moved within her, slow and steady, she felt like he was part of her.

They caught their breath and he tenderly cupped her nape. Their eyes met and he swallowed. 'Sophie, I think I'm in love with you.'

Her eyes teared up as she gazed at him, his searching eyes dimming as she failed to respond. She took a deep breath. 'I *know* I'm in love with you.'

There was a spark of hope. 'Stay with me, stay here. Don't go. Help me do this.'

One tear escaped, running down on to her pillow. 'I can't. You have to do it for yourself. And you know what you need to do. What I want you to do.'

'Survive the rest of the season, the last month, without you.'

'Yes, and make up with your family. No matter what they've done.'

'I need to forgive them before I leave.'

'And that's one more thing.'

'What?'

'You need to really think about where your future is. Your family is here, your friends are here, your rugby career for the next few years could be here.'

'You won't be here.'

'No, I have a life back in London.' The tears were slipping freely down her face as her heart continued to fracture. 'I still have to figure out what to do with it.' She smiled through her tears. 'You're not the only one who needs to sort things out.'

They made love sweetly. He moved slowly within her one more time, held her so tenderly. She kissed every part of him she could reach as her eyes dripped bittersweet tears and her heart shattered.

They fell asleep wrapped together, bodies entwined.

It was strange entering the stadium and knowing it would be for the last time, and not even for the whole match. They held hands as they walked towards the players' entrance.

'So this is it.' Marcus stopped by the side of the doors.

Sophie tried to smile. 'Good luck today, although I don't think you'll need it. You'll smash 'em.

'Thanks to you.'

'No, you're the one who's done all the hard work, remember?' she scolded lightly, summoning all her willpower to stop herself from grabbing him and refusing to let go.

He cupped her cheek and smiled at her. 'You take care. Don't end up in another strange hospital.'

'I won't.' She pressed her hand over his as he bent down and gave her a slow, sweet kiss. It ended, but her throat was choked and she couldn't talk any more. All she could do was hug him.

His name was called, and her arms dropped away.

'Bye, my *liefie*.' One last kiss, and he reluctantly turned and disappeared.

Sophie closed her eyes, willing tears back and trying to keep her composure. All she wanted to do was curl up in a ball and sob. Instead, she wandered around the stadium by herself, waving at Todd and his horde before joining his friends.

'You're definitely going?' Kara gazed sadly at her. 'I'll miss having you watch with me.'

'Yep, we're leaving at half time. A month more of travel, then I'll be back in the UK for the start of the Harford Park season.'

They took their seats to watch the team run out, and cheered them on. Marcus scored a try just before half time, a well-timed interception from within their half.

'Are you going down to speak with him at half time?' asked Kara as she hugged her goodbye.

'No, he doesn't need me.' His team were gathering together to head into the changing rooms.

She said her final goodbyes and made her way out to the end of the row of seats as Marcus joined his teammates.

Somehow, amongst the cheering, boisterous crowd, he managed to spot her. She nodded. He smiled ruefully, then a waving flag broke their gaze and his attention returned to the coaches.

She took one last look at the man she loved, on the pitch he loved, before she turned and walked away.

On arrival at the airport, Klaus must have been able to tell that she needed some time to herself. 'Listen, I've checked in already, but there's some gear I need to ensure is either on this flight or the next. We're a little early, so take your time. I'll see you in the departure lounge?'

Sophie gave a weak smile. 'Yeah. See you in a bit.'

As she walked towards her check-in desk, she glanced up at one of the TV screens and did a double-take. There was Marcus, *her* Marcus, running in a try as part of a rugby highlights reel. The full time scores came up: M. Coetzee had scored another hat-trick. Sophie laughed as her eyes teared up again. There was even a clip of him being interviewed, smiling and joking with the woman holding the microphone, who looked to be half-swooning at his beautiful, blond presence.

All his fears had come to naught. He was fine without her. He didn't need her.

She checked in on autopilot, her rucksack rolling away from her on the conveyor belt. There was no point in delaying, so she headed towards the departure lounge entrance.

As she reached the front of the Security queue, she heard a woman call, 'Sophie! Sophie! Stop!'

She turned to see Bridget running towards her, out of breath and handbag flapping.

'Sophie! I need to talk to you!'

She stepped out of the shuffling queue, to meet Marcus' sister. 'Hi.'

'Hey.'

There was an awkward silence. Sophie didn't know what to expect after their last meeting.

'I only found out you were leaving at the end of the match, from Todd.' Bridget paused, uncertain for once. 'Can we ... do you have time for a coffee before your plane leaves?' she eventually asked.

Sophie shrugged and checked her watch. 'Not coffee.' Bridget's face was crestfallen. 'I'm planning to nap on the plane. I can manage a juice.'

'Good.' The brunette smiled with relief.

They found seats at a place along the concourse, and Bridget fetched a couple of drinks.

Bridget stared into her cup. 'I'm so sorry about everything. I should've stood up for you, I should've welcomed you.'

'Maybe you should have.'

'You've done so much for Marcus. He's like the brother I remember from when he was younger. He's more confident and happier, even playful, yet more mature at the same time. He smiles more than I've seen for years. We treated you so badly. I tried calling you to apologise, but your phone was turned off.'

'I've said my goodbyes and it's a South African SIM card, it won't work where I'm going. I have a new one waiting for me at home.'

'Oh. Can I have your UK number please? Marcus' agent said he's been offered a Premiership contract after the match today. I can let you know how he gets on.'

'I'm not sure that's a good idea. If he's not returning to Harford, I'd like to make a clean break of it. Keep the memories intact. Unless I bang my head again,' she added wryly.

'So … you're definitely splitting up.'

'We were never together to split up in the first place. It was a holiday fling.'

Bridget stared into her coffee. 'He loves you.'

Sophie sighed. She wanted so much to believe it, but she had to be realistic. 'You don't know that. We have great chemistry, but I'm not sure he really loves me. He did love someone else not so long ago, so perhaps for him, love is a transient feeling?'

'You love him though.'

Tears ran gently down Sophie's cheeks, but she was at peace with herself. 'You know the expression, "If you love someone, set them free"?'

'Aren't they lyrics?'

'Yeah, but there's another part. To paraphrase, if he does not return, he was not meant to be mine. If he does return, and he wants to be with me, I'll love him as hard as I can for the rest of my life.'

'But what if …'

'I'm only just learning that I can be my own person, that I can stand up for myself, I don't have to rely on anyone else. And no one else need rely on me.'

As the plane took off, Sophie dried her eyes. She knew she would see him again, she knew it would be a better time for them to start from scratch, as stronger, less-damaged individuals. But she also knew that if she didn't, it would hurt like hell, but it would not be the end of her world.

There had been no audio when Sophie had seen the highlights, nothing about what Marcus had actually said to the smitten interviewer after he received his man of the match award. As Bridget made her way out of the airport, she heard her brother's voice echoing from another TV.

'This is for someone I've recently realised I love very much, who I love being with, love watching, and love loving. Someone who had faith in me, supported me, and let me be myself, but didn't hesitate to give me a much-needed kick up the arse. Sophie, in a month's time, I'm coming after you. I'm coming to get you, wherever you may be, and you're not going to get away.'

If you want something very, very badly, let it go free. If it doesn't return, it was never yours to begin with. If it comes back to you, it's yours forever.

Toria Lyons

The Scarlet Series

CARIAD

For more information about **Toria Lyons**

and other **Accent Press** and **Cariad** titles

please visit

www.accentpress.co.uk

Lightning Source UK Ltd.
Milton Keynes UK
UKOW04f1829291115

263780UK00001B/13/P